BESET BY GHOSTS

HAUNTED TOWN SERIES BOOK 1

E.K. CARMEL

PERSISTENT IRIS PRESS

Beset By Ghosts
Haunted Town Series Book 1
Copyright © 2017 by E.K. Carmel
Cover by Laura Putorti

For Andre.
My best friend, biggest cheerleader,
and love of my life.

CONTENTS

1

I woke up this morning with a bad feeling in my gut.

The first time I felt that hallow, quivering uneasiness was when I was seven years old, just before Bobby Caruthers stuck his tongue down my throat. He got a black eye for his trouble and I learned a valuable lesson about my senses. For many years, I trusted that feeling. But it's been so long since my body's last early warning signal I ignored it and got ready for work.

Should have known it would bite me in the butt later.

Opening the front door of my apartment building, I stepped into a sauna. The air conditioning in my rusty black Honda blew hot air, making me feel like a lobster in a pot of boiling water. I gunned it out of my complex and, a half mile later, the cold air finally kicked in.

Braking for a red light, movement at the corner of my eye made me look at the faded two-story houses lining the street.

A fluffy, light-colored dog, probably a terrier and poodle mix, bounced down the front steps of the closest house on my right. After a moment, an elderly lady appeared on the porch, yelling after the dog. He scooted between the overgrown front bushes toward the back of the house. The lady leaned over the railing, watching him, then turned back to the door.

Images flashed through my mind like a video: a barking German Shepherd leaped over lawn furniture, running toward me, its teeth bared.

A car horn pulled me out of the scene, my heart hammering. "Jeez Louise." The light had turned green and the cars ahead were gone. I pulled into the next driveway, parked with a jerk, and jumped out of the car, knowing I was too late.

Fierce barking and female shouts came from behind the houses.

Pushing through the bushes toward the backyard, I saw a slight blond woman and young boy struggling to hold back a lunging German Shepherd by its collar. The elderly woman from earlier dropped to the ground beside a small mound of fur only a couple feet away from the big dog.

Crazy lady.

"I'm so sorry, Mrs. Jankowsky," the blond woman cried, fighting the dog. "I don't know what happened. He was perfectly fine a minute ago!"

Stumbling out of the bushes, one of my clogs caught on a root and my ponytail swung around, catching in a branch. As I tugged at my hair, the dog snapped his head around and started toward me, jerking the blond woman and boy. I froze, wondering how long before the collar gave way but they kept the dog from advancing.

"My name is Kenna Tierney," I called, over the

barking dog. "I'm a vet tech. Can you get your dog in the house and bring out towels?" I gave one last yank and freed myself from the bush.

The woman nodded, not even questioning me. Maybe it was the scrubs I wore.

The shepherd was having none of it, though. Despite the woman and boy pulling back with all their strength, he gained ground.

I opened my mind and both dogs surged in. The small one was in a spiral of fear and pain. The big one howled worse than any two-year-old deprived of his favorite toy. Kind of like conflicting conversations going on in my head at the same time. I winced. Since the shepherd was still dangerous and unpredictable, I focused on him and his "voice" came through clearer.

My yard. My people. You don't belong. He continued to bark.

I know I don't belong here, I thought toward the dog, *but—*

The shepherd lunged closer. *You don't belong. Small, annoying one doesn't belong. This is my territory.*

The blond woman gasped.

I wanted to jump back, but braced myself. *I'll take the small dog away if you stop this noise and go inside.*

The shepherd barked his frustration. Then baring his teeth and growling, he ran toward the house, hauling the surprised woman and child behind him. I waited until they were inside, then knelt beside the elderly lady.

The dog shivered in her arms. I couldn't see much the way she held him but when I touched his head and focused, I felt hot pain lance my side and neck and sucked in a quick breath. Closing my mind to him, I checked his eyes. Clear. But his gums were bright red, his breathing shallow, and heart rate rapid. Early signs of shock.

His owner looked at me, tears running down her seamed cheeks. "He's hurt bad, isn't he?" she whispered.

"I won't know for sure," I hedged, "until we get him to the clinic. The sooner, the better."

She nodded but looked like she didn't believe me.

A door slammed. The boy ran up, dropping an armful of towels beside me. "Will Clyde be okay?" he asked, staring.

"I'll do my best," I said, covering Clyde in Mrs. Jankowsky's arms with a towel.

The boy's mother returned and helped me settle the woman and dog in the back seat of my car. About ten minutes later, I pulled into the driveway of a large, one-story square building. The clinic always reminded me of a drug store with its fake brick siding and huge sign, Syracuse Animal Clinic, in friendly, cursive lettering. I drove around back, hustled them inside, and into an exam room. It was still early, so Clyde was the only patient besides the ones that stayed overnight in the kennel.

Mrs. Jankowsky was tiring, having trouble holding Clyde up, so I transferred him to the exam table. "I'll be right back." She nodded, her shoulders hunched.

I quick-walked to Reception where a heavy-set woman with curly brown hair in a messy bun sat typing at a computer, her back to me. "Pat, I've got a BDLD in room three. Where's Doc?"

BDLDs, short for "big dog, little dog," don't usually end well. When a bigger dog tangles with a smaller dog, it results in massive injuries to the smaller dog.

Pat swiveled toward me, her granny glasses half way down her nose. "He's not in yet." She reached for the phone. "What happened to you?" She turned to punch buttons.

I looked down, surprised to see dirt smudges in random spots on my scrubs and a tear near the knee. "It got a little intense."

She turned back. "I guess so. How bad's the dog?"

"He's in shock."

"I'll be down with the paperwork." She put the phone to her mouth. "Hello, Doc?"

"Thanks, Pat," I called, sprinting back to the exam room.

Pulling the stool over to the exam table, I got to work. "Okay, let's see what we've got." Clyde's eyes were wild-looking. I rubbed the top of his head. "Hey, sweetie, I'm going to unwrap you." As I lifted the end of the towel, he whimpered. So did Mrs. Jankowsky. Blood matted Clyde's fur around his neck. Typical in dog fights, where they went for the throat.

A soft knock at the door made Clyde growl but when Pat entered, he stopped.

"Doc'll be here soon," she said, setting a clipboard on the counter. She gave Mrs. Jankowsky another clipboard, explained how to fill out the required background information, and left.

I pulled the towel back further. More blood on Clyde's side. He shivered. Listening with the stethoscope, I noted his increased heart rate, then took his temperature. He didn't squirm. It was slightly elevated. Laying the towel back over him, I wrote down his stats.

"So, just to get the chain of events recorded, what

exactly happened? How did Clyde come to be attacked by your neighbor's dog?"

Mrs. Jankowsky puckered up, then took a deep breath. "I don't know what got into Clyde this morning," she said, her voice wavering. "I went out to get the newspaper, like I do every morning, and he just shot between my feet. I almost fell. And that other dog barks all the time." She scowled. "Had to call the police a couple of times at night. Decent people can't sleep with all that noise going on. But he never went after Clyde before." She shook her head. "You know, we're lucky you happened to be nearby. Did you hear the noise?"

I smiled and nodded. Yeah. That was it.

The door burst open and Susan, one of the veterinarians, walked in. "So, what do we have?"

Clyde growled.

Susan wasn't the most thorough vet and I didn't want her anywhere near him. "Doc is on his way," I said.

She pressed her lips together. "Well, I'm here now." She smiled at Mrs. Jankowsky. "Let's see what's going on." She pushed me aside but Clyde showed his teeth. "Why doesn't this dog have a muzzle on?" she snapped.

"He was fine a moment ago," I said.

"Well, get one." She looked at me like I was an idiot.

I gritted my teeth and deliberately looked in the wrong cabinet drawers.

The door opened again and tall, gray-haired Doc stepped in.

Clyde stopped growling.

"Thanks," Doc said, nodding to Susan. "I've got this."

Her expression froze. Doc was the head vet and she

had to give in. "Of course," she said, her tone controlled, and left the room, back stiff.

I hid my relief and tried sending Clyde calming thoughts, but he was in too much pain.

Doc looked at Mrs. Jankowsky. "Hello, I'm Dr. Corday."

I made introductions and he sat on the stool in front of the exam table. "Hello, Clyde," he murmured. "I understand you were in an altercation with a larger dog. Let's take a look at you."

Clyde whimpered.

Mrs. Jankowsky touched his head. She repeated her story as Doc lifted off the towel and gently searched through the long fur to see the extent of Clyde's injuries. He asked questions about Clyde's general health, since he wasn't a regular at the clinic.

I always learned something by watching Doc. He had a careful but assured touch, something I hoped to develop. He also talked to Clyde, unlike some vets who treated the pet like an unfeeling lump and their support staff like lesser mortals. Doc was one of the good guys and I was lucky to work with him.

From what I could see, Clyde had a long laceration from the left side of his neck around to the back and another along his side. With so much fur, it was hard to tell for sure but it matched what I'd learned my way.

Clyde turned his head to the side, staring at something across the room. In the exact moment I followed his gaze, I felt a sensation like a heavy blanket dropping over my head and shoulders. This was another unwanted feeling I hadn't had in many years and was quickly followed by an I'm-in-deep-deep-trouble chill in my chest.

A small woman in her early 60s stood next to the supply cabinet. She had short, curly, bright-red hair, wore a long, flowered house dress, and was not human. She was a ghost.

She didn't say a word, which was unusual, but she looked surprised.

Me too.

Last I knew, Ma was alive and well, living at home in Hurlbutt.

2

___

Declan settled deeper in the shabby chair that hugged his old body just right, savoring the wry humor of Mark Twain.

The whispers began again.

"*...just cannot see...*"

"*...talking. Now listen to...*"

"*...you...better...I...*"

Ice ran through his veins, raising goose bumps on his thin skin. *A Connecticut Yankee* fell to the floor. The bright sunlight streaming through the windows dimmed. He hunched over, his heart beating like a caged animal fighting for its freedom. He fumbled for the remote, turning on the TV, even though it was just talk shows and soap operas at this hour. He increased the volume. Louder. Louder still.

The voices faded.

But the talk show host asked such intrusive questions. And the guests eagerly told their most personal secrets.

He clasped his trembling hands together. "Our Father,

who art in Heaven..." At the end, he didn't feel the peace he usually found in prayer. Was this his life now?

"Hey!" A voice shouted behind him.

Thank God.

"You hard of hearing, or what? Been calling since I walked in," Brian said, his face red from exertion. "Turn that damn thing down. I can't hear myself talk."

Declan didn't even mind the bad language. He pressed the volume button several times.

Brian waited for the volume change, then said, "Katrina sent over food and I put it in the 'fridge. I've got what I need to fix those steps." He stared. "You alright? You look like you seen a ghost."

"Didn't *see* any." Declan's throat spasmed and he swallowed past the lump. "But I *heard* several. Now that you're here, though, I'll be fine. For a while, at least."

3

I stared. No. This was not happening again. Not after all this time. And Ma?

"Kenna?"

My attention snapped back to Doc. He and Mrs. Jankowsky stared at me. "I...I'm sorry," I stammered. "What did you say?"

Doc stood up. "We have to check Clyde's other side."

"Oh, right. Of course." Idiot. Nothing like making a fool of yourself in front of the boss.

"Easy does it, now."

Together, we attempted to roll Clyde over but he whimpered and stood up on his own for a moment before sitting down.

I casually peeked across the room. No ghost.

Relieved, I let out a breath. Maybe it was a trick of the light. I used to see ghosts but that part of my life was over. And thinking one was my mother? Lately, I'd been working a lot of hours and last night I'd stayed up late again watching a movie. I was overtired and probably coming down with a cold. That was it. Just put the ghost stuff out of my mind and pay attention to the emergency in front of me. I focused on Clyde and Doc.

After finishing his examination and checking the clipboard, Doc said, "Well, it could be worse. I don't see any deep puncture wounds. He's going to need surgery, of course, to close up those lacerations. We may find something more when we get in there, but he's relatively young and seems in good health and that's in his favor." He wrote instructions.

Mrs. Jankowsky's whole body relaxed. "Thank you, doctor. I've just been so worried."

"It's lucky Kenna happened to witness the attack and got you here quickly." He handed me the clipboard and nodded. "She'll give you more information on what's to happen."

The next hour was a blur, answering Mrs. Jankowsky's questions and prepping Clyde. Once he was sedated and the damaged areas shaved of fur, it revealed the laceration along his side was quite ragged. That would take some work to close up.

I loved the challenge of assisting in surgery. Today, I was in the zone. Each time Doc asked for an instrument, I anticipated him. There was minimal internal damage, nothing a couple stitches couldn't handle. The lacerations, though, required a lot of suturing. In the end, the surgery was a success, and Doc complimented my work. I was on a high.

While Clyde recovered in the good hands of another tech, I explained to Mrs. Jankowsky and her son, who'd joined her in the waiting room, about Clyde's condition and what we expected would happen next. "You should go home," I told her, "and get some rest. We'll let you know if there are any problems but I don't expect any. And you can call in the morning for an update."

"Thank you so much Kenna," Mrs. Jankowsky said, her eyes bright.

I headed to the break room with a little bounce to my step. I felt like I could take on the world.

A sales rep must have visited today because the smell of pizza and wings hit me before I walked into the room. Nice. It saved me a trip to the convenience store down the road. I went to my car and grabbed the energy drink I'd left there with all the excitement this morning. Mmm, warm pop. When I lifted the pizza box lid, however, only two tiny pieces with a little cheese were left. And no wings.

I sighed. Better than nothing.

Four tables with chairs stood in the middle of the break room. A couch occupied one wall and a couple cushioned chairs with a small table between them were on the adjacent wall. All the comfortable seating was taken, as usual, so I zeroed in on an empty table on the other side of the room.

"Hey, Kenna. Heard you tangled with the she-devil today."

Gossip got around fast. Best to cut it off at the knees now. I stopped at a table occupied by two other vet techs, both younger than me and fresh out of college. "No tangling involved," I said. "Doc came in and took over the case. I didn't have anything to do with it." I started to move away.

"That's not what we heard."

I turned back. They grinned at me, then at each other like the naughty frat boys they probably had once been.

"You better be careful," said the one with spiky blond hair.

The one with dimples said, "Yeah, or she might have you cleaning maggots out of a dog's ass."

So, they had no real information. I smiled, with an edge. "Like she did when you screwed up the lab results last month?"

"Well..." Dimples tried to smile his way out of it.

Blondie snickered.

"There you are!" said a testy, female voice.

"Speak of the she-devil," I muttered, turning around.

Susan pointed at Blondie.

I let out a relieved breath and slipped away to the empty table.

"I told you," she barked, "to prep and sterilize surgical kits."

"I...I thought you meant after lunch," Blondie whimpered. He bolted from his chair.

Susan followed him out, hounding him all the way down the hall.

While chewing cold pizza, I thought back over the steps of the surgery. Then, the one disturbance in the Force of my day popped into my mind, ruining my fantastic mood. Had I really seen Ma or was I just imagining it? I felt my forehead with the back of my hand. No fever.

My gut twinged again and I put my hand over it. First, the gut, then the whatever-I-saw in the exam room. Either I was going nuts or something was definitely wrong. But if something happened to Ma, my sister would have called me. She's Ma's emergency contact.

I dropped my gnawed pizza crust.

What if no one knew yet?

Not wanting to open that particular can of worms but seeing no other alternative, I pulled out my cell phone. Then hesitated. I did not want my co-workers over-hearing me. I threw away my half-eaten lunch, left the building, and stood under a big maple tree across the parking lot that offered shade and distance from any curious listeners before dialing Ma's number.

She didn't pick up. Normally, this wasn't surprising. We—my brother, sister, and I—had bought Ma an answering machine years ago, but teaching her to use it was a nightmare and we finally gave up. My sister, Nora, had also set up voice mail for her, but Ma called the phone company and disconnected it. Don't even get me started on cell phones.

I rarely called Ma, because, honestly, we don't get along. I tried again and let it ring at least twenty times with no answer. She was probably just outside or shop-ping or something. What more could I do?

Returning to work, I checked on Clyde. He was still out of it but his vitals were all good. He was a tough little survivor.

Between immunizations and infected scratches, I still had that nagging feeling in my gut and called Ma again.

No answer.

I didn't want to imagine the worst, but had to know for sure. There were a couple ways I could play this. I could go full steam ahead, call out the police, the ambu-lance, and the SWAT team, which would be overkill by anyone's standards. Or I could make the two hour trip to Hurlbutt after work. Not my favorite option. Sixteen years ago, after a huge fight with Ma, I left home, promising I'd never be back. And I hadn't. Ma and I had sort of patching things up, at least enough to talk on the phone, but I did not want to go back.

Either way, if everything was fine with Ma, I'd never hear the end of it.

For years.

It reminded me of this past February. In the early morning, a train hauling crude oil derailed outside of Hurlbutt. One of the tankers split open and exploded, causing the evacuation of everyone in a five mile radius.

My sister, Nora, lived in Texas and had frantically tried to contact Ma. Our brother Jim was stationed in the Middle East so he couldn't do anything. That left me, the only sibling still living in New York State but I was working. Besides, with the evacuation, I figured I'd never find her in the chaos, and if I did, she wouldn't thank me. Once things settled down and I got through to Ma, the first thing out of her mouth was, "What's the matter with all of you? It was just a train wreck. You'd think the whole town went up in flames or something."

I went back inside the building, but all afternoon I imagined the worst. She could have slipped in the tub and hit her head or accidentally cut herself, fainted, and was bleeding out. Then again, maybe she was just visiting someone, probably from church. Certainly not family. From what we kids could pry out of them, as soon as our parents married, they moved across the state and hadn't talked to their respective families in New York City again.

They never explained about why they split with their families or whether it came before or after the marriage.

I clenched my fists until my stubby nails caused a satisfying pain in my palm. As usual, anything having to do with my family was complicated.

Back at my apartment after work, I couldn't stand it anymore and called Nora. She was closest to Ma. If something was going on, she would know. Of course the one time I actually wanted to talk to her, I got her voice mail instead. I rolled my eyes at the Texas accent in her greeting. After the beep, I said, "Hey, Nora, it's Kenna," attempting to sound unconcerned. "I tried calling Ma today but she didn't answer. Is she away visiting someone or something?" I didn't want to raise alarms if there was no need and wasn't about to tell her I had one of my feelings. But I knew just the suggestion would be enough to get Nora, the bloodhound, on the scent. "Well, anyway, talk to you later."

I reheated some leftover pork fried rice and collapsed in front of the TV, but after one bite, set it aside, too anxious to eat. Nothing on TV sounded interesting, so I looked through my movie collection. Usually, I could cheer myself up watching Deadpool, but not even the Merc with a Mouth cut it tonight.

I gave up and went back to the clinic to check on Clyde. We had techs on duty after regular business hours, but I always felt responsible for the surgery cases I'd assisted. They were my patients, too. Clyde was laying in his cage wrapped in a blanket, sleeping. I checked his clipboard. Vitals all normal.

"How's he been acting?" I asked the tech.

"He growled a little in between meds, but he's mostly been sleeping."

"Good." I checked my cell phone. No messages or missed calls. It was 7:30.

What kind of daughter was I?

For a moment, the old guilt reared its ugly head before I squashed it like a bug. What kind of daughter? One who'd been doubted and ridiculed from an early age. However, it occurred to me that if I didn't do something and Ma died as a result, I'd be haunted by her the rest of my life.

Literally.

Twenty minutes later, I was on my way west, heading to Hurlbutt. Just before reaching the Thruway, my cell phone rang. Nora, of course. I pulled into a strip mall parking lot. "Hey, Nora," I answered, trying to sound normal.

"Well, she's passed."

"Uh—"

"She didn't answer her phone. As far as I know, she didn't have anything going on this week." Her clipped tones were at odds with her soft Texas accent. "I called Alice Keenan. You remember, the Church School teacher with the lazy eye? She said Ma hadn't been to Mass today. You know Ma. If she doesn't go to Mass, something's wrong. So, Mrs. Keenan and her husband went to check on her. The house was quiet. They banged on the doors for quite a while, I guess. They called the police, who broke open the kitchen door and found her on the floor with a broken neck. They think she fell off a stool. Though, what she was doing up on a stool at her age, I can't imagine."

"I knew something was wrong." As soon as the words slipped past my teeth, I cringed. Now I'd done it.

Nora was silent for a heart beat. "They're taking her to a funeral home."

I breathed out, slowly. Safe.

"Apparently," Nora continued, "Buchanan's went out of business. The police gave me a couple other names and I just picked one." Sounds of shuffling paper came through the phone. "Here it is. Jamison Funeral Home. Since you're right there would you call and make sure everything is okay?"

"I'm not exactly 'right there,' Nora. I'm two hours away."

"Closer than me or Jim. In fact, just handle the arrangements with the church and the cemetery too."

Before I could protest, I heard a child's voice in the background.

"I'll be right there, darlin'," Nora called. "I have to go," she said to me. "Here's the contact info."

I scrambled through my glove compartment, finding an expired insurance receipt. As she rattled off names and phone numbers, I jotted them down in the margins.

"Call me," Nora said, "when you have all the arrangements made. Talk to y'all later." She hung up.

Staring at the cell phone, the urge to throw it against the windshield grew until I noticed something else.

My gut now felt fine.

4

Listening to Mass in St. Brendan's again was uncomfortable. It wasn't because it was for Ma's funeral or because I was last here for my father's funeral.

No. It was because my parents wouldn't shut up.

"Jim, I feel so underdressed," Ma said, looking down at her flowered house dress.

"Darling, you're a ghost." This was my father's deep voice now. "No one can see you." They stood to the left side of the sanctuary in the cool stone church.

"It doesn't feel right, is all."

I liked it better the first day when Ma didn't speak. She'd been so surprised to find herself dead and in spirit form, it shocked her silent. Well, not anymore. At some point she met up with Dad and I hadn't had a peaceful moment in the last week and a half.

"It's a shameful turn out!" Ma complained.

I watched the faces of people sitting in the pews nearby. No one else could hear this conversation but me, of course. I breathed in, pulled on the lapels of my suit jacket, and smoothed the skirt, trying to ignore them.

"Stop fidgeting," Nora whispered, ever the mother hen. As kids, she'd taken advantage of the almost two year age difference between us to boss me around. She flipped her salon-colored blond hair behind her shoulder as she returned her attention to the priest.

I clenched my teeth. Together for only a few hours and already she was getting on my nerves. I just had to survive a day or two with my siblings.

"What's the matter with everyone these days?" Ma asked. "Don't they have a shred of decency to pay their respects? Why, if that had happened—"

"Evelyn, my dear," said Dad. "You, of all people, know to be more respectful in church."

How right he was. If I'd ever spoken during Mass, Ma would have beaten me at home afterward. From then on, she was quiet. But what she said was true. Only about twenty people attended, making the large sanctuary feel empty and echoing.

My brother, Jim Jr., walked to the lectern, looking sharp in his crisp Army uniform, crew cut graying at the temples. He began with a funny story. At the age of twelve, he and a friend had stolen a fresh-baked blueberry pie from the kitchen. When Ma discovered them, forks in hand, eating it behind the garage, she chased them with a wooden spoon. They ran too fast for her to catch them but late that night, when Jim sneaked in, she let him have it.

"I couldn't sit for a week," he said, smiling at the few chuckles from the congregation. "She was tough but fair," he said. "I was a handful and deserved it."

I picked lint off my skirt. I didn't remember any fairness. After that, my attention drifted. The church seemed smaller and darker, though the beautiful stained glass windows were the same. Remembering my first communion, I reached for the tiny gold cross on a chain around my neck, separating it from the other necklace I wore. Fingering it, I became aware of subtle movement throughout the sanctuary. Ghosts popped in and out of the confessional, others genuflected and sat in pews. I closed my eyes, trying not to see them but I could still feel them. Returning to my hometown was bad enough for normal reasons like seeing people I knew from high school. But after picking up Jim and Nora from the airport in Rochester and arriving in Hurlbutt, I noticed ghosts everywhere.

The headache I'd had off and on all day pounded behind my eyes. I furtively rubbed my temples to relieve the pressure but it didn't work. I couldn't wait to finish things up here and get back to my cozy little apartment and the job I loved.

Nora blew her nose as Jim returned to his seat and the priest concluded the Mass. Afterward, we shook hands with people. I recognized Mr. and Mrs. Keenan, the ones who checked on Ma for us and called the police. I avoided looking in her lazy eye. Others were parishioners I barely remembered from my childhood. Everyone looked so old. Spotting a white-haired lady marching toward us in a blue blazer and matching skirt with a white blouse, I elbowed Nora. "Look out," I whispered.

"What?"

"Saints preserve," Ma sang out right in my ear,

making me flinch. "It's Maida Maglennon. Now, if she could show up, why not anyone else?"

Years ago, Mrs. Maglennon had been the overbearing head of several church committees. Maybe still was. For as long as I could remember, she and Ma had a polite contempt for each other.

Mrs. Maglennon took Jim's arm. "What a lovely eulogy, James."

Her voice, though thinner than I remembered, still had the power to turn my insides to liquid.

"Mrs. Maglennon." Jim immediately covered her knobby hand with his larger one. "How nice to see you."

Her parched, orange-red lips spread into a smile. "Evelyn was so proud of you, always speaking of your accomplishments in the service."

Ma sniffed. "How would she know? Haven't bothered talking to her in years."

"Thank you, ma'am."

Mrs. Maglennon's sharp gaze shifted. "And Nora, I understand you have a family now. Down south someplace?"

Nora smiled, tucking her hair behind one ear. "Why, yes, in Houston. My husband's company moved us there a few years ago."

"You have children?"

"Joseph is ten and Lily, eight." She leaned in, patting the old lady's arm with her manicured hand. "You know, Mrs. Maglennon, you are such a sight for sore eyes. It's wonderful to be home again. I've missed it."

There she was, Perfect Nora, sucking up like when we were kids. Some things never changed.

"Good." Mrs. Maglennon's smile faded as she aimed

her sights on me. "Kenna. I understand you are in Buffalo, working at a coffee shop?" From her tone it was obvious she felt that was only one step up from garbage collector.

"I—I'm in Syracuse now."

Her eyes narrowed. "And what do you do?"

"I'm a vet tech." At her blank look, I clarified. "Veterinary technician."

She frowned. "A Veterinarian?"

Feeling like a trapped deer facing a hunter, I stammered, "N—not quite. I...assist the vets. Run tests. Assist in surgery. That sort of thing." Why was I still intimidated by this woman? I was an adult now.

"I see." She pursed her lips like she'd sucked on a lemon. No doubt disappointed I had a respectable job.

"Ha!" Ma said. "Serves the old busybody right."

Behind me, Dad whispered, "Takes one to know one."

I almost peed my pants.

We went to the cemetery where Ma's body would be laid to rest next to Dad's. Her physical body, that is, because her spirit was yakking away again.

"It's absolutely mortifying the way they found me, Jim."

"I know, dear."

It was hard not to roll my eyes. This had to be the tenth time she complained about how she was found. Enough already. I was just relieved I wasn't responsible for her death when I delayed contacting anyone. She had died immediately after the fall.

"All I wanted was to take a flower arrangement to church. The roses were just starting to bloom and were so pretty. I got up on the kitchen stool to get a vase out of the high cabinet, like I've always done. Then, I saw something move out of the corner of my eye."

That got my attention. She hadn't mentioned this part before.

"I was afraid it was mice but it was a young man standing there! Scared me so bad, I slipped and fell."

"Who was it?" Dad asked.

"I don't know. I only saw him for a second but he looked old-fashioned, with his wire-frame glasses and suspenders. Like pictures from when my parents were young."

"You never saw him before?"

"No. And he disappeared as soon as I fell."

Nora grabbed my arm. "Come on. It's about to begin." She dragged me over to the casket, but my mind was still on my mother's words. I thought I knew who scared her.

When I was seven years old, a car hit me as I rode my bike. Luckily, I only had bruises and a broken arm. But the night I got home from the hospital, I woke up to see a young man with glasses standing at the foot of my bed, watching me. I screamed. Everyone in the family came running, but the man was gone. They searched the house, top to bottom. The door locks were still in place. The windows weren't jimmied. They just thought I had a nightmare.

The next night, it happened again. They searched and found nothing. By the third night, Ma told me to stop my blathering and go back to sleep.

But sleeping terrified me. He would be there, watching me. Each night, I pulled the covers up, hiding. After days of little sleep, I grew exhausted and confused. One night I cried out, "Who are you?"

The man said his name was Henry and he'd lived and died in the house long ago. When I told my family about him, Ma thought I was making up stories to get attention. Now, years later, Ma saw a man who fit the description, causing her to fall to her death. It could have been Henry, the ghost she never believed was there. The irony almost overrode my sense of vindication. Almost.

Brushing sweat from my upper lip, I regretted wearing pantyhose and a suit jacket. As the priest spoke, memories gripped me. The last time I'd been to this cemetery was for Dad's burial. He died when I was seventeen, after a nasty struggle with cancer. It was heart-wrenching, even for someone who saw ghosts, knowing they sometimes stick around to visit. After all, he was right there, next to Ma, listening to the priest, and I still felt choked up.

Fighting the sensation, I looked out over the grassy landscape. At various spots in the cemetery, ghosts watched our group. Why so many? And why, after successfully ignoring them for years, did they bother me now?

~

AFTER MA'S BURIAL, WE HAD AN UNEVENTFUL MEAL prepared by the ladies of the church. And, oh, can they cook. It was just what I needed to recharge my batteries. After Nora dumped the funeral arrangements on me, I'd spent the last week and a half on the phone, worried about every detail, and arguing with her about expenses. We still had to sell the house, but the most emotional and draining part was over.

After eating seconds, I needed to get away from all the stares and Nora's stupid complaints about the food. I snuck down a hallway, then another, trying to remember where the back door was. A woman emerged from a room, closing the door behind her. She turned and jumped a bit when she saw me.

"Oh, goodness! You scared me," she said, smiling, hand to her chest. "Are you lost?" She was taller than me, plump, with silver-gray hair tied in a bun and soft brown eyes. She looked familiar.

"Kind of. I need a little fresh air but it's been so long since I've been here..."

She smiled. "Of course. You just got yourself turned around is all." She guided me back to a different hallway and out the back door. "If I don't see you in a while, I'll come looking for you, in case you get lost again."

"Thank you," I said, to be polite, but hoped she didn't. I needed to get away from everyone. It wasn't meant to be, though, because the minute I stepped out of the church, I felt my parents' presence.

My father had been a bigger-than-life figure, always telling jokes, with a great big laugh and a dimpled smile. Ma had always been muted and serious though I suspected she colored her hair that hideous shade of red to compete with Dad. When I felt them now, it was that same sense of fun and games followed by a grim determination. Bizarre. I could never figure out what kept them together.

"Time to go, my Kenna," said Dad.

Relieved, then feeling guilty at the relief, I asked, "So, you guys are crossing over?"

"No," Ma said. "Not yet. We plan to keep an eye on you children for a while."

Lucky us.

"But first," Dad said, winking at me. "We're going to travel a bit, see some of the places we didn't get to before."

"Vacationing ghosts, huh?"

"That would be right. So, you may not be seeing us for a while."

Okay by me. "Have fun you crazy kids. I love you, Dad. Ma."

Ma seemed lost in thought and didn't notice.

"Love you, too," said Dad. "Now, don't be too hard on Jim and Nora."

I snorted. "They owe me after this."

He laughed the big, booming laugh I remembered and my throat tightened.

"Go on, Evie," Dad prompted Ma.

Ma rested her fists on her hips. "Do I have this to look forward to for eternity? You pushing me, again?"

Dad smiled his best 'convincing Ma' smile, dimples showing and blue eyes full of mischief. "We have things to do and you need to talk to Kenna first."

"Honestly, I thought dying would be more peaceful!" She looked at me, then cleared her throat.

Funny, the little human gestures we keep, even after death.

"Well, Kenna, I suppose an apology is in order," Ma said. "I didn't know about this." She flapped her hands at her incorporeal body. "I'm sorry I didn't believe you when you said you saw ghosts...and I'm sorry about the house."

Then she disappeared.

I glanced at Dad. "She didn't let me say anything."

Dad chuckled. "Probably for the best, don't you think?"

I shrugged. "I suppose." Besides, I didn't want to fight with my mother in public. Someone might think I was a prime candidate for the psych ward. Bad enough it looked like I was talking to myself. A quick peek around relieved my fears on that score.

"Be good Kenna, my dear."

"No guarantees, Dad." We laughed at the familiar words we used to say to each other. "Love you, miss you."

"Love you, too, darlin'. Always."

And then he was gone, too.

I stared at the spot where they had been, listening to the crickets sing. I don't know how long I stood there, thinking about my mother's words. An emptiness crept over me. So many wasted years.

But I didn't want to think about that now.

Standing straighter, I walked back into church, wondering what she meant about the house.

5

———

Before returning to our hotel, I convinced Nora and Jim to stop at the old house. By that point, Ma's little comment bugged the heck out of me.

None of us had been back home in several years. Driving through town, it looked smaller, shabbier than I remembered. "Ma mentioned things were hard lately," said Jim, his six-foot-tall frame folded into the passenger seat of my little Honda. "But I had no idea how bad it was."

That reminded me of something I'd heard. "Yeah. A few years back the village dissolved its...incorporation? I think that's what they called it. The fire, police, and school had to consolidate with others in the county."

"The school closed?" Nora asked from the backseat. "That's terrible!"

I sniffed. "Yeah, well, no big loss there."

"Hey," she tapped me on the shoulder. "Some of us have fond memories of school!"

"Heaven help us from former cheerleaders," I grumbled.

"Consolidating services isn't good," Jim said. "With a bigger area to cover, response time takes longer." Jim's head swiveled from one side of Main Street to the other.

There were a lot of empty storefronts.

I braked at a stop sign. "Didn't there used to be a stop light here?"

"Yes," said Jim.

I was just about to turn left onto Mason Street when I saw a guy wearing jeans and an army jacket. He leaned on a light pole, smoking a cigarette. "That guy has got to be boiling hot dressed like that."

"What guy?" Jim asked.

I pointed. "The one leaning against the light pole."

"I don't see anyone," Nora said.

Then I felt the sensation of a blanket settling on my head and shoulders and realized my mistake. He was a ghost. Apparently my ghost-detecting ability was a little rusty or he was too far away. And now he looked right at me, his cigarette half-way to his mustached mouth. One second he was there, the next he was gone.

I tried to recover. "Oh, he was there a second ago. Must have walked away." I turned onto the side street, wanting to get away from there before they caught on.

Nora looked out the back window. "I don't see anyone, anywhere."

"He was wearing a heavy jacket and jeans. I thought it was weird in this weather, that's all." After an uncomfortable few seconds, I pointed at a house to the left, slowing down. "Hey, isn't that the old Cranston place?" Nora had been friends with the eldest daughter, so I hoped it would distract her.

The two-story clapboard house was in bad shape. Paint peeling, shutters missing or hanging by one corner.

"What a dump," Nora said. "I haven't heard from Cammy since graduation. She just fell off the face of the Earth."

Crossing the railroad tracks that cut the town in half, I felt ghosts in the abandoned warehouses beside them. When I was a teenager, I used to explore those buildings looking for ghosts, testing my abilities.

The stupid things we do as kids.

When we got to the house, we stopped talking. The immaculate blue two-story house was now weathered gray. Jim examined the crumbling cement front steps with his foot.

I felt a presence in the house. Henry, no doubt.

Jim produced a key to the front door, but when he unlocked it and pushed, the door wouldn't budge. He strained against it.

"What's the matter?" I teased. "G.I. Jim not strong enough?"

He cupped his hands, looking in the window, trying to see beyond the drapes. "I think there's something in front of the door."

We walked around the house. The lawn was shin-high and weeds had taken over the gravel driveway.

"Hello!" called a female voice.

We all turned. A blond woman waved from the end of the driveway, holding a leash. Her small dog yipped, trotting up the driveway, his owner following.

"Hi, I'm Gloria Stanley. I live across the street."

Up close, she appeared to be in her thirties and wore white jean shorts and a tight red tank top. Jim introduced us as we all shook hands.

Her dog, a Pomeranian, sniffed around my feet, so I squatted down. As I pet him, I noted he was young and in excellent health. It was nice to see his people took good care of him. He wriggled his stubby little body in delight, getting his front paws up on my knees.

Hi. Hi. Hi. Hi. Hi.

"Ralph!" Gloria tugged on the leash and the poor dog coughed. "Get down." She looked at me. "I'm so sorry. He knows better than to do that." She picked him up.

I stood. "No worries. I love dogs."

"But your skirt!"

I looked down, brushing at the little bit of dirt on the black material. "No damage done."

"Oh, good." She flashed a brilliant smile. "You must be Evelyn's children. I'm so glad to meet you. She talked about you all the time! You know," her smile disappeared. "I felt just awful the way Evelyn died." She began to tear up. "Normally, I'd pop over to have a little chat if I saw her in the yard, but it had been a busy two weeks getting my kids ready for sleep-away camp, getting my husband, Barry, ready for a big business trip, and the Garden Club's annual competition is coming up, so I was trying to get the yard in shape and I feel terrible I never noticed she wasn't out and about and then, when the police arrived, I was horrified..." She finally took a breath, but it came out as a sob.

"Awww," Nora rushed over, giving Gloria an awkward hug with the dog between them.

"To think she was just across the street, alone, and needing help."

Nora fished a packet of Kleenex out of her purse. "That's OK. I know how busy a family can be. I have two children, too." She handed a tissue to Gloria, who put Ralph down.

Jim scanned the street, looking uncomfortable.

Ralph trotted back to me, so I squatted down to pet him.

Nora and Gloria pulled out their cell phones to exchange numbers. I rolled my eyes at Jim. He shrugged. By now, dusk was falling. Enough of this Soccer Mom moment. "Well, it's getting late," I said. "It's been a long day for us, but we wanted to check on the house before going back to our hotel."

"Oh, of course!" Gloria wiped her eyes. "It was so nice meeting you. You'll be back?"

"Yes," Nora answered.

Gloria beamed. "Good, I'll see you later, then!" She left, fluttering her fingers goodbye and tugging on Ralph's leash.

Ugh.

Turning back to the house, my stomach twinged.

Jim unlocked the side door, cautiously opening it. A disgusting, rotting smell rolled over us. "What the hell?" he said.

Nora made a face. "What is that?"

"I don't know," said Jim, "but I'm about to find out."

"You go right ahead," Nora said, backing away. "I'll stay out here, thank you very much."

I covered my nose and mouth with my sleeve, following Jim. Immediately inside the door was a short landing. Straight ahead was a set of stairs leading to the kitchen. To the left, stairs went to the basement. I felt a ghost down there in the dark but got an odd chill instead of the welcoming feel I expected from Henry. I didn't linger long, since Jim had already reached the top of the kitchen stairs. I hustled to catch up just as he opened the inside door.

The stench made my eyes water. He flipped the light switch. When we walked all the way in, a nasty surprise awaited us.

Now I understood why Ma apologized about the house.

Jim didn't say a word. He just shook his head as we passed the sink filled with dirty dishes soaking in gross water.

"Witch on a stick." My mind didn't want to believe what I saw.

There was stuff piled on all the counters right to the bottom of the cabinets. Bulging garbage bags lined the floor. Only a narrow path led through what had once been a spacious kitchen. We followed it, trying not to touch anything.

Jim turned on the lights in the dining room. Ma's sewing machine sat on the drop-leaf table, surrounded by piles of fabric and half-finished projects. Boxes, bags, and clothing covered the floor. We could barely see the buffet on the other side of the room for all the junk piled on and in front of it.

Another narrow path led through to the family room. It looked to be in much the same condition, as did the hall leading to the front door and stairway to the second floor.

A prickly sensation on the back of my neck made me stare hard into dark areas created by the shadows of towering piles.

Jim grunted, turning off the light. "Let's get out of here."

I was happy to comply. On the way out, I grabbed a pile of unopened mail sitting on the corner of the counter.

We stumbled outside, shocked into silence.

"Well?" Nora looked back and forth between us. "What is it? What's wrong? What is that awful smell?"

"Ma was a hoarder," I said.

Nora had to see for herself. It didn't take long. She ran out, coughing and retching. Jim made her sit down on the step. Once she caught her breath, she said, "I can't believe it. She never let it get like that before."

I snorted. "She didn't have us to do chores anymore."

Nora shook her head. "There had to be a good reason for it."

"Did Ma have any health problems?" asked Jim.

We both looked at Nora, who shook her head. "Nothing that would explain this."

Jim stared at the house, rubbing his chin. "Well," he said, turning back to us. "We have some cleaning to do."

My brother, Captain Obvious.

Hurlbutt didn't have a hotel, so we drove to the Comfort Inn about ten miles away in Bartlett, the closest city. Actually, it was a very small city when compared to

Buffalo, the next closest to the west or Rochester, to the east.

In Nora's and my room, Jim stretched out on my bed, a beer can balanced on his stomach. I sat cross-legged on the desk chair, comfy in my shorts and tank top. Behind me, the air conditioner blew full-blast. Nora was doing her "evening beauty routine," though it looked like a lot of work to me.

A stack of opened mail sat on the desk, including several past due bills amounting to almost two thousand dollars. We felt sure there were more and these were just the latest. We had an appointment with a lawyer the next day to discuss Ma's "estate" as Nora kept calling it. The mortgage was paid off but, looking at the bills and knowing the condition of the house, I wondered what other surprises were in store for us.

"God knows what's in that house." Nora stood, rubbing white cream on her face. "Obviously, something is rotting and there are probably mice." She walked into the bathroom.

"The worst of the smell," Jim said, crossing his ankles, "is coming from the garbage bags. Get those out and the rest may not be so bad. As for the mice, well, we can buy traps." He took a swig of beer.

Nora emerged from the bathroom again. "We should hire a company to clear it all out. Some specialize in that sort of thing."

Jim swallowed. "Great. How do you suggest we pay for that?"

I smirked. "Since it's Nora's idea and she's wealthy, she should pay for it."

Nora glared at me and I tried not to laugh. She resembled the Phantom of the Opera with most of her face still covered in white. "Well, bless your heart," she said, stalking back to the bathroom.

I glanced at Jim. "The words sounded pleasant, but the tone didn't." I reached for another beer.

"I believe that was a Texas 'fuck you.'"

I made a face, popping the tab. When we were kids, Ma washed our mouths out with soap for swearing. For some reason, I still found it hard to cross that line. It was the only rule of Ma's I actually followed.

Nora stepped back into the room, wiping her face with a washcloth. "I will *not* bankroll this insanity. We are equals in this and I refuse to pay more than my share of it."

I almost blew beer out my nose. "Oh, c'mon, Nora! I was just kidding."

She glared at me. "Well, it was in bad taste and I won't have it anymore."

After smoothing her ruffled feathers, the previous conversation continued. We played around with various scenarios, but kept returning to Jim's idea of cleaning the house ourselves. It made sense to me, though it would mean taking more time off of work. Nora didn't like it but she wasn't willing to part with any more money than she had to. After another hour of verbal wrangling, we agreed to split expenses until the house sold and the bills paid. Then we'd evenly divide up what remained. If there was anything left.

Nora assumed responsibility for keeping track of the expenses. Jim and I let it go because she'd drive us nuts if we didn't.

6

After we met with the lawyer the next morning, I called Doc to beg off work for a while. Then, because we wanted to get started cleaning the house, went back to the hotel to change clothes. Jim and I did, anyway. Nora refused to change out of her silky capris, a knit tank top, and rhinestone sandals.

"You're going to clean house dressed like that?" I said. "You look like you're going to a garden party."

She frowned. "As if I'd wear this to a garden party," she said, a distinct chill to her voice. "Where did you find that?" She pointed at me. "Salvation Army?"

I looked down at my faded Goo Goo Dolls t-shirt and cut-offs. Perfect for a dirty job. "You know, Nora, it would be a shame if you ruined your nice clothes. I have some stuff you can borrow."

Nora stretched her lips a fraction. "Not necessary." She sauntered out of the room.

Jim made a bet with me on how long it would take before her designer outfit got its first splotch of gunk.

In Hurlbutt, I stopped at the Kwik Fill to gas up and buy more coffee, despite refills at breakfast. Tiredness had dogged me the last couple days. I returned to the car with a large covered cup and two energy drinks.

"Good Lord!" Nora said, an expression of horror on her face. "That stuff will kill you, you know." She pointed at the energy drinks.

I started the car. "No, they will not. I don't guzzle ten of them a day, which is where people are getting into trouble. There are some beneficial ingredients, too."

"Energy drinks are awful for your body. There are documented cases of increased heart rate and blood pressure, vomiting, and sometimes death. "

"Okay, Nora." I drew out her name the way she hated. "You've given me your public service announcement. I'm an adult and can do what I want with my body."

She sat back in a huff and didn't say another word, which was fine by me.

Jim had managed to track down a buddy from high school and arranged to borrow a pickup truck. After dropping him at the friend's house, Nora and I stopped at Hanley's Market.

Entering the grocery store was surreal. As kids, we rode our bikes here to buy pop and candy. Now it was dirtier and much smaller than I remembered.

Nora pointed to a card and gift area. "Didn't the produce section used to be here?"

"Yup."

Nora looked through the cheap kids' toys, cutesy garden signs, and ceramic frogs with a sour expression.

A young guy walked by in khakis, with his shirt

buttoned up to the neck, and slicked-back hair. Who gelled their hair anymore?

Facing the far wall, he turned, grasped several things I couldn't see, then set the non-existent things on nothing. No tables or shelves. Right. A ghost. Stocking a produce table that was no longer there. Why did I keep seeing them? I turned away and almost ran into Nora standing behind me.

"What are you staring at?" she asked.

I flinched. "Just...remembering. Fruit used to line the wall here, didn't it?" Good save.

"I guess." She checked her slim, expensive-looking gold watch. "We better get going or Jim will be a drill sergeant when we get back."

"He will anyway."

"True." She pushed the cart like she owned the place.

We headed for the aisle with cleaning supplies, choosing disinfectant, bleach, garbage bags, and mouse traps. Latex gloves, too, because, as Nora put it, "I'm not about to put my bare hands on anything there."

I had to agreed with her, for once.

She chose brand name products until I reminded her of our money situation. She rolled her eyes but switched out the items. In the next aisle, she held up a paisley bandanna. "I could tie this over my nose to block the smell."

"Good idea." I grabbed two more.

Thinking ahead, I picked out a Styrofoam cooler, bottled water, and three sub sandwiches. It would take too long to stop working and go to a restaurant. Besides, we would be gross after cleaning the disgusting kitchen. Nora replaced hers with a salad.

Topping it off, I added a bag of miniature candy bars. With all the family fun times ahead of me, some chocolate therapy was prudent.

While standing in line at the checkout, two women ahead of us talked non-stop and loud enough to be heard across town. Nora huffed, looking daggers at them but I shrugged and scanned the impulse items.

"Weird shit's been happening," said one of the woman. "Tools and small equipment got moved around at night."

"Kids?" asked the other.

Nora wrenched a magazine from the rack.

"That's what they thought, so they hired security. But it kept happening and the security guys swear nobody broke in. They're setting up cameras next."

I yawned. "It's strange being back here."

Nora nodded, not looking up from reading Cosmo. "It seems so sad, though. Old, and, I don't know, less, somehow."

I agreed.

Returning to the house, we set the cooler in the backyard under the trees, filling it with ice, drinks, and food. I threw the candy bars in last.

Nora surveyed the overgrown lawn. "I don't sit on grass," she said.

"Of course you don't." I plunged on, despite her frown. "Let's see if there's lawn chairs in the garage." Darn my mouth. Things could get ugly so fast with Nora.

The garage was as full as the house. We found some rusted old chairs, their webbing torn in places. "Better than sitting on the ground, right?" I asked.

Nora curled her lip.

"Watch out or your face'll freeze like that." I teased.

Nora stalked back to the house.

What was wrong with me? I was reverting back to my bratty childhood.

I followed Nora into the kitchen where she had already tied her bandanna on. Jim refused the one I offered, but I tied mine on. I don't know if it helped much. The smell was still bad. We opened the kitchen windows, but there wasn't much of a breeze to get rid of the stench. Jim hauled two garbage bags to the truck, which disturbed flies and ants and other insects. Nora shrieked, jumping away from the creepy crawlies. I searched under the sink, grabbed an old can of insect spray, and sprayed the floor and air.

"I'm going to look for papers for the lawyer," Nora said, leaving the room.

"I wondered how long she'd last," Jim said, grabbing two more bags.

Together, we cleared the rest of the garbage out in no time. Then Jim opened the fridge, grimaced, and closed it again.

I handed him a garbage bag. "Good place to start. Here ya go."

He gave me a look, shook the bag out, and began throwing containers of moldy food, condiment jars, and expired milk in the bag as fast as he could.

I pulled on latex gloves and fished for the drain plug in the disgusting water in the sink. Once found, water slurped down the drain.

We worked until the pickup was full, then took it to the dump.

When we got back, the kitchen faucet was on. Jim,

who was the first through the door, turned it off. "You need to be more careful, Kenna."

I stared at the faucet. "I didn't leave it on. Nora must have." She hadn't gone to the dump with us.

"I must have what?" Nora asked, entering the kitchen.

"Left the faucet on," Jim said, pointing to it.

"I've been in the other room the whole time," Nora said. "It wasn't me."

"Well," Jim said, gaze swinging between the two of us. "Let's be more careful from now on."

I wouldn't have done something so dumb and didn't bother to answer.

After mopping the floor and cleaning the counters, Jim and I checked out the rest of the house. It wasn't as bad as it had looked in the dark. Ma was short and had piled things only as high as she could reach. Still, it covered most of the floors, every surface, and blocked windows and doors.

In the family room, Nora showed us piles of sheets, blankets, and Ma's clothes stacked on an easy chair. "I think she slept here on the couch. These were already folded and look at that," she indicated a tissue box, prescription bottles, glass of water, emery board, and nail clippers on the coffee table. "All neatly lined up."

I shook my head at Ma's odd behavior.

"And those," Nora pointed at two cardboard boxes stuffed full of papers. "Are bank records, old tax returns, and other papers. I still haven't found the deed to the house."

We didn't want to pay a fee for a title search company so were hoping to find it in the house. This room alone had to hold at least fifty boxes and a whole lot of loose items. "It could be anywhere," I muttered, feeling discouraged.

A noise overhead made us look up at the ceiling.

"Sounds like something fell upstairs." Jim said. "Let's check it out."

Nora opened a box. "You go right ahead."

We hadn't explored much of the house yet, but I hoped it wasn't the same all the way through. As Jim and I climbed to the second floor, though, we had to turn sideways. Baskets, boxes, and other stuff occupied every stair. At the top, it didn't get any better.

I peeked in Ma and Dad's old bedroom at the top of the stairs. A path from the door to the bed indicated Ma still slept there at some point. Mounds of clothing occupied the other side of the bed, both dressers, and a chair. We couldn't reach the closet for all the piles of boxes topped with loose clothing.

We checked the next room, the one Nora and I had shared. We could just make out the posters on the walls above all the stuff. On a small empty patch of floor sat an overturned box of paperback books.

"Here's the culprit," I said, righting the box and tossing books back in it. "Ha. The Baby-Sitters Club." My life had been such a paranormal nightmare, reading those books about normal kids had been my escape. "Why would she keep all this stuff?" I stood up, surveying the room. "What was she thinking?"

We looked at each other, then continued on.

In the bathroom, boxes filled the tub and personal care items covered the counters and toilet seat.

Jim's old room was as bad as the rest. I sighed, leafing

through a box of folded street maps. "This keeps getting worse and worse."

"That's because you're looking at the big picture." Jim left the room and I followed. "You only see the whole job and how big it is. If we break it into smaller pieces, it won't be so bad."

I didn't think so, but said, "Maybe," while inching around a precarious pile in the hallway.

We found Nora on the couch, picking through a box, crying. She held up a plastic ducky. "There's a whole box of things she must have bought the kids."

I hesitated. Nora was a pain to deal with but I hated to see anyone cry. Sitting next to her, I searched through the box. It held a bunch of cheap dollar store toys—purses, baby dolls, fire trucks, board books, etc. All designed for preschool-age children. Way too young for Nora's kids.

"She must have bought these, ready for a visit, but we never came." Tears ran down Nora's blotchy face. "We talked on the phone and I sent her pictures, but we never visited."

Nora had finally cracked.

"Oh, come on," I said. "We don't know what happened. She may have collected those for a charity. You know she was always doing stuff for the church."

Nora sniffled. "Maybe."

I grabbed the tissue box from the coffee table, handing it to her. "There's no sense in beating yourself up over something we have no way to know for sure."

She blew her nose.

I described the massive clutter upstairs. Nora's expression was bleak. "It's an illness," she said. "I read somewhere it's an obsessive disorder, like hand washing or counting things. She couldn't help herself. I wish I'd known. I could have gotten her some help."

"She hid it," Jim said.

The light on the side table flickered and went out. Jim reached over but it went back on before he touched it. "Probably just the wiring," he said, examining the lamp. "Hey, I made this in shop class." The lamp had a square, dark metal base and round shade covered in dust. Jim blew on it and began coughing as the dust flew in his mouth.

Nora scrubbed her hair back from her face. "I'm ready for a break. Let's eat lunch."

They walked out of the room, but I hesitated, peering into corners. Faucets turning on by themselves? Boxes falling over? Lights flickering? I shook my head, leaving the room.

7

After lunch, while Nora and Jim worked on the living room, I stood at the top of the basement stairs. My heart beat like I'd just run a race.

"I can do this," I whispered.

Jim had mentioned checking the plumbing and electrical later. As much as I didn't want to deal with ghosts, I had to find out what it was I sensed here before Jim started poking around.

Turning on the light, I began to descend. "Henry?" I whispered. "Are you here?" I had a good grip on the railing, which was the sole reason I didn't plunge to my death when a strong push came between my shoulder blades. It scared the bejesus out of me and I sat on a step. Gulping in air, it took every ounce of courage in me not to bolt.

This was not Henry.

Once I had my nerves somewhat under control, I continued down the stairs, hands clutching the railing.

Nothing happened. So far, so good.

The basement consisted of the large main room and a smaller, narrower section toward the front of the house. At the bottom of the stairs, boxes surrounded the stairway, stacked so high and deep only a narrow path led through. How did Ma stack them so high? Maybe she had help.

I walked ahead four or five feet when something hit me from behind. Falling, I made myself into a ball but boxes fell on me from every direction. The sharp corner of a box jabbed into the middle of my back. I shifted to relieve the pressure.

This ghost was strong.

"Who are you?" I asked.

No response.

"You don't belong here. You need to go."

Nothing.

Levering myself up, I stared at the tumbled boxes and into dark corners. On the right, a clothesline ran between two metal posts. Dozens of dresses, blouses, and slacks hung from the line, some still in shivering dry cleaner bags. Watching the remaining hall of boxes, I picked my way forward, afraid they'd topple on me again.

Around the corner at the end of the boxes, I stopped, my mouth hanging open. Along the side wall of the house, an enormous mound of stuff piled up almost to the height of two small, high rectangular windows. It's like Ma just threw stuff on the pile.

As I focused on that, I walked into a spider web strand. Batting at the web, my foot hit something, and my momentum carried me down again. I put my hands out to break my fall and tumbled, scraping my ribs on a big, blue plastic box sitting in the middle of the path.

It had not been there a few moments before.

A slow burn started in my belly. Scrambling up, I kicked the box out of the way. "Alright, that's it. This stops now," I said, fighting to keep my emotions in check. Ghosts used human emotional energy. I took a deep breath. "You aren't welcome here. You're dead and you need to move on. You cannot stay here any longer."

Movement on my head made me swipe with my free hand then shake my head like a dog. Ick, ick, ick. I may have been calm earlier with a can of bug spray in my hand but I still had a deep dread of crawling things, particularly when they crawled all over me. Lots of them.

Yeah, I ran. Screaming like a banshee. Up the basement stairs and out the side door. Dancing around in the yard, slapping at my hair and clothes.

Bet it was quite a show for the neighbors.

Jim and Nora followed me. "What's wrong?" Jim asked, his eyes scanning the yard.

"Spiders," I shrieked. "Get them off. Get. Them. Off. Me."

They both looked, turning me around.

"There aren't any on you," said Nora.

I pulled in a ragged breath. It was only my imagination, but I shuddered at the lingering sensation of millions of tiny, segmented legs swarming over my head and arms.

Why couldn't this be easier?

"What happened?" asked Jim.

"I was in the basement. It felt like a whole nest of spiders fell on me."

"I am not going down there," Nora declared.

Jim grinned. "They're gone now. You probably just

walked into a web. What were you doing? I said I'd check there later."

I shrugged, thinking fast. "I heard something and thought it was mice."

Nora made a face. "Ugh. I'm not setting one foot down there."

"Well, we better get back to work," Jim said. "Plenty left to do."

My skin still crawled. "If you don't mind, I think I'll stay out here for a while."

Jim laughed. "You two are pathetic."

He and Nora went back in the house.

I ripped my ponytail holder out, smoothed my hair with shaking hands, and retied it. Great. I'd hoped to deal with whatever was in the basement before it went past the prank stage, without Jim and Nora finding out. But whatever or whoever it was, it was strong and my gut wouldn't relax.

AFTER I CHILLED OUT, WE MADE ONE MORE TRIP TO THE dump. The house began to smell better, though that may have been because Nora sprayed air freshener everywhere.

The ghost was quiet. I suspected it had expended all its energy earlier.

"A-ha."

In the living room, Jim held a file-sized box. "Important papers, I think."

On the coffee table, I slid Ma's meds and things to the side, clearing a space. He set down the box and I grabbed some papers off the top. Greeting cards, letters, receipts, paid bills. I tossed the pile back in.

He lifted out a big envelope tucked in one side, pulling a large stapled booklet from it. "This is the deed to the house." He dug deeper. "Looks like bank statements, too. I'll put this in the car with the others to check through at the hotel."

Nora and I looked at Ma's sewing stuff in the dining room. Lots of fabric pieces, trimmings, scissors, pins, etc.

"There must be someone," Nora said, "who would love all this."

"Maybe someone at church?" I asked. "We could talk to Father what's-his-name, see if he knows anyone."

"Good idea." She picked through a pile of old clothes, not looking at me.

I didn't trust this change of attitude but she seemed sincere.

A loud banging started at the side door. We looked at each other before I ran into the kitchen and down the stairs. When I twisted the door handle, it didn't move. Locked. I unlocked it and turned the handle, but the door still wouldn't open. The deadbolt was engaged. I turned it and opened the door.

"Why was it locked?" Jim demanded.

"I don't know. The deadbolt was over." We both looked at the handle.

"How the hell did the deadbolt slide over by itself? Are you playing with me?"

"No. I wouldn't do that."

"Kenna was with me the whole time," Nora said from the top of the stairs.

"Well, a deadbolt doesn't just slide over on its own,"

Jim said, fiddling with the mechanism. "I kinda slammed the door behind me on the way out. Maybe it fell in place." He opened and banged the door shut a couple times, but it didn't work. "Weird," he mumbled to himself.

It seemed the basement ghost had energy for one more trick.

"Oh, puh-leez," Nora drawled. "This house is old and Ma neglected it. It's no surprise things are falling apart."

"Yeah, but—"

"And you're spending time we don't have on something that doesn't matter."

"Maybe, but—"

"Oh, give it up, Jim." Nora planted hands on hips. "It's a waste of time. Or," she glared at him, "are you doing this on purpose?"

The old Nora was back.

I saw a muscle in Jim's jaw leap but then he cleared all emotion from his face. He'd learned control in the Army. He took a step up. "Doing what on purpose?" he asked.

"Sabotaging this clean up." Nora turned back into the kitchen.

Jim eased past me on the stairs and I followed him. This was getting interesting. When we got to the top, Nora leaned against the far counter, arms crossed. "If y'all don't want to do this clean up—"

"Hey," I said. "Don't drag me into this."

"Honey," she drawled but her eyes didn't waver from Jim's. "You're already in this up to your eyeballs so hitch up your big girl pants." She paused. "Let me know now if you don't want to do this and I'll call up the professionals.

We won't get as much for the house but this may be one of those times it's worth taking a loss."

She was trying to weasel her way out of cleaning. As expected. But there was no guarantee selling the house would cover all the bills *and* the cost of professional cleaners. Nora was wealthy and Jim didn't have a family so he had money socked away but I wasn't willing to use up my own small savings account. Not when we could do it ourselves.

"Maybe you can afford it," I said, "but I can't."

Jim stood still, watching Nora. Neither said a word. I couldn't breathe. It felt like the walls were closing in on me. "This is nuts," I said, shaking my head. "*You* are nuts. I've got to get out of here." I turned around.

"That's right," Nora called after me. "Run away again. And as for you..."

I slammed out of the house, memories of similar scenes from my childhood cycling thorough my brain like a bad movie.

Nothing like gettin' the band back together.

8

Outside, I snagged the half-empty bag of candy bars from the cooler and ate one in two bites. At the front sidewalk, I looked back. Nora's shrill voice continued on and on inside. "That's it," I muttered, heading up the street and eating another candy bar. At the end, I turned left, toward downtown and the metropolis of Hurlbutt.

After a block, I calmed down enough to notice them. Ghosts. In many of the houses along the street. "What the —" A weight pressed down on me, my body heavy. Drained. I locked my knees to keep from falling. Two ghosts hovered beside me with more closing in. I didn't feel any malicious intent but a deep hunger. For recognition. For energy. They'd suck me dry if I let them.

Panicking, I closed my eyes, imagining my body as a closed container surrounded by pure, white light. I felt shadows gathering around me. "Go," I whispered. "Go away. You aren't wanted here." Repeated it, over and over.

When I felt a slight easing of the energy drain, I imagined the light growing stronger, warmer. Repelling the ghosts.

Once they left, I opened my eyes. A woman's face was so close to mine I could see her pores. Startled, I stepped back and would have fallen on my butt except she grabbed my arm.

"Are you okay?" she asked, concern in her voice.

My heart danced the Macarena. "Yes, I'm fine. Thank you." I stepped around her and hurried away, adrenalin pumping. Not good. That kind of energy only lasted so long and then I'd collapse.

Up ahead, I spotted Dad's favorite pub.

A faded sign saying "Mickey's" hung from the sagging porch roof of a peeling tan, two-story house. Neon signs lit up windows on either side of the door.

I checked my shorts pocket and found the twenty dollar bill I like to keep on me for emergencies.

Things were looking up.

My legs felt wobbly as I climbed the porch stairs. Inside it was dim and cool. I wiped sweat from my upper lip. Thank goodness for air conditioning.

A long, wooden bar ran the length of the back wall. Three guys occupied the left end. People sat at two of the scattered tables filling the rest of the space. Altogether, there may have been ten people, most of them men. A few looked up as I entered.

Feeling underdressed in my dirty shorts and t-shirt, I ducked into the Ladies' Room. After washing my hands and face, I pulled my ponytail holder out, stretching it over my wrist like a bracelet. Fluffing and finger-combing my dark hair, I sighed, looking at my reflection. "Too short, too thin, and too pale," I said. But the green on my t-shirt brought out my green eyes, my best feature. "Good enough." The adrenalin was starting to wear off so I popped another candy bar in my mouth. Still chewing, I walked to the bar and picked a stool on the opposite end from the group of guys. They looked like construction workers from their boots and the tape measure hanging off the belt of the closest one. I sank into the red cushion, setting my bag of candy on the bar.

"What can I get you?" The bartender had an impressive handle-bar mustache, something I hadn't seen in years.

Hot and thirsty after my walk, I ordered ice water and, because I needed something with a little kick, a whiskey on the rocks. "Do you serve food?" I asked.

He slid a bowl of peanuts toward me.

"Thanks." It was better than nothing.

While I munched and waited, more people entered, talking and laughing. Someone sat next to me, smelling like he'd bathed in cologne. He bumped me and I ignored him.

"Sorry," said a male voice.

"No problem," I said, not turning or making eye contact, but feeling the stare. I pulled a handful of peanuts from the bowl and ate them one by one.

The bartender brought my order.

"Thank you." I rubbed the peanut salt from my hands and slid the twenty to the back of the counter. As I chugged the water, the guy whispered with his friends.

Not a good sign.

When the bartender brought my change, I left him a tip and shoved the remainder in my pocket.

The guys ordered a pitcher of beer. "Can I buy you a drink?" the guy asked me.

I sighed and looked over. Three guys, barely over the legal age, stared at me. Naming them Larry, Curly, and Moe to myself, I said, "No thanks. I've got what I want here."

"What's with the candy?" asked Moe, the one closest to me, pointing to the bag on the counter.

The bartender set coasters and glasses in front of them.

I finished the last of the water to give me time to think. I wasn't in the mood for where this conversation was heading. Time to shut them down. "Blarney-bait," I said.

They looked confused.

"What's that?" asked the blond one, Curly.

Jumping down from the stool, I flashed them a big 'ol grin. "That's so I know who to avoid." It wasn't a very good joke but the bartender smirked as he brought the pitcher.

Picking up the whiskey, peanuts, and the candy bag, I walked away.

A moment of silence fell over the group, then crowing laughter. "She got you, dude."

I shook my head, steering toward a table in the corner. Never did like having my back to the door. As I passed a table of four elderly men, one raised his glass to me. I returned the gesture. At the corner table, I ate peanuts and swirled the whiskey around the ice cubes.

Two young women in shorts and tank tops entered, sitting between the two sets of guys at the bar. Soon after they ordered, Larry made his move but the women weren't interested. They stared at the construction workers, who were oblivious, arguing baseball. Curly leaned over, saying something I couldn't hear.

A loud clink and then shattering glass.

Curly yelped, jumping off his stool. He wiped at his shirt, while Larry and Moe pointed and laughed. The bartender handed him some napkins.

The old guy at the other table stood up. "Nothing to be scared of, lads. It's just Fergus, the ghost, wanting his nightly beer."

Then, I felt it. I'd been so wrapped up in the drama, I'd missed it. An extra person stood behind the bar. One not altogether alive. And "Fergus" was a she. The ghost wore a low-cut red blouse showing a lot of breast. A former barmaid, maybe?

"This town is full of ghosts," continued the old guy. He sat down, his friends nodding their heads and slapping him on the back.

One of his companions cackled, "You tell 'em, Brian."

Curly blotted his shirt with napkins as the bartender cleaned up the spilled drink and glass shards. Hands on her hips, the ghost watched the activity with satisfaction. Then she looked straight at me, nodded, and disappeared.

Huh.

Now, I needed the drink. I learned from Dad, at the tender age of sixteen, the proper way to sip whiskey. True to his Irish heritage, my father enjoyed "a wee little nip" or several, depending on the occasion. But he didn't abuse it in public and made sure we kids learned at home and not out binging with our friends.

When sipping whiskey, you don't want to taste the

alcohol with your whole tongue. That ruins it. Avoiding the tip, you let the whiskey roll to the back of the tongue and feel the warmth as it goes down your throat. This had more of a woody bite at the end than I preferred, but it hit the spot.

A group of young women entered the pub. A ghost followed them in, looking tired and worn. It seemed attached to one of the women in particular, a pretty redhead.

The Stooges must have known them. They gave their stools to the women and ordered drinks. Larry put his arm around the redhead and she snuggled up to him.

"Hey. Hey you. Leave her alone!" The raggedy ghost hauled back to take a swipe at Larry.

The ghost barmaid materialized next to him, grabbed his collar, marched him to the front door and tossed him through it. Apparently this was her place and she kept things from getting out of hand.

I sipped my whiskey, amused by the show in front of me.

"You're pulling our legs," said an elderly man at the other table.

"It's the God's honest truth," said the one who raised his glass to me earlier. "Declan said they're all over town now."

"That what's been knocking garbage cans over?" said a third one with glasses.

"Eh, it's probably the damn kids again," said the first guy.

A fourth man, smaller than the others, with a full head of snowy white hair, leaned forward. "But why are there so many ghosts?"

"All I know," Brian said, "is he's been seeing them worse than when we were kids."

There was no getting away from ghosts today. I took another sip. An interesting bit of information, confirming what I'd observed since arriving in town. It was also the main reason I disliked small towns. Your business was not your own.

What was going on here? In a flash, several things fit together in my mind. It had been so long since I worked with ghosts, I'd forgotten basic things like daily protections. Sure, I wore necklaces with grounding and protective properties but for sentimental reasons now. I'd gotten out of the habit of meditation and closing myself off to energy-sucking ghosts. My tiredness and need for caffeine should have clued me in but with Ma's death, funeral and the house, I'd missed it.

I finished my drink. Enough spirits, ethereal or alcoholic, for today. Grabbing my candy bars, I left, checking my cell phone as I walked. Nora had tried to call but left no message. Good. I didn't want to talk to her yet anyway. I chose a different way to get back to the house.

Crossing the street, I felt watched. From the corner of my eyes, I checked out the houses on either side of the street, but didn't see anything unusual. I glanced behind me. A tomcat sat in the middle of the sidewalk, washing his paw. I continued on. After three more houses, I looked back. The same cat sat about six feet away.

Oh no.

A Bicolor Domestic Short Hair, he was white with small black patches on his head and tail, though the white was dingy with dirt. He was also skinny, had a scab above his eye, and a chewed ear. A fighter, this one.

"Go on," I said in a stern voice. "I don't have time for this now. Go back home."

He ignored me.

I walked. He followed.

Tuning into his thoughts, I noted a feeling of interest and curiosity, but that was it. I tried to chase him away, but as soon as I turned around, he trailed after me again.

Nearing Ma's house, the woman across the street waved. What was her name? Georgia? No. Gloria. I held up my open hand, but didn't stop. Half way up the driveway, Nora and Jim's voices drifted from the backyard and I followed them.

They sat on the lawn chairs, talking as if nothing had happened earlier.

"Hi, Ma," I said, walking toward them. "I'm home." I couldn't help it.

"Think you're funny?" Nora snarled. "Where were you?"

I sat in the empty chair. "Awww. You do care. What's up?"

"What do you mean, what's up? Why didn't you answer my call?"

I wasn't interested in starting a fight, so I shrugged. "Went for a walk and stopped at Mickey's. I couldn't hear the phone ringing."

Her eyes bugged out. "You were at a bar? Oh, my God. You've been drinking?"

I smiled, to show her I didn't care about her little interrogation. "I had one drink and a glass of ice water. What's it matter to you?"

Jim snorted. I thought Nora would blow, but she didn't. I offered them the candy bag and Jim took one. I guess things were back to normal again. At least until the next catastrophe.

Jim looked beyond me. "Who's your friend?"

The tomcat sat a short distance away, washing his paw again. I sighed. "He followed me."

Jim raised his eyebrow. "That still happens?"

"Every once in a while." When I was a kid, strays used to follow me home but Ma never let me keep them. Even then animals knew they could trust me. "These days, I usually find homes for them through work, but this guy is on his own."

"He looks like he can take care of himself."

I agreed.

We went back to work and by the end of the day, Jim and I were hot, tired, and nasty-smelling. Nora, on the other hand, hadn't gotten a single spot on her fancy clothes, so neither Jim nor I won our bet. I don't know how she did it, since I wanted to burn my own clothes.

THE NEXT DAY, WE HAD ANOTHER APPOINTMENT WITH THE lawyer to sign papers and didn't get to the house until late morning.

Before starting work, I went into the back yard. Sun filtered through the maple trees and cicadas sang. Children in the neighboring yards laughed and played.

I called out, in my mind, to my parents, hoping they'd help me with the ghost in the basement. I waited awhile, but they didn't answer my call. Still vacationing.

To say I was nervous was an understatement. With a couple exceptions, the ghosts I'd noticed around town were mostly just leftover psychic energy but this ghost in the basement wasn't messing around. As much as I wanted to, I couldn't ignore it. It didn't want us here and would cause escalating problems as we continued to work on the house.

I hadn't tangled with a strong ghost in years, so I procrastinated by cleaning. The entire time, though, my mind teased apart the problem. Preparation was important if I had to face the ghost but I didn't have any supplies and didn't expect to find a metaphysical store in the area. At the very least I needed bundles of whole leaf sage. When set on fire then blown out, sage creates a smoke that cleanses a person, object, or space of unwanted spiritual energy. But that was after the ghost was sent on and how could I do it without Jim and Nora knowing?

I'd figure it out later.

When we ran low on cleaning supplies half way through the afternoon, I volunteered to go to Hanley's Market. The selection of herbs was limited. The only dried sage was in small containers but it at least contained pieces of the dried leaf. It wasn't ideal but would have to do. Then I found a long-handled barbecue lighter. The last thing needed was something heatproof to burn the sage in, but there should be a bowl or something at the house.

Throwing garbage bags into the cart, I noticed movement out of the corner of my eye. About ten feet down the aisle, an elderly man stared at the shelves of toilet paper, twitching and mumbling.

That wasn't the strangest part, though.

Ghosts surrounded him. Two and three deep. I'd

never seen anything quite like it. And the poor man knew they were there. He grabbed a package off the shelf, threw it in his cart, and pushed off like monsters chased him.

What was happening in this town?

My heart went out to the old guy. How awful. I should help him. But it gave me a squirmy feeling just thinking about telling someone I could see ghosts. On the other hand, what kind of person leaves an elderly man alone and scared, doing nothing to help? I took a deep breath, trying to calm the panicky feeling rising up my throat.

I hurried through the rest of my list, catching a glimpse of him now and then. As I finished at the check-out, he approached the line. Turning quickly, I left the store and crossed the parking lot. After throwing the bags in my car and shutting the door, I forced myself to calm down. The man needed help. It was the right thing to do.

I returned to the store on shaky legs.

9

———

The ghosts crowded close, whispering.

Declan dropped a box of tea in his cart. A few more things and he'd be done. Then the walk home. His breath came in little gasps.

Stupid not to wait for Brian but he resented his dependence on his older brother.

Somehow, he got through the checkout without alarming the cashier, though she did look concerned. He left his cart at the corral, walked two steps away and stopped. He shook his head and returned, pulling his one bag of purchases from the cart.

"S-sir?"

Declan jumped.

"I'm so sorry," said a husky, female voice.

He looked over and then down at the young, dark-haired woman beside him. A tiny little thing, reminding him of Granny's tales of the fae.

"I—hello, my name is Kenna and—" she leaned in,

lowering her voice. "I see you've got a ghost problem. I can help."

He stared at her, not sure he had heard correctly. "Pardon me?"

"I can help you with your ghost problem."

"You can see them?"

"Yes."

"I feel them, hear them." He felt dizzy and clutched her arm. "They're so close, I can hardly breathe."

A vehicle roared to a stop in front of them. "Hey. Leave him alone."

Always the big brother. "Brian, it's alright. She's helping me."

"Right. Thanks." Brian said to the young woman. "I can take care of things from here." He opened the truck door, finally looking at Declan. "Why didn't you wait? I told you I'd do your shopping."

"I wanted to do it myself." He swung the bag onto the seat, grabbed the door, and levered himself into the truck.

"Wait." The woman stepped nearer. "I can see the ghosts around him, teach him how to make them leave him alone."

Brian crossed his arms over his barrel chest. "For how much?"

She shook her head. "For nothing."

Brian was going to be stubborn again. Well, not this time. "Please, Brian?" He loathed pleading almost as much as being dependent but enough was enough. "I can't stand it anymore."

Brian looked back and forth between them. "Fine, but can we get out of the way here?"

Shoppers stared at them. "Yes. Please."

The young woman followed Brian's truck and they parked around the corner. It was cooler in the shadow of the building. She got out of her car and stood next to the open truck window but wasn't tall enough to see in well. She climbed on the running board and smiled, but then it faded.

"Wow," she said. "Ghosts are crowded around you like a movie star at a premier."

He didn't know what to say.

"I'm Kenna Tierney, by the way."

"I'm Declan Quinn and this is my brother, Brian. Don't mind him. He watches out for me. A little forcefully, perhaps." It was so tiring, this small talk.

"Pleased to meet you, Declan." She ducked and waved. "Hi, Brian. I think I saw you last night at Mickey's."

"I remember."

"Brian." It came out sharper than he intended.

Brian scowled. "Oh, alright. Nice to meet you. So, what can you do for him?"

"I've been able to see and speak to ghosts since I was a kid. I've learned how to make them leave me alone and I can teach Declan how to do it, too."

"You can?" Her words gave him hope.

"Tierney, eh?" Brian said, rubbing his chin. "Big Jim Tierney would have been your father?"

Jim Tierney had worked with him and Brian at the shirt factory years ago. A tall, muscular man fond of telling off-color jokes in a thunderous voice. Everybody had known Jim Tierney.

"Yes."

"Thought so. Er, sorry about your mother."

"Thank you," she murmured.

Of course. How could he have forgotten? "I would have been at her funeral," he said. "Except for all these ghosts."

"Yeah," said Brian. "And I only go to church when my wife drags me there by my nose hairs."

"I understand," Kenna said to him, ignoring Brian.

"You don't live here, do you?" Brian continued, oblivious, as usual. "I would've recognized you if you did."

She frowned and glanced over. "No, I live in Syracuse."

Brian nodded. "You can go ahead, now."

The small woman pressed her lips together and returned her gaze to his. "You can tell ghosts to leave you alone, but you really have to mean it." Her eyes were a beautiful jade green.

He sighed. "I have, but they keep coming back."

"You're afraid of them, aren't you?"

Of course he was.

"You try not to see—I mean, hear them?"

He nodded.

"Have you talked to anyone about this?"

"No." What a thought. "I never told anyone but Brian. He's the only one I trusted."

She glared at Brian a moment then refocused on him, smoothing her expression. "How long have you felt them around you?"

"I was real young at first. Back then it scared me so bad, I would pray for God to make them go away. After a while, they did. For years." He shrugged. "But a few months ago, they came back, so much worse this time. It's like I'm in a crowded room, even when I'm by myself. Can you help me?"

"I'll see what I can do." She hesitated. "First, you need to ground yourself. Close your eyes."

He didn't know what grounding himself meant, but he did as she asked.

"Imagine your feet sinking down into the ground." Her voice reminded him of Lauren Bacall.

Brian snorted.

She frowned. "Whether you believe or not, this'll help your brother."

"Okay, okay," Brian said, palms out. "I'll be quiet."

Kenna touched his shoulder. "Please, let's try again."

He fidgeted in his seat then leaned back, closing his eyes again.

"Good. Take a deep breath and let it all out."

He could listen to her voice all day long.

"Another deep breath now. In...and out. Feel your legs sink down into the Earth. It feels warm and safe. Allow it to take your weight, to support you. Accept the energy of the Earth, let it flow up your legs and throughout your body. Feel the strength."

He visualized the Earth's energy as a stream of electricity around his body.

"Now," she said, "to protect yourself, you need to get a little space between you and the ghosts. Imagine light surrounding your whole body."

Brian muttered, "For crying out loud. What a bunch of..."

"If you learn this, Declan," she raised her voice, "they won't bother you so much, I promise."

He hoped she was right. "I'll try."

"Good. Above your head, imagine a ball of pure, white light. It begins to move down over the top of your head, making you feel safe, secure. It flows over your shoulders. It's warm, full of love and protection. Over your chest and arms, down your torso and legs to the tips of your feet. The light covers you, keeping you from any harm."

Warmth flowed over his body. He filled his lungs. The weight pressing in on all sides lessened. "It feels as if they've moved out a ways. And they aren't quite as loud, rather muffled, actually."

"You're doing real good, Declan. Now, even when you open your eyes, you'll still feel the protective light around you and the ghosts will keep their distance."

First, he squinted, then popped his eyes open. The spirits weren't gone but had moved a little ways off. "It's a miracle. What a difference. Thank you." Tears threatened. "Thank you so much."

She smiled. "You're welcome but we aren't done yet. You need to be able to tell them to leave, too."

"Finally, we're getting somewhere," Brian said.

Kenna ignored him. "We're going to talk to the ghosts now, okay?"

He frowned. Talking to ghosts seemed sacrilegious, but he desperately needed help and she appeared to know what she was doing. "I understand."

"I know you're scared, but I want you to try to relax. I won't let anything happen to you. Do you feel three ghosts together in a group near you?"

"No, they're all jumbled together."

She was quiet for a moment. "You hear and feel them,

so maybe close your eyes. Sight may confuse your other senses."

He followed her instruction. It was certainly easier to concentrate. "Now what?"

"Kind of push your awareness out away from you. The same as when you visualized the white light except imagine going beyond your body."

So strange. Yet, the idea was appealing. He felt his body, then imagined he pushed out from it, as if walking forward a step. It took him several tries until he did it. Then he took another step. And another. He was doing it! "This is ama—" He ran into something and gasped.

"Declan?"

It was a wall of ghosts. He skittered back, feeling foolish. In the excitement of learning something new, he'd forgotten them. "There's so many. It's hard to separate them." He focused on finding three ghosts together. Then, suddenly, they were there. "Oh. Yes, I found them."

"Good job," she said. "You three. We want to speak to you."

It was so strange. He couldn't explain how, but when he felt the ghost step away from the wall of ghosts, he "saw" a form, in his mind, move toward them. He felt/saw it as a gray, roughly human-shaped figure. Nothing distinguished it from the others.

"Madame," said the figure. "My name is Ambrose Blakeley. May I present my wife, Elma."

It had a British accent.

"I'm Kenna, and this is Declan."

"We were traveling to the home of a dear friend, Jonathon Wood, and seem to have lost our way. Would you be so kind as to direct us? Though, we have misplaced our carriage as well."

After all this time, he heard an actual conversation, not a mishmash of whispers. Did it say, "carriage?" His fear vanished and was replaced by excitement.

Another form approached. "And I was walking along the forest road. But I don't recollect where I was headed."

This one had a British accent as well, though didn't sound as pompous as the first one. They had to be from the early eighteen hundreds when this area was first settled. How wonderful to be talking to someone who had been alive two hundred years ago. The stories they could tell would be—

"Declan?" Kenna asked. "Did you hear what they said?"

He opened his eyes. "Yes, I did."

"Great." She addressed the ghosts again. "I'm sorry to tell you this, but, you all have passed on."

Declan shut his eyes again and concentrated on the energy forms.

"I beg your pardon?" the pompous one said. He seemed to be a spokesman of the group.

"You. Are. Dead." Kenna enunciated each word.

"That is impossible."

"It's true. You died long ago. You've been pestering this poor man for no reason. He didn't know what to do for you."

"Miss?" the other ghost said. "Will we go to Heaven?"

"Yes. Do you see a bright light or a doorway or something? Heaven is beyond it."

"But," Declan interrupted. "What of the historical significance? Can't we talk to them for a while?" The next moment, a feeling of peacefulness flowed over him, different than anything he'd ever experienced. It came from somewhere above and to his left. Drew him. He felt someone glide toward it and he floated behind in a bubble of calm. Of love. As if love were a tangible thing. Felt it envelop him and soothe him. He was home.

"Hey. What's going on?"

Brian sounded agitated. He wondered why but then lost his grip on the thought.

"What did you do to him?"

"I didn't do anything. Declan? Can you hear me?"

He should respond. He wanted to respond but couldn't quite form the words.

"You better do something quick."

"Sir," Kenna said. "You must cross over."

"I refuse to believe," said a man with a foreign accent, "that I have ceased to exist."

Ah, yes, the ghost. Kenna had been speaking to the ghost. But where there had been three ghosts before, now two remained. Where did the other one go?

"You haven't," Kenna said. "You're on a different level of existence. There's more to come but you must walk through the doorway to get there."

"Who are you, dressed like a trollop, to tell me what I should do?"

"Calling me names won't get you out of this situation."

"You must then be a witch."

"Really, now? That's what you're going with? Well, sorry to break it to you, buddy, but I'm not a witch."

Kenna sounded angry. She shouldn't be angry. Couldn't she feel the love?

Brian laughed.

"Look around you," Kenna continued. "Things are very different, aren't they? It's been a long time since you were alive and the world has changed. I know what I'm talking about."

The two ghost forms turned toward each other.

"My dear," a female voice said. "I believe it is time to leave."

The other ghost was a woman. His wife, perhaps.

"Is it?" The pompous ghost asked, in a loving tone of voice.

"Yes, indeed."

The ghost forms went toward the doorway. He was happy for them. They did the right thing. After they passed through, the door shut.

It was as if all the joy in the world had disappeared. Shocked, he opened his eyes. Sunlight stabbed him and he shut them again. Sweat prickled his torso and goose-bumps raced across his arms.

"And that's how you cross ghosts to the other side," Kenna said. She sounded pleased with herself.

"About time," grumbled Brian. "What happened to him? Are all the ghosts gone now?"

Declan squinted. He couldn't see well, but grabbed for where he thought Kenna's arm would be. "Is that," he pushed through trembling lips, "what it's like in Heaven?"

"I don't know if it's Heaven but it's powerful."

"Yes."

"Will somebody talk to me?"

Brian hated to be left out of conversations.

"I'm sorry," Kenna said. "What did you say?"

"What happened? Is he going to be okay?"

"Of course he's okay. When the ghosts were ready," Kenna explained, "the door to the Other Side opened. It's hard to describe but it's, well..."

One word came to Declan's mind. "It was glorious."

Kenna smiled at him.

"But the ghosts are gone?" Brian asked.

"Some are," Kenna said. "Declan has more, but they're keeping their distance and now he knows what to do." She touched his shoulder. "Are you alright?"

Despite feeling light-headed, he smiled. "Yes."

"You have to eat after this type of thing. Ghosts drain you. With so many around, I'm surprised you aren't exhausted all the time."

"He is," Brian said. "He hasn't been himself the last few months."

Declan shrugged. "I thought I was just getting old. You mean it could be these ghosts?"

She nodded. "Oh, yes. Go home, eat a big meal, and get some rest. Be firm with them, like I showed you. Be careful. Don't let the door pull you in. And not all will want to cross over. Encourage them to, but if they resist, at least tell them to go away and leave you alone. And before you go to bed, ground yourself and imagine the protective white light. Do it every morning and night."

Brian pointed at her. "Why don't you come and show him?"

Despite Brian railroading her, she tried to beg off. He almost felt sorry for her but he needed her. He just didn't feel up to doing all this himself. What if he drifted off again?

They settled on her visiting Declan's home later that evening.

10

One of my mother's favorite sayings came to mind: "No good deed goes unpunished."

Soon after I got back from the store, Jim grabbed the garbage bags and went to the basement. I wasn't prepared to deal with the ghost yet but grabbed two cereal bars. Already low on fuel from helping Declan, I needed more for the inevitable confrontation. I shoved most of one bar in my mouth when Nora and I heard a series of heavy thuds.

Something fell down the kitchen stairs.

I bolted, Nora following close behind.

Jim was on his hands and knees on the floor of the basement shaking his head. I took the remaining stairs two at a time.

He glanced my way. "Why'd you push me?"

"I didn't push you," I said around my mouthful of food.

We helped him up and over to the stairs. He sat and rubbed a shoulder, then a hip. "But—"

"You know I wouldn't push you," I said.

"Well someone sure as hell did." He stood, *bonking* his head on the ductwork hanging from the ceiling. "Damn it." He was a big guy and the ceiling wasn't high.

"I was upstairs. Right, Nora?"

Nora was on the landing, not willing to come any further. She shrugged. "I suppose."

I ground my teeth together. "I was and you know it. I'd never push Jim down the stairs." I leaned over, looking him in the eye. "But I know what did."

"Oh, yeah?" he said.

"A ghost."

"Lord, help me," Nora spit out. "I thought you were over that nonsense years ago."

Jim rose, remembering to duck before hitting the ductwork. "Ghosts? Bullshit." As he spoke, a pile of boxes toppled on him and he went down again. It took plenty of energy for a ghost to use that much force. Of course, we'd been feeding it a lot of emotional energy lately.

Nora stomped up the stairs and out the side door.

Jim crouched, eyes darting, ready for a fight.

"Stop, please." I said. "You had a pretty good knock on the head and I want to look at it in better light. Let's go upstairs, okay?"

He grunted and began backing up the stairs, watchful until we reached the top. I directed him out of the house and into the back yard. Nora was already there, pacing. He sat in a lawn chair, swearing as his hip made contact.

I examined his scalp through his bristly hair. "There's no blood, you're good." I stared at the house, hating to go back in. Finally, I said, "Stay out here for a while. I have work to do and I don't need you two antagonizing the...situation."

"I'll go where I darn well please," Nora said to my back.

She didn't follow me in, though.

Before facing the ghost, I devoured another cereal bar and guzzled water. But not too much. Didn't want to have to pee at a crucial moment. Rooting around in the cupboards, I discovered a heavy glass ashtray and emptied one bottle of sage into it, then put it and the lighter at the top of the basement stairs.

I grounded myself and did the white-light visualization, feeling its protection like a big, warm robe on a snowy morning. But it had been so long since I had a regular practice it felt strange. And here I was doing it twice in an hour. When I felt calmer, I said, "Dad? Ma? I could use your help." I waited, listening.

Silence.

I squared my shoulders. "In can do this."

The ghost had a lot more tricks ready, I was sure, but it didn't shove me. In fact, the basement felt empty. Had it gone? My experience told me the opposite.

I shoved the fallen boxes away from the stairs. For a second, a faint presence developed near the front of the house, then was gone in a heartbeat. "Now you're playing games with me." Suddenly, clothes flew off the clothesline to my right. I slapped them away. Shoe boxes, belts, and other things shot at me from all directions. I ducked.

"Who are you?" I asked. "Why are you here in this house? Show yourself now."

An old man appeared beside the furnace, stomping his feet, his hands clenched in fists. "Get out. Get out. Get out. This is my house." He flapped his arms, shooing me away.

"Nope," I said, standing. "You're the one who has to go."

He disappeared.

At a popping sound near the hot water tank, I turned. Water spurt from the pipe connections, and I scampered out of range.

The ghost expected me to run.

"Not this time, buddy," I murmured.

More clothes darted from the line, sailed through the water spray, and slapped into me. I peeled them off. Something cold slithered over my foot and I flinched but it was water from the tank.

"What the hell?" Jim stood on the stairs.

"I told you I've got this," I called over the noise of splashing water and things flying through the air.

"I see that," he said, surveying the scene, hands on hips. "But I'm no quitter."

I could see the wheels turning in his brain. "Hold on there, G.I. Jim. This is my battlefield."

"You need help. I'm here."

"So you believe me, now?"

"I'm gathering Intel."

A clay pot shot at his head and he ducked. It smashed on the stairs. He'd either be a bigger target than me or harder to drop. Either way, he could take care of himself. Maybe with the two of us, the ghost would split its energy and tire easier.

I turned to see a chair shoot toward me. Too fast. I screwed my eyes shut and crouched, covering my head. Water splashed on me. I peeked. The rusted metal kitchen chair lay at my feet. I stared at it. Then, every-thing in the air dropped to the floor, splashing us from every direction.

"What the—" Jim said.

"Are you alright, darlin'?" Dad's rich baritone flooded me with relief. Behind him, Ma glared at the condition of the basement.

It was a mess.

"Too close," I said. Dad and Ma's presence must have scared the ghost. It wouldn't last long, though.

"No shit." Jim muttered, moving to the water heater. It had stopped spewing water and he played with the valves. "Must be empty."

The old man ghost didn't reappear, but my gut flip-flopped. I stood. "Can you help me with the ghost?" I whispered to Dad.

"Of course," he said, next to my ear. "But he's a feisty one. You need help."

"Yeah, that's why I'm asking you."

"No. You need to bring in the big guys."

"I don't know—" But I did know. He meant my spirit guide and other helpers. And Angels. "I can't...I mean...I don't do that anymore."

"From everything you've told me, it's never too late, my dear."

Maybe. Years ago, I had a good relationship with my guide, the once-human soul assigned at my birth to watch over me. Then, I abandoned him and all the rest at the same time I refused to acknowledge ghosts.

Lights flickered. Sopping clothing lifted from the floor and whirled like dervishes, spraying us with dirty water. The old man ghost was at it again. One of Dad's old shirts flew at my face as I was hit on the back of the head with a wet thunk. I peeled the shirt off me, looking backward. Rotted brownish-yellow insulation puddled at my feet. "Dad," I hissed. "Can you distract him?"

"Workin' on it."

"Aren't you the expert on this ghost stuff?" Jim called. "Can't you do something?"

"I am," I answered, "but it's a little hard to concentrate here."

Sparks shot out of the ceiling near the stairs and a black electrical cord with exposed wires dropped toward the flooded floor.

Jim bounded over, grabbing it before it fell into the water. He pushed it up over the ductwork.

Now or never. Standing very still, I closed my eyes and took deep, calming breaths.

"Look out," Jim shouted.

Losing focus, I crouched and covered my head again.

Another splash.

"Gotcha," rumbled Dad.

A metal watering can lay on its side next to me. I don't know what Dad did, but he kept the can from hitting me. "Thanks." My heart pounded but I tried again. Deep breaths. I sent my thoughts out, asking my guide for help.

And heard something odd. "Jim, did you hear a dog bark?"

He was turned away from me now and had found an old metal baseball bat. He hit another clay pot and it exploded into pieces. "Nope." He swung at a pair of garden clippers.

Since Dad was protecting me, the ghost had focused on Jim. This had to stop.

I heard another bark. It sounded like it originated inside my head. "I'm so out of practice." This was psychic hearing. Since I'd asked for help, this probably had to do with the ghost. I hoped, anyway. Interpretation was always tricky.

In a flash, the electrical cord Jim had tucked onto the ductwork slithered out and wrapped around his neck. He pushed his finger under it before it pulled tight but I had to act fast.

"Hey, old man," I screeched. "Someone you know's waiting for you on the Other Side."

The ghost appeared, yanking back on the cord and Jim choked.

"If it's any of my family," the ghost shouted, his face a contorted, angry mask. "They can go to hell."

Dad reached for the ghost but it disappeared before he got to it.

The cord around Jim's neck went slack. He ripped it off, holding it like a poisonous snake.

"My poor baby," Ma cried.

Dad looked mad enough to kill.

A name popped into my head. "It's Fluffy," I yelled.

No response.

Now I knew what to say. "Fluffy's waiting for you. Don't you want to see her?"

Silence.

I licked my lips then gagged, forgetting I'd been splashed by nasty water. "You can't stay here anymore. We'll hound you until you leave. Do you really want to keep roaming? You'll have to start over, be the new kid on the block. Wouldn't you rather see Fluffy?"

The ghost appeared near the stairs, his face screwed up in disgust. "You had better not be lying to me, missy."

Ma made an angry noise and flew toward the ghost but Dad caught her and held her.

"I'm not," I said, feeling the door to the Other Side opening, steeling myself against its hypnotic pull. A dog barked and not only in my head. "See? I didn't lie to you."

The ghost's hate-filled expression changed to surprise, then wonder. He moved nearer the door. A white Cockapoo paced excitedly at the door's threshold. The ghost rushed at it. The dog launched itself into the old man's arms. His expression changed to sheer happiness, laughing as the dog licked his face.

The feeling of love was infectious but my initial smile faltered.

"What happened? Who's Fluffy?" Jim asked. He couldn't see or hear the reunion going on.

"The spirit of the ghost's dog," I said. "Must be the only thing he ever loved in his miserable life."

"Dogs have spirits?"

"Of course. All animals do."

Jim grunted.

The door closed and emptiness filled me. After a moment, I whispered, "Thank you," to my parents.

"You're welcome, my Kenna," said Dad. Then he and Ma left.

I sighed, remembering I'd wanted to discuss the house with Ma.

"Is it gone?" asked Jim.

I nodded. "Yeah."

We stared at the mess in silence. It was like a hurricane had ripped through the basement. My gut spasmed. "Wait."

Jim froze.

I looked toward the front of the house. "Who are you?" I asked.

An area near the breaker box seemed hazy until it coalesced into a figure of a young man with dark hair and wire-rimmed glasses. The top half of him, anyway. "Hello, Miss Kenna."

Relief flooded through me. "Henry, where've you been?"

He looked the same as I remembered, still dressed in a white button-down shirt with suspenders. "The other spirit asked for sanctuary. Once I gave him permission, he bound me, took my energy, and kept me from calling out to you." He smiled. "Thank you for releasing me."

I smiled. "You're very welcome."

"Who's Henry?" asked Jim.

"He's a ghost. But a good one. He's been in this house for over a hundred years. He said the other ghost bound him and drained his energy. No wonder it was strong."

Jim hesitated. "Aren't you going to get rid of this one, too?" His tone was almost mocking.

"Absolutely not. Henry doesn't cause problems. In fact, he protected me when I was younger. I won't make him go unless he wants to. Do you want to cross over, Henry?"

"No, thank you, Miss Kenna."

"There. He said 'no, thank you.'"

"Well," said Jim. "As long as he's polite about it."

"I must leave for a while, Miss. I'm very tired." Henry's figure faded as he waved to me.

"'Bye, Henry." I waved back. "He's gone now to build his energy back up."

"What is he, your mascot?"

At the top of the stairs, the outer door flew open, hitting the wall behind it. Nora peeked over the railing. "The door was stuck again and I couldn't get in. Oh. My. *Gawd*. What happened?"

Jim and I looked at each other. He shrugged. "Well, you start hauling stuff out on the lawn," he said. "I'll shut off the water and see if there's a pump in this mess."

"I'll get right on it," I said. "After I burn sage."

I wasn't sure if Jim believed in ghosts yet, despite what he just saw. He kept his thoughts to himself while we worked.

Nora didn't believe my explanation, but couldn't say much because Jim backed me up. Sort of. He agreed the hot water tank blew but shrugged at the rest. He said he didn't understand it but "all hell broke loose." She was furious with the damage to the basement. I wasn't happy about it myself but she wouldn't leave it alone until Jim told her to knock it off.

He found a sump pump and got it started. We called it quits for the day, went back to the hotel to shower, and then out to eat. I was starving and ignored Nora's whining as I planned how to help Declan with his ghosts.

Later, I dropped Nora and Jim at the hotel with an excuse about meeting up with old friends.

By the time I bought more snacks and drove out of

the city of Bartlett, the sun was low on the horizon and I slipped on sunglasses against the glare.

It was hard not to compare Bartlett with its traffic, plenty of pedestrians, a busy Main Street, and sprawling commercial district with Hurlbutt. It felt alive and my sad little hometown boasted fewer cars and pedestrians, dirt in the gutters, and weeds growing out of cracks in the pavement. In front of an empty storefront on Main Street, teenagers passed a cigarette back and forth. Right out in the open. What next, pot?

I turned left and crossed the railroad tracks, officially entering my side of town. The Irish have always lived on the south side of Main Street, within convenient distance to the factories and other heavy business employing most of them. All closed now. With the train tracks paralleling Main Street to the south, you could say we also lived on the wrong side of the tracks.

Yeah, I never heard that one growing up.

While gawking at the changes to the buildings, I drove into a monster-sized pothole. Hoping it didn't damage my car, I slowed to a crawl, watching the street till I stopped at Declan's house. It was narrow but deep, and pretty big for an elderly man. It was also one of the best looking in the area with a recent coat of white paint on its clapboard siding.

After parking at the curb, it hit me. Heaven above, what was I doing? Last week I was at home, caring for animals, a job I loved. Maybe I didn't have many friends or much of a social life, but I was doing something important. When I looked into their eyes, the animals trusted me, and I knew, just knew, I belonged there. Not chasing ghosts in Hurlbutt.

Then again, there was a little matter of a promise made to Declan. But what if I messed up? What if I made things worse for the poor man?

I leaned my forehead on the steering wheel. "Oh God," I whispered. "Please, please, please, let me do this right and please let us finish the house and sell it so I can get back where I belong." A lapsed Catholic I may be, but saying the words comforted me.

Sitting back and closing my eyes, I breathed deep to compose myself, imagining light surrounding me like a shield.

When I knocked on his door, Declan and his entourage of ghosts answered. "Hello, Miss Tierney. Come in." He sounded out of breath.

"Kenna, please," I responded but my attention was elsewhere.

Inside, his house was like a rave. Ghosts sat on furniture, stood and stared, walked from room to room, waving at us, trying to get our attention. It felt claustrophobic. Uncomfortably warm, too, with fans only blowing the hot air around.

"Can I get you something to drink?" Deep circles traced underneath Declan's bloodshot eyes.

I hoisted a water bottle I'd brought with me. "I'm good, thanks."

He tried to smile, but looked uneasy. "I'm not sure how this works."

The sheer number of ghosts hanging around was distracting. "Declan, what does the house feel like to you?"

He sighed, hugging himself, as if trying not to touch anything. "Full."

"I hope you had a big dinner," I said, attempting to sound cheerful. "Because we've got a lot to do but let's sit down and talk first." This was going to be a long evening.

He showed me to his living room which contained floor to ceiling bookcases, chock full of books.

"I don't get out much," Declan said. "I prefer to read. Always have."

He seemed embarrassed, so I said, "It's a nice collection. I bet you never get bored."

A faint smile appeared on his weary-looking face. "That I don't. Please, sit."

The furniture had seen better days, but looked comfortable. He sat in a recliner facing a small TV set on a metal rolling stand. A couch was perpendicular to the chair and I chose the end closest to him.

The room already contained several ghosts, and more followed us in. How was he still upright and coherent?

"Many people," I said, "believe in wearing amulets and holy items to protect them from ghosts and other entities invading their space." I pulled my necklaces out from the neck of my t-shirt. "This," I held up a tiny cross on a thin gold chain, "was a gift from a dear family friend for my first communion." I smiled, remembering "Uncle" Leo, a bear of a man who had always been kind to me. I let go of the crucifix and held up a man's ring threaded on a stainless steel chain. "And this was my father's. It has an onyx stone, good for grounding and a defense against energy drain. The metals in the ring and chains also have protective qualities. Do you have anything you could use?"

Declan thought for a moment. "Somewhere, I have my mother's rosary."

"Perfect. Anything else holding religious significance for you will help, too. Things like medals, a bible, holy water, or praying."

He nodded, seeming to absorb the information.

"Learning to clear your mind and stay calm under pressure will help. Lots of people meditate, but it doesn't always work for me. Sometimes, I do what I showed you earlier, be still and visualize a warm, bright light to wall off outside forces."

"I tried to after I got home, but the ghosts didn't stay away long."

"It's like a muscle," I said. "It'll get easier the more you practice. And I think this is party central here. We need to clear the whole house for it to be effective for any length of time."

Declan found his mother's rosary and seemed to gain confidence by its presence.

Once we grounded, visualized, and were calm, we got to work.

First, we focused on the ghosts surrounding Declan himself. A motherly ghost felt it was her duty to take care of him. We could use her to our advantage. There were others, including a factory worker, a flower shop girl, and an elderly female who said she was in love with Declan. Of course it mortified him.

Lover Girl and Mother bickered back and forth so bad they gave me a headache. "You need to tell your lady friend to leave," I said.

His face flushed and he hesitated, his Adam's apple jumping up and down.

Holding back a laugh, I said, "You can do this. You don't want her to stick around, right?"

His eyes widened. "No. Not at all."

"Tell her she has to go. You don't love her. She makes your skin crawl. Whatever it takes."

He had to clear his throat a couple times. "Well, um —" He stopped. "Ah, I—" He cleared his throat again.

I suspected Declan had never married.

"You have to go," he told Lover Girl, almost whispering. "I need the quiet."

"I can be quiet," she said, sauntering toward him. Good thing he couldn't see her. She did a good Jessica Rabbit impression.

"I don't lo—" his voice cracked. "You need to go on to Heaven where you'll see your family, those who truly love you. This is no place to spend eternity." Then, with a little more force, he said, "I want you to go. I don't care for you. Cross over, as they say. Now."

She looked surprised, then angry. The door to the Other Side opened and she left without a word.

Declan felt it. "Thank God," he sighed. But even after the door closed, he faced the doorway.

"Declan," I said sharply, startling him. "Remember what I said about the door? You have to pull yourself away and ignore it?"

He took a deep breath and gave me a thin smile. "Yes. Of course. I'm fine now, thank you."

That was just the beginning. Time to shut this house party down.

11

"Let's see," Miss Tierney said, "how many ghosts you can handle on your own."

Declan was eager to get started. As they went from room to room, she coached him. He told the ghosts they weren't welcome in his home and to leave. A good half the crowd departed, though not through "the doorway to the Other Side," as she called it. They disappeared into thin air. This worried him. "Won't they come back?"

"Maybe," she said. "But this time, you're prepared. Your house will be cleansed so it won't be easy for them to return and I'm teaching you how to keep it that way. Plus, you'll ground yourself every morning and night. If you keep up these protections, you'll be okay."

It sounded reasonable. He hoped it worked.

Next, they focused on stubborn individuals. One woman from the early 1900s didn't want to cross over because she was afraid her abusive husband was waiting for her. Miss Tierney explained how, on the Other Side, he wouldn't be able to hurt her. She still wouldn't leave.

Several other spirits were reluctant as well. In the end, two helpful ghosts took charge. After much persuasion, they all went together.

Miss Tierney did the bulk of this kind of "ghost busting," then he did a few on his own. As they "cleared" each room—he got a kick out of all the new words she taught him—she burned dried sage, getting rid of negative energies. The resulting smoke smelled terrible but it worked.

Halfway through, she insisted they take a break. He was grateful for the rest. He made himself a sandwich and glass of milk and she ate meat sticks and granola bars she brought with her. It didn't seem terribly substantial but she turned down his offer of a sandwich.

Despite the fact the spirits still frightened him, they also fascinated him. He was surprised to discover the process of crossing them was quite educational. He so wished he could see them. They represented every period in Hurlbutt history, each with a different story, reminding him of the town's historical events. As they ate, he told Miss Tierney about the founding of their fair town by Nicholas Hurlbutt III, a story he'd always enjoyed, but she nodded off. The poor girl was exhausted.

Jerking awake, she rubbed her face. "Declan? You mentioned yesterday the ghosts didn't bother you for years, then a few months ago you had this." She indicated his full house. "Do you know what caused you to see the ghosts again? Did you have an accident or lose someone close to you or was there some other kind of change? Those things can cause a person's intuition to open wide."

"I've wondered about it, myself. Last Spring we had a warm-up in March and Brian and I went fishing. Brian was in a bad mood. Stood right up in the row boat and tipped us over."

"Really?"

"I haven't been swimming since I was young. The water was so cold." He gazed out the front window, remembering the bone-chilling cold. With a shiver, he returned his attention back to his delightful guest. "Quite a shock, I can tell you. I caught a chill which developed into pneumonia and kept me down for weeks. Still haven't got all my energy back."

She rubbed her chin. "I'm so sorry to hear that happened to you. Did you hit your head?"

"No."

"Has someone close to you died?"

"No. Not recently. Actually, I was wondering when *you* first started seeing spirits? I can't imagine it was easy with so many of them around. Just one or two scared me near to death as a youngster."

"Well, when I lived here, there weren't as many ghosts." She described a bicycle accident when she was young and seeing a spirit called Henry. "At first, I didn't know I could make ghosts go away by telling them to. After I learned who he was and got used to him, he was comforting to have around. I got the feeling he sort of watched out for me."

"You were lucky, then. Was your family understanding about the ghosts?"

She made a face and her striking green eyes darkened. "No. My father came around, but my older brother and sister still don't believe. My mother thought I made things up to get attention." She gripped her plastic water bottle until it snapped.

His heart went out to her. He understood about family judgment.

"Things got real bad when I was a teenager so I left right after high school."

"What did you do then?"

"Oh, I stayed with a friend, working at a gas station, then I was a waitress. I even worked one summer at the Renaissance Festival in Sterling. I sold food, though I got to know some of the fortune tellers. One was a real psychic and I learned a lot from her." She smiled. "It was a great summer. I dated one of the security guys. He was from Buffalo and when the festival closed up, I moved there with him. It didn't last long, but I stayed and met a great bunch of people who helped me set myself up as a psychic medium."

"Is that what you do now?"

She smiled. "Nope. I ran into some problems so I went to college, moved to Syracuse, and now I'm a veterinary technician."

This young woman was full of surprises. "Growing up, we had a dog or two around. They're so calming."

"By the time I see them, they aren't calm, but I can make them relax." She paused. "I can communicate with them, mind-to-mind, know what they're thinking and feeling. I'm not sure if it's related to being able to talk to ghosts or not." She sighed, shaking her head. "I probably shouldn't have said anything. Please, don't tell anyone."

"You're secret is safe with me."

She looked embarrassed. "Thanks."

Before Declan could ask her more, the kitchen door banged shut. "Hey," Brian called. He walked into the living room where they sat. "Good Lord, what stinks?"

He couldn't keep his nose out of things.

"Sage," Declan explained. "It keeps the ghosts out when we clear a room." He peeked at Miss Tierney for verification.

She nodded.

"So you're getting rid of lots of spooks?" Brian waggled his eyebrows. "I heard there used to be some at the old train depot they made into a restaurant. That's why they shut down, you know. But leave Fergus at Mickey's. I like him."

Miss Tierney sat straighter. "As a matter of fact, there isn't any Fergus. A barmaid spills the drinks."

"Oh, yeah? Does she have..." He pantomimed a large bosom.

"Brian," Declan scolded. He could be so crude.

Miss Tierney frowned. "I'm not about to give you material for your fantasies."

Typical of Brian, he didn't take any notice of her indignant tone of voice and laughed. Declan saw a quarrel brewing and wanted to prevent it. "I think it's time we got back to work."

Miss Tierney bit her lower lip. "You're right. It's getting late and we have a lot to do." She stood up.

Brian watched them as they talked to the spirits. He smirked but didn't say a word.

As the evening dragged on, Declan grew tired. His reflexes and speech slowed but he insisted on continuing. He'd given up on too many things in his life and needed to finish this. Brian stepped in at one point, acting like the protective big brother. He found the energy to argue but felt guilty for wasting it on his brother.

Miss Tierney pointed out the need to clear the whole

house or he'd have the same problem to deal with later. Brian wasn't happy but gave in. Though it seemed to take ages, they finally cleared the house, the motherly spirit taking the last batch with her to Heaven. Though Miss Tierney kept calling it the Other Side, he was sure it was Heaven.

"How does the house feel to you now?" she asked, sweat rolling down her face.

Declan collapsed in his chair. He smoothed down his hair and shirt, feeling unkempt but pleased beyond anything. "Blessedly empty. Thank you so much, Miss Tierney."

She grinned. "Kenna. And you're most welcome."

"Ach. Enough of the nice-nice, you two." Brian stared hard at Declan. "You look whipped. Time for some shut-eye."

Miss Tierney seemed concerned. "He's right, but eat something first. Got to keep up your strength, remember? And don't forget to ground yourself before you go to sleep."

After she left, Brian warmed up a bowl of Katrina's beef barley soup. The smell made Declan salivate and he dug in with gusto.

Brian sat across from him, fidgeting with the salt and pepper shaker. "So, the ghosts are gone?"

Declan patted his mouth with a napkin. "Oh, yes. They're gone." He listened to the quiet. Tomorrow, he'd start on *A Connecticut Yankee* again.

"And you say there's ghosts all around town?"

Declan focused on Brian. "What are you planning?"

"What?"

"You're planning to do something. What is it?"

Brian opened his mouth in surprise. "I am not."

The indignant act was a little too exaggerated. It hadn't worked when they were kids and it didn't work now. But a wave of heaviness hit Declan's body and he let it go.

He was going to sleep like a baby tonight.

12

The last few days I'd felt beaten down, but Declan's simple "thank you" made me feel I could scale a mountain.

Maybe not.

Leaving the house, I checked my phone. It was close to midnight. Helping Declan hadn't been as awful as I thought it would be.

At the stop sign at the end of Declan's road, I swung my head, picking up on an unusual animal mind. At my job, I have to close myself off because of the large number of animals in one place. When not on duty, I've learned to tune them out, similar to ignoring someone's car radio as they pass by you on the street. This animal was different. A deer or a fox, maybe. It wasn't unheard of for wild animals to sniff around a rural community at night. I yawned. It had been a long day and I had to drive back to Bartlett. I put the animal out of my mind and got on the highway.

Back at the hotel, I tried to be quiet entering the room

but found I shouldn't have bothered. Nora was awake and on the phone, talking to her husband. As soon as I entered, she retreated to the bathroom.

The sounds of her alternating between whining and crying lulled me to sleep.

The next morning, my eyes felt gritty as if I'd walked in a sand storm and I moved in slow motion. Yesterday's ghostly double header had wrecked me. Jim, on the other hand, looked refreshed and ready to tackle the day. I wanted to punch him in the throat but I'd settle for coffee. Gallons of it. And food.

Nora's mood had not improved. "It's your fault." Nora pointed at Jim and I as we left out motel rooms. "You should pay for the basement damage."

I put on sunglasses. "We didn't have any control over what happened."

Nora shrugged. "You both were there and I wasn't."

I snorted, unlocking the car. "The house is old. The hot water tank could have broke at any time." Not wanting to start World War III, I avoided the ghost issue.

"Keep it down," Jim growled next to me.

Two people standing outside their door stared at us.

Nora glared at the spectators. "Well, they can mind their own business."

The two men turned and walked toward the office.

Jim shrugged. I sighed and got in the driver's seat.

Nora slammed the back door shut. "The mess will cost us time and money to fix." She clicked her index finger nail on Jim's headrest. "I wasn't anywhere near it and I refuse to pay for it."

"We made an agreement." Jim's voice was firm. He looked straight ahead, the nerve in his jaw twitching.

"Do you honestly think we'll sell the house, much less have anything left over? Have you not seen all the "for sale" signs? Hurlbutt was on its last leg twenty years ago, after they closed the shirt factory. It's just taking a while to die."

I pulled out of the parking lot. "Jeez, Nora."

"We should abandon the property," she continued. "We'll have to put much more money into it than we can ever get out of it."

"But that's our family home."

She eyed me in the rearview mirror. "When did you become so sentimental? You took off as soon as you could."

"So did you."

"Hold on," Jim said. "Hurlbutt is in bad shape because people abandoned it. We have the means, between us, to clean up the house. It's the right thing to do. I never pegged you for a quitter, Nora."

She shrugged. "I'm not about to throw good money away on a bad investment. Be realistic. In a few years, Hurlbutt won't even exist anymore."

I had no words and we were all silent during the ride to the restaurant, through breakfast, and my stop at a convenience store for energy drinks.

At the house, the tomcat slipped around the corner of the garage as I pulled in. As I got out, he rubbed up against me. "Still hanging around, huh?"

He purred.

The first thing we did was check the basement. Thanks to the sump pump, the standing water was gone but wet piles of clothing and unidentifiable garbage remained. Jim started inspecting the plumbing and electrical and told me not to worry about the other stuff until later. Nora began packing boxes with dishware from the kitchen. Wanting to get away from her, I started on the stairway going to the second floor. By lunchtime, I was sweaty but had several bags sorted into donations, stuff to sell, and garbage.

At the diner in town, the cool air revived me and my stomach snarled at the smell of food. I was still working on an energy deficit from the previous day.

The waitress, a woman with short, curly gray hair and an efficient manner brought us menus and silverware. Jim and I ordered burgers and fries.

"Are the vegetables in the Cobb Salad organic?" Nora asked.

I rolled my eyes.

"No," said the waitress, her pen poised above her pad of paper.

"What about the chicken?"

The waitress waited a moment. "What about it?"

"Is it organic?" Nora enunciating each word.

"No, it isn't."

"Is anything organic here?"

The waitress straightened her back. "This is a diner, not a country club."

I dipped my head, hiding a smile.

"Obviously." Nora's tone dripped sarcasm. "I guess I'll have to make do. Cobb salad, no onions or croutons, and oil and vinegar dressing on the side."

The waitress took the order without another word.

Nora looked pinch-faced. "This is unacceptable. I was afraid there'd be nothing decent to eat here. I can feel the chemicals rushing through my system and I'm bloated." She smoothed the shirt over her stomach.

"Maybe you're getting your period," I said.

Her mouth dropped open. "I can't believe you said that."

She was so easy to wind up, even when I wasn't trying hard.

Jim gave Nora a look then swung his attention to me. "Did you have fun with your friend last night?"

Nora subsided, but continued to glare at me.

Visiting a friend from high school was my excuse to help Declan. "Yes," I said, "and her daughter is adorable. Pudgy cheeks to die for." To change the subject before Nora started questioning me, I asked, "So, what do you think it'll take to fix up the basement?" A look between Jim and Nora set alarm bells ringing in my head. "What?"

"Because of yesterday," Jim said, "the plumbing and electrical are all screwed up. I can fix it, but it's going to take a while, particularly if I'm doing it alone. I've got a friend who can help on the weekends, but it puts us behind with the rest of the house. Then, of course, we have to have it inspected. All of it takes time."

"Crudballs."

"Yeah," Jim said, "and I have to leave at the end of next week."

"I may leave before then," said Nora, examining her nails.

I sat up straighter. "What? *Nuh-uh.* We can't get everything done in one week."

"It's more like a week and a half but I've got no choice. Uncle Sam tells me to go and I go." Jim propped his elbows on the table. "And, Nora, you promised me you'd stay."

Nora sighed and crossed her arms. "I never promised anything."

"Come on," I said. "You guys can't leave me with everything. I have a life to get back to, too, you know."

Nora shrugged. "You're the closest. You can return on weekends."

So, they'd made plans behind my back. Well, I wasn't feeling generous. "No way. We can get someone to finish it, then."

"Kenna," Jim said. "I'm going to be half way around the world and Nora will be in Texas. I thought we already decided it'd cost too much to hire a company?"

His reasonable tone made me feel ten years old again. "It's not fair."

"No, but we still have time. We can get a lot done."

Everything would get dumped on me while they went back to their lives, free and clear. "This sucks my big toe."

Nora rolled her eyes.

After we ate, in silence for the most part, we walked to the register to pay. One guy at the counter had long, tied-back hair and seemed familiar. "Nate?" I blurted out. "Nate Brewer?"

The guy turned. He squinted at me a second, then a huge smile lit up his face. "*Kennaaaaaah*. Hey, how are ya?" He bounded off the stool and hugged me.

I hugged him back, not even caring about the dried grass and dirt clinging to his faded jeans and t-shirt. "Doing good. How are you? Wow, that's some beard."

He laughed, scratching his scraggly brown beard.

"Yeah. Doing good. Hey, this is trippy. Haven't seen you in forever."

"We're here to sell my parents' house. Oh, this is my brother, Jim, and sister, Nora."

Jim shook hands but Nora just waved.

"Hey, sorry about your mom," he said, a look of sincere compassion on his face.

"Thanks," I said, wanting to get past the emotional stuff. "We're here a few more days, getting the house ready to sell. So what have you been up to?"

He grinned. "Just keeping it real. Today, I'm mowing lawns. Yesterday, I fixed some leaky pipes. Tomorrow, who knows? Something'll show up. It's all good."

In high school, Nate was one of the few who moved from group to group and seemed to always belong. He was quirky and fun, definitely not a threat to anyone. And Nate knew everyone in town.

"We're looking for a place that buys furniture and collectibles. Do you know any?" I asked.

"*Hmm.*" He stroked his beard, thinking. "There's nothing in town but there's an auction company in Bartlett. Give me a couple days and I'll try to work something out."

"Thank you so much. Let me give you my number."

He lifted his hands. "Sorry. I don't have a phone. How about we meet here at noon in two days? Okay with you?"

I looked at Jim.

He shrugged.

"Sure," I said. "If you need us, we'll be at our parents' old place on Caro Street during the day. You remember it?"

"Sure." He glanced at a clock on the wall. "Hey, gotta

bounce. Yards to mow." He pulled money out of his pocket, counted out a couple bills and some change, and put it on the counter. He hoisted a camo-colored back-pack from the floor and slung it to his shoulder. "Later, *Kennaaaaah.*" He hugged me. "Nice to meet you." He waved at Jim and Nora, then hurried out the door.

"Wasn't he interesting?" Nora raised her eyebrows. "Who doesn't have a cell phone?"

What a snob. "Plenty of people, I'm sure," I said. "He's a good guy, and was always a friend to me."

"Yeah, but you haven't seen him in a long time," Jim gave his receipt and money to the young waitress at the register. "He probably smoked a little too much weed in school."

"Who, Nate?" asked the waitress. She seemed younger than me, with dirty blond hair in a high ponytail but I didn't recognize her. "Maybe. But I've never seen him stoned. He's a hard worker. His mom died owing a lot of money and he's been paying it back ever since. "

"Oh, no." I said.

The waitress nodded her head as she rang up Nora's bill. "Yeah. He does whatever jobs come along. But I'll tell you what, he always leaves a tip, which is better than some people with a lot more money." She glared at a table of businessmen in suits.

The older waitress passed behind her with an armful of dirty dishes. "You don't get paid to gossip," she said.

"Yes, ma'am." The young woman winked at us.

The older waitress then deposited the dishes further down behind the counter and bustled in the kitchen.

"Don't mind old Bonny," the waitress murmured,

glancing at the kitchen pass-through window. "She's had her panties in a twist for years."

Jim and I left a tip, but Nora refused, saying something about rude service. I threw an extra dollar on the table.

~

WHEN WE GOT TO THE HOUSE, NORA WENT UPSTAIRS, where it was clean and dry, Jim went to buy PVC pipe, leaving me with the general basement clean up.

Oh, joy.

I found a shovel and a garbage bag. "This is so wrong." My sneakers squishing in muck as I began shoveling something I tried not to identify off the floor into a bag that kept collapsing closed. After filling the bag, I hauled it up each step—it weighed a ton—and outside, left it on the lawn and went back to the basement for more fun.

My hair worked its way out of my ponytail, stuck to my face, and itched, reminding me of the fake spiders the basement ghost had tricked me with the day before. Suppressing a shudder, I brushed at my shoulders and over my head.

Three bags full uncovered a small area but I was ready to keel over. Holding the shovel with one hand, I pulled backwards with the other, trying to move the bag to another area. My foot slipped in the slime and I fell on my butt. Gasping, I scrambled up, but the damage was done. Gross stuff oozed down my bare legs and my seat was wet.

"Son of a biscuit." I slammed the shovel down, splashing myself again. *"Aaarggghhhh."*

"Kenna, what did you do to yourself?"

I whipped around. Ma and Dad hovered a few feet away.

"Saints preserve, what a mess." Ma said.

"Yeah, well, now I've got the fun of cleaning it up."

"And you're doing a good job of it, sweetheart."

"Thanks, Dad," I said, with a harsh edge, as I picked up the shovel. "Sorry, I'm frustrated. Ma, why did you let the house get like this?"

She looked ashamed. "It just sort of piled up. I never meant for it to get this bad."

"No kidding." I leaned on the shovel handle. "Hey, do either of you know why there's so many ghosts around here?"

"Where?" Ma asked, as if they were congregating in the basement with us.

"All over Hurlbutt. I've been seeing them in Henley's, people's houses, and Mickey's."

My father smiled. "Ah, Mickey's. I've missed it. Maybe I'll stop in later."

"Why go there?" Ma puffed up, ready for a fight. "It's not as if you can drink anymore."

"So? I may not drink but—"

"Excuse me? The ghosts?"

Dad and Ma stopped mid-sentence.

"Will somebody please tell me what's going on here?"

"Right." Dad said. "As a matter of fact, there are a few more ghosts than usual." He frowned. "Some are real scrappy. You be careful."

"I'm always careful."

At the same time, Ma said, "What is it, dear?"

Dad frowned. "Nothin' good, I'm afraid."

They started arguing again.

I lost my cool. "What is it?"

"What are you yelling about?" Jim stood at the bottom of the stairs, holding a cardboard box with PVC pipe fittings. "Who are you talking to?" He stepped closer, eyes zeroing in on me. Scary calm.

I didn't know what to say. How much had he heard? Oh, well. Might as well rip the Band-Aid off. "Dad and Ma." I stood up straighter. I refused to feel intimidated, even when he looked at me like I was the enemy.

He shook his head, putting the box down in a clear spot by the hot water tank. "How 'bout you help me unload the pipe?" He started toward the stairs.

"Wait. We need to work this out, once and for all."

He sighed, turning. "There's nothing to work out but there's a shit-load of work to do."

"Ask him," Ma interrupted, "what he did with my canner."

One summer, Ma's porcelain enamel canner disappeared just as we had bushels of beans to preserve. Ma had been livid. I always thought it was Nora, trying to avoid the long, sweaty, canning process, but apparently Ma suspected Jim. "No way."

"We've got a deadline to hit, remember?" Jim sounded testy.

It drove me nuts trying to follow two different conversations.

"Ask him," Ma said.

"Ma wants to know what you did with her canner." I called out because Jim had started walking away again.

He stopped halfway up the stairs. "Leave it alone, Kenna," he said, then continued up and out the door.

"Give me something else," I said to Ma. "Something I couldn't know about."

"Tell him Dan Anderson is fine." Dad said.

I rushed up the stairs and outside. Jim was rummaging in the bed of the borrowed truck. "Dad says, 'Dan Anderson is fine,'" I said when I reached him.

He turned fast, with an intense look on his face. "Say that again."

I stepped back. "Dan Anderson is fine?"

"Dan Anderson is dead," he spit out.

Nearby, Dad said, "Tell him he wasn't alone that day."

I repeated what Dad said.

Jim shook his head. "You don't know a damn thing." His voice was cold enough to raise goose bumps on my arms.

A video ran in my mind of Jim and three other soldiers, in full gear, driving along a dusty road. Then, a loud explosion. The vehicle bucked and everything turned sideways. Yelling and screaming. Blood. Jim was pinned back against his seat but wore no seatbelt. Loose items and his buddies tumbled inside the vehicle. But not him.

Now, I understood. "You were the only survivor, weren't you?"

His lips pressed tight for a moment. "Yes," he whispered.

"Dad was with you. He's watched over us for years and Ma's learning how it works. They're here, right now." In fact, they stood near the garage, watching, Ma clutching Dad's arm.

Jim followed my gaze. "You're telling me they're—Jesus, Mary and Joseph." He leaned against the truck and rubbed his face. "This is crazy."

"Think of it like...ghosts emit radio waves and I'm a radio."

He stared at me.

"Just go with it for a minute, okay? You can't hear radio waves. You need an antenna to catch them out of the air and an amplifier to change them into sounds we can hear, right?"

"There's more to it, but, yeah, basically."

"Well, ghosts give off a type of energy we'll pretend is like radio waves. There are some people who can tune into the ghosts' wavelength, and I'm one of them. Okay, it's not a great analogy, but you see where I'm coming from?"

Jim lifted his eyebrows and grunted.

At least it wasn't a complete rejection.

Dad and Ma began talking at once, distracting me.

I touched his arm. "They send you their love."

"Um...come on. Help me get this pipe downstairs." He pushed away from the truck, breaking our contact.

I had to be content with baby steps. At least he didn't totally shut me out this time.

13

Needless to say, we hired Nate. He wasn't as expensive as a cleaning service and we needed all the help we could get, especially with the basement. After the mess the ghost left behind, little was salvageable, so we made lots of trips to the dump. Nate also knew plumbing and electrical work. Jim was impressed by his skills, if a little exasperated by his conversation.

When we first saw the house, I was worried we had a situation like you see on those hoarding shows on TV. Luckily, Ma didn't have any pets or problems with leaky pipes and we didn't find any rodent damage either. Ma just had a lot of stuff. The kitchen and downstairs bathroom were in the worst shape, but a thorough cleaning made a big difference. We hoped the house would sell before anything else happened.

Nora talked to Realtors. She started with ones in Buffalo and Rochester, but they wouldn't touch the house with a hundred-foot pole. One said it was because properties in Hurlbutt didn't sell. Nora was ready to bail but we convinced her to check with local real estate agents. She found one in Bartlett which was a friend of hers from high school so she stuck it out a little longer.

We were happy to hear from Nate's auction house buddy, however, it would be a couple days before he could come out to assess the situation and longer to auction it.

Restaurant bills were getting expensive so we began stocking Ma's now-clean fridge and making simple meals there.

We couldn't lose Nate's help, though, so Nora and I set up a garage sale to raise some money to pay him. Normally, I'd rather gouge my eyes out with red hot pokers than haul things out on a lawn, sit in the hot sun, and dicker with a bunch of strangers over prices. We put out stuff the auction house didn't want. Absolute junk. And, wonder of wonders, Nora was all for it, haggling like a pro.

Even the local hippie church, The First Church of Peace and Love, visited us. These days, they were more mainstream. Instead of the wildly-colored clothing and doped-up ramblings I recalled from my childhood, the man and woman who crashed our garage sale were dressed conservatively in a suit and dress.

I first noticed them talking to one of our customers, thinking they were overdressed for a hot Saturday afternoon. Our customer shook her head, changing direction. They followed her, continuing to talk, and she abruptly got in her car and drove away, depriving us of a sale.

Snagging Nora, I whispered, "See what's up with those two. They drove off one of our customers."

Nora spoke with the man and woman for a while,

then stiffened. They quoted scripture at her and she quoted back at them, following up with, "This is not the place or time for this discussion and I would like you to leave."

"When is a more convenient time for you?" asked the woman.

"Never," said Nora, smiling. "We aren't interested in your church. Now, do I need to call the police to forcibly remove you or will you leave on your own accord?" She never raised her voice, but left no doubts they were to get off our property. Nora's a pro with the genteel, Southern way of politely telling people off.

Gloria, who'd been hovering for a while, chuckled and nudged me with her elbow. "I'll remember that when the First Church bunch come around to my house." She watched Nora with admiration.

"Right," I said, then turned to the next customer wanting to pay for a pile of clothing.

Surprisingly, we got rid of a lot in two days and made about four hundred dollars. For the time Nora and I invested, I didn't think it was worth it, but it did pay for Nate's help and a few meals.

There was so much to do, but we ran out of time.

The night before Jim and Nora left, I called my boss to ask for a few more days. Doc wasn't pleased.

"I'm truly sorry about your mother's death," he said, "but the office is swamped. I need you back by next Monday or I'll have to get someone else."

Less than a week? I'd have to return on weekends to finish after all.

The next morning, when Jim and Nora handed in their keys at the motel, I downgraded to a single.

"I'm still not convinced it's worth it to clean up the house and sell," Nora said. Jim gave her another one of his looks. "I know. I know," she said, waving him away. "But since you are, despite my advice, you need a plan. You don't have experience with this and I do, so here is a list of what needs to be done." She handed me a sheet of paper. "The Realtor's phone number is on top. Any questions or problems, ask her."

"I'm really gonna miss you guys," I said, "particularly when I'm in the garage, sorting through all those containers of nuts and bolts Dad kept."

"Yeah, well you're capable enough." Jim gave me a big bear hug. "Besides, Nate will help. He seems to know what he's doing."

"Thanks for that ringing endorsement, G.I. Jim," I joked, then got serious. "Be safe." I worried about him being in a war zone but knew he was watched over. We hadn't spoken of ghosts again and I didn't want to push our truce.

"I will." He took his and Nora's luggage out to the car.

"Nora," I said. "Thanks for staying as long as you did. I'll muddle along. Tell Craig and the kids I send my love."

"Don't forget to call the Realtor," she said, checking her hair in the mirror. She gathered up her purse and carry-on and walked out to the car without a backward glance. I should have known leaving on good terms was pushing it with Nora but it still felt like a failure.

After dropping them off at the airport, I drove to Hurlbutt.

I missed my life. Just five more days, though. Come on, Monday.

~

As soon as I stepped out of my car, Gloria pounced on me. She was weeding her garden. I saw her, hoping I could get in the house before she noticed.

"Hello," she called, crossing the street. "You all have been so busy over here. It's nice to see the old house get cleaned up. Who knew there was so much stuff in there?" She upped the wattage on her smile, like she was in a toothpaste commercial.

"Yeah, look—"

"I hope you can sell the house. You know, I was talking to my friend, Addy, the other day—our kids are in the same swimming lessons—and she said her husband —he's a banker—told her several families have been evicted lately for defaulting on their mortgages. It's so sad, don't you think?"

"Yes, but—"

"We're so lucky Barry has such a good job. I wish he didn't have to travel so much."

"That's too bad," I said, rushing to speak before she did. "I need to get back to cleaning but thanks for stopping by."

"You bet," she called, as I turned to leave. "Anything I can do, let me know."

I waved, walking toward the house. The tomcat shot out from the bushes and rubbed against my ankle, almost tripping me. "Well, hello there." I rubbed around his ears, noticing a fresh gouge on his head. "Quite a scrapper, aren't you?"

He leaned into my hand. *Itchy.*

Using the pads of my fingertips, I dug into his back,

from his neck to the base of his tail and back up. I felt kind of guilty. "I have to leave soon, cat. Go away for good. What'll you do then?"

He purred, all his attention on the kitty massage I was giving him.

I continued for a few more minutes, checking him for fleas. Surprisingly, he didn't have any. "Sorry, buddy, but I gotta get back to work."

He tried to follow me in, but I gently held him back, closing the door. He meowed, then scooted under the bushes.

Each time I opened the kitchen door now, it gave me a thrill of accomplishment. All the garbage and piles on the counters were gone. It was scrubbed, top to bottom. Same for the bathroom. The linoleum was discolored and cracked in places but it was a huge improvement. The dining room, family room, and hallway to the front door contained just furniture and boxes of things good enough to go to auction.

I was stoked.

Someone rapped on the side door and I clattered down the stairs. "Hey, *Kennaaaaah*." Nate said when I opened the door.

"Hey, Nate. It's you and me now, bud."

Nate looked down, embarrassed. "Yeah, about that. I'm kind of behind in my mowing. A couple people were asking. Do you mind? I'll be back bright and early tomorrow."

I'd forgotten he had other responsibilities. "Of course. I'm sorry we kept you from your regular business."

He smiled. "No *problemo*. See you tomorrow."

For the next hours I worked upstairs sorting clothes,

shoes, old perfume and, I kid you not, paintings of kittens on black velvet. After eating a container of yogurt for lunch, I felt antsy, needing some fresh air. I grinned at a sudden idea and grabbed my car keys. Instead of a walk, I'd check out Rogers Lake.

The lake was southwest of Hurlbutt on property owned by the Rogers family. However, they allowed generations of locals to use it for swimming and fishing. At night, teens used to party there, though I'd only gone once. Mostly it was a bunch of losers getting wasted. The police had made regular sweeps of the area to discourage it. Not that it ever lasted for long.

Outside Hurlbutt, woods full of maple and pine lined both sides of the road, broken by the occasional open property with a house and outbuildings on it. It felt good to get out of the house and drive.

When I reached the turn-off to Rogers Lake, goosebumps skittered across my skin. Weird. I continued on, the need to see the lake from my childhood growing strong. Bumping along the long, rutted driveway, I noticed a crawling feeling in my gut. I tried to pinpoint the source but then the trees ended, opening onto the lake sparkling in the afternoon sun.

I braked hard, my seatbelt pulling tight on my chest. I couldn't reconcile the serene view in front of me with the dark feeling pressing on me, taking my breath away.

"What the—"

Strong emotions washed over me. Fear. Shame. Blinding rage. Clawing hunger for retaliation. These weren't my emotions, but they were strong, pulling at me. I'd never felt anything quite like it.

"Oh, no," I groaned. Ghosts. Dozens of them.

∾

I UNSNAPPED MY SEATBELT, AND GOT OUT. IT WAS STUPID, and I knew it, but it was like a wreck on the side of the road. I had to see, had to feel, what was going on. Walking toward the lake, the storm of emotions grew stronger.

At the water's edge, I wavered between my self and some *other*. I resisted, clinging to the scrap of me. A tug of war went on until I pushed back as hard as I could and fell backward, hitting the ground with an *oof*. Lay there, stunned, battered by the emotions.

"Get...up," I said, through clenched teeth. Slowly, I rolled onto my side, in a fetal position, and up to my knees. Once on my feet, I lurched toward the car. Dizziness sent me stumbling into the side mirror and I clung to it until the feeling passed. Tearing at the handle, I got in, put the car in gear, and floored the accelerator. It lurched forward, though, toward the lake. I slammed on the brakes, shoved it in reverse, doing a wide, jerky, three-point-turn. At the highway, I almost collided with a pickup. Slowly, I edged out onto the road.

In Hurlbutt, I roared into the driveway, stopping in a cloud of dust. Shaking badly, I turned off the ignition. Resting my head on the wheel, I listened to the ticking of the engine.

Oh crud, oh crud, oh crud.

Too stupid to live. That's me. I felt something wrong but followed my nose, not taking any precautions to protect myself.

Stumbling out of the car, I staggered across the yard to the door. My hands shook so bad I dropped the keys.

Finally getting the door open, I tripped up the kitchen stairs, through the house, and collapsed on the couch, clutching a pillow. Drenched in sweat. Tried not to think. Tried to put it all out of my mind.

It didn't work.

Once the shakes subsided, I was exhausted and fell asleep, but bad dreams woke me up. After my heart rate returned to normal, my stomach wouldn't stop growling so I fixed two sandwiches, chips, and a Pepsi. While I pigged out, the stacks of boxes in every room seemed to crowd closer, taunting me.

To stop myself from thinking about what happened at the lake, I went back to sorting and cleaning in my parents' bedroom, but it didn't help. I dragged a chair over to the open window. A slight breeze stirred the edges of the curtains, cooling my sweaty face. I tried to do breathing exercises and visualize the protective white light. Stuff I should have done when I felt the first pangs in my gut earlier.

Stop it. Beating yourself up won't help.

Starting again, I was able to get through the whole routine. Now, I could think about the experience without feeling panicky.

As a kid, I'd been to Rogers Lake lots of times and never experienced anything unusual. Where did the ghosts come from? Maybe I was overreacting. The last few weeks had been stressful. There were a lot of ghosts at the lake, but there'd been a lot at Declan's too. What was the difference? The ghosts at Declan's had been more...what? Like regular people? The lake ghosts seemed to be all raw emotion. Something bad must have happened to them.

Guilt gnawed at me. I could have helped them if I hadn't let the emotions overwhelm me. I knew better but needed to get back in the practice of protecting myself and handling ghosts.

I shook my head. I wasn't going to be in Hurlbutt much longer.

Movement outside the window made me look into the front lawn below. Cats. A bunch of them sat on the grass, facing the house. As I watched, more wandered into the yard and sat. Some groomed themselves. Some looked around with interest. A couple stared up at me.

Bizarre.

Concentrating on one, then another, I got the impression they were attracted to something, but didn't know what.

I clattered downstairs and opened the front door, expecting them to scatter. But they didn't. I counted twenty-three, with more arriving through the adjacent yards. Different breeds and different ages. A few watched me with interest. None moved. Fur brushed my ankle.

The tomcat twined himself around my legs. He sat in front of me and washed his paw, as if to say, "What? I don't see anything."

I've always loved animals. Ma wouldn't let us keep a pet, but I walked elderly people's dogs and fed my neighbor's cat when they went on vacation. And animals seemed to feel the same way about me. That's why I chose veterinary medicine, though this kind of attraction was ridiculous. Every cat in the neighborhood had to be sitting on the lawn.

The tom stood, arched his back and let out the most blood-curdling yowl I've ever heard.

My person. My house.

A few of the cats took off right away. Some seemed startled, but wary, watching the tom.

He leaped off the stairs, stood his ground, and yowled again. And again. Hissed. Waved his paw around, claws extended. *Go away. Mine.*

He was magnificent in defending his territory, even if he was mistaken.

When he had chased the last one out of the yard, he returned, rubbing against my ankles. How could I not give him some attention? For the first time, I picked him up. He nestled under my chin, purring. "I am so in trouble," I murmured. He allowed this contact for about one minute before using my chest as a springboard to jump down.

I sat on the top step and rubbed my face. My life was such a mess. First, I found ghosts all over town, then the lake, and now this. What was going on around here? Even the domestic animals were acting weird. It was like being trapped in one of those horror movies I'd loved as a kid, stalked by a supernatural monster.

But without the sex.

In that trope, with my abilities, I should have been the "expert." But I didn't know what to freaking do.

The cat rubbed up against me and I pet him. His fur was coarse and his skin scabby, either from insect bites or fighting.

"Let's take a peek here, big fella." Picking him up, I quickly examined him. He was around two years old, malnourished, and neutered. He'd been someone's pet once, so he probably had his first set of vaccines at least. He squirmed away and wandered behind me, over to my other side. I gave him another massage, head to the base of his tail. He arched his back, standing on his tippy toes, almost drooling, then crawled into my lap.

Well.

When there's a purring cat in your lap, it seems all is right with the world.

Except it wasn't.

Later, on the way back to the motel, I bought a six pack of beer. For a little while at least, I tried to shake the feeling things were just cranking up in Hurlbutt.

14

Light streamed through the partly-open curtains of my motel room, shining right in my eyes. Rolling my tongue around my dry mouth, I snuggled deeper under the covers, but my internal alarm clock wouldn't let me fall back to sleep. And it felt like someone was hammering on my skull.

Once under the hot shower, a few brain cells revived. Nate would be back to work today, so we'd finally tackle the garage. Well, maybe I'd cut him loose with it and find something quiet for me to do.

I guzzled water on my drive to Hurlbutt. Food was the last thing on my mind but I was in desperate need of coffee. Since the car was low on fuel, I stopped at the Kwik Fill. After pumping gas and cringing at the cost on the credit card receipt, I went inside.

As I filled my cup with extra-caffeinated goodness, the attendant talked to another customer, their babble flowing over me. I added creamer and sugar so the coffee wouldn't eat a hole in my stomach and grabbed two energy drinks. They stopped talking as I approached the counter and the customer moved aside. I paid, putting the change in my pocket. Just as I was about to leave, the customer stepped in front of me.

"Hey."

I looked up, registering the fact a pimply-faced teenage boy stood there. "Uh...hi." I said.

"Aren't you the psychic lady? When are you going to exercise the ghost?"

My brain was still a little fuzzy. "Pardon me?"

"You're the psychic, right?"

How did this kid I'd never met in my life, know me, much less know that? I stared, my brain not making the connections needed to deal with the situation.

"Dip shit."

I whirled on the attendant, who didn't look much older than the kid. "What?"

"Not you, ma'am," the attendant held his hands up.

Great. Not yet thirty-five and already getting called "ma'am."

"I meant him." The attendant pointed at the kid. "It's 'exorcise' not 'exercise' the ghost." He shook his head. "Go on, get out of here," he shooed the teenager out. "Don't mind him. Everyone's talking about what happened and he got a little excited."

"What happened?"

"You didn't hear?" He grinned. "A bunch of kids were at Rogers Lake last night. Partying, you know? Then, well, there's a lot of different stories going around, but some of them were beat up pretty bad and scared. A couple said it was ghosts did it."

I felt like I'd been sucker-punched. "Oh."

He shrugged. "Yeah, well, anyway, that's why he asked if you were going to exorcise the ghosts."

"Right." That was my cue to get out of there. "Thanks."

"Sure. Have a nice day and good luck with the ghosts."

Walking to my car, I felt light-headed. Settling in behind the wheel, I took a huge gulp of coffee and burned my tongue.

Did I stir up the ghosts going to the lake yesterday? Was I responsible for what happened to a bunch of kids?

The jackhammer in my brain grew worse.

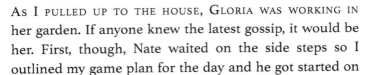

As I pulled up to the house, Gloria was working in her garden. If anyone knew the latest gossip, it would be her. First, though, Nate waited on the side steps so I outlined my game plan for the day and he got started on the garage.

Then I ambled across the street.

"Hi, Gloria. How are you?" I called from the sidewalk.

She was cutting dead flowers, putting them in a huge brown paper bag. She turned, smiling, but it seemed forced. "Hello. Fine. How about you?"

"Good, thanks."

She smiled and went back to cutting plants. Strange. Every other time I'd talked with her, she gave me her whole attention. Like any good gossip.

I moved a little closer. "You know, I heard something strange happened out at Roger's Lake last night."

"Is that right?" She glanced at me, then went back to her flowers.

That was it? "I was wondering if you'd heard anything," I said, trying to continue the conversation.

"No." She looked at her watch. "Oh, my." She dropped her clippers. "I forgot an important phone call I have to make. So sorry, but I have to run." She pulled her garden gloves off, dropping them as she hustled to the door.

Gloria's odd behavior was proof to me the Hurlbutt rumor mill was hard at work. But who started it? While crossing the street, all the pieces of the puzzle fit together. "Son of a—" It would have to wait, though, until I finished work for the day.

Nate had an old lawn mower, a snow blower, and boxes of greasy oil cans and rusted mechanical parts pulled out of the garage. He was humming.

"Hey, Nate. How's it going?" I tried to sound cheerful.

He turned with a big grin on his face. "Great. There's some awesome stuff here." He pointed to the mower and snow blower. "I'm not sure how long these have sat. Could be all they need is to drain the old gas out, put new in, clean them up, an' they'll run just fine."

"Good." I made an effort to sound interested, but I'd never mowed in my life. My father or brother did the lawn care at home and then I lived in apartments. "What else is in there?" I peered in the dark garage.

"Bikes and garden tools and boxes of nails and pipes and electrical fittings."

Apparently, Nate found his happy place. He had worked hard this last week and a half helping us. Most of the stuff in the garage was supposed to go to auction, but

I saw a way to save myself some immediate cash and help him out too.

"Would you be interested in trading?" I asked. "Instead of today's pay, you can have whatever you want from the garage?"

His eyes lit up again, but he frowned. "That's nice of you, Kenna, but I don't want to take advantage. Some of this is worth a lot."

How refreshing. "OK. How about two or three days' pay? Whatever you think is fair."

We agreed he would work one day without pay and once he got the mower working, maintain the lawn until the house sold. He would then keep the mower, oil, and spare parts for himself. We were both happy.

Since I didn't know much about mechanical stuff, I left Nate to it. Not long after, the doorbell rang.

An older guy stood on the front step. "Hello, are you Kenna Tierney?"

What now? "Um, yeah. Can I help you?"

"I hope so." A smile touched his lips, then was gone. "I'm Greg Adams. Are...are you the psychic?"

Once again, my brain froze.

"You see," he hurried on, "I've got a problem with my wife...well, I think maybe it's a ghost, but it's affecting my wife. It only seems to happen to her, never me, and I can't stand seeing her so...so...well, can you help?"

Great. I gave up my former life and friends and kept my abilities hidden for years. Now, everyone in town knew and I felt naked.

"Sorry, I can't help you." I began to close the door.

"Please," he pleaded. "I don't know what else to do."

His desperation was obvious. I cracked the door

wider, studying him. He was older, with silver in his sandy hair and crow's feet around his eyes. He hadn't shaved but was dressed in a clean polo shirt, shorts, and sandals. Really, how can you not trust a guy wearing sandals? Bare feet always seem so vulnerable to me.

Lordy. My headache was not going away any time soon.

"Mr. Adams? Why don't we sit on the steps and you can tell me what's happening."

He looked relieved. "Sure, and call me Greg." He backed up and waited for me to sit before he did.

A car drove by on the street, music blaring from its speakers.

"Well," he hesitated, one knee bobbing up and down. "A couple months ago, my wife misplaced keys or the checkbook, you know? She'd look all over the house, then I'd come in and find them sitting in plain sight. We joked about senility, which, considering our ages, wasn't smart." He laughed without humor then rubbed the back of his neck. "Anyway, a couple days ago, she told me about other things she'd kept from me. Noises she heard in other rooms or in the garage but there wasn't anything there. She claims the pictures on the walls changed positions, though I never saw it myself. Suddenly we'd be out of coffee or sugar after she had bought some." He shrugged. "I didn't know what to think. When we were away from the house, she was her old self again."

"Have you considered other possibilities, like electrical or structural problems with your house?"

He nodded his head. "I did and was about to look into it, but, with what's been going on in town and the kids last night and then I heard about you, I wanted to rule this out first."

Unusual, wanting to rule out the paranormal before the mundane. "What's happened in town?"

"A couple businesses reported vandalism. Nothing was stolen, but items were moved. And people, in general, have been on edge for a while. Combined with what happened at the lake, what do you think?"

Interesting. "It's possible." I stared at the street, listening to kids shrieking in an adjoining yard. I'd already helped Declan, but he was different, an overwhelmed fledgling psychic who would've gone crazy without my guidance. Greg's problem could be something with the house or even his wife developing Alzheimer's disease. If it was a haunting, I was nervous facing another ghost. And if I was successful sending it on, he'd tell others and I'd never get out of town.

"I'll pay you," he said.

I shook my head. "Look, I'm not a professional psychic doing readings for money. I don't know how accurate I'd be or even if ghosts are your problem."

"Listen, I'm really worried about my wife. She's always been a tough lady, but, now..."

Holy moly, the guy looked miserable. I felt backed into a corner but the guy's wife was probably a basket case. *Yay*, me. "Alright. I'll take a look but no guarantees, okay? Is your wife home?"

The guy's whole face lit up. "Yes."

"Also, I want your word you won't tell anyone else about me."

He raised his eyebrows but said, "I promise."

"Okay, let's go."

15

I threw the last container of sage, the ashtray and lighter into a bag and let Nate know I'd be back later.

Greg and I drove separate cars. I wasn't stupid. He could be a serial killer for all I knew, sandals and vulnerable tootsies be darned.

The house was a nice little ranch in a newer section of town built when I was a kid, before the factory closed and everyone lost their jobs. Lots of "For Sale" signs here, too, but the houses were in better shape. It must have been garbage day because cans lined the road, except those in front of Greg's house and those on either side of him.

Greg pulled into the driveway but I parked at the curb. I grounded and protected myself, using the technique I'd talked Declan through. Looking at the bag of supplies, I decided to leave it in the car. It was embarrassing carrying that stuff. If I needed it, I'd get it. Climbing out of the car, I noticed Greg scooing garbage back into the cans.

"This wasn't a mess earlier," he grumbled. "When I

get my hands on whoever keeps doing this. Sorry, it's frustrating." He placed the lid back on the can and dusted off his hands, leading me to a side door.

"I would be too," I said. "How long have you lived here?"

"We built the house in '95."

"It's not an old house. Has anybody died here?"

"No." He opened the door, leading me into a kitchen so clean it belonged in a magazine spread. "Honey," he called, washing his hands at the sink.

A tall woman with short, golden-blond hair walked from a side room, folding a towel. "Greg...oh, hello." She was thin and tired-looking, but, otherwise, seemed alright.

"Honey, this is Kenna Tierney, the psychic I told you about. Kenna, this is Jackie."

"Hi," I said. Movement farther in the room caused me to glance over her shoulder. The ghost of a young boy waved at me. He bounced up and down.

Cute little guy.

Jackie didn't look so friendly anymore. "I don't believe in ghosts," she said, her voice chilly.

"You should. There's one right there." I pointed to the doorway behind them.

"What?" They both said, turning.

"He's about five or six and has shaggy red hair. He's wearing overalls without a shirt and bare feet. And he can't keep still."

The ghost grinned and ran toward the couple but they continued to stare at the doorway. He shifted to me. "You can see me?"

"Yes, I can see you," I said.

The couple turned back.

"But they can't," I said, for their benefit. "Now, what's this I hear about you playing tricks on these people?"

The ghost pushed out his lower lip. "I didn't mean ta scare 'em. I gots nobody ta play wif."

"What's your name?"

His whole attitude changed. "Johnny. An' I'm a handful. That's what Mama used to say."

"I'm sure you are, Johnny. Have you always lived here?"

"Nah. I used ta lif where there was aminals. I liked the hogs bestest." He grunted and giggled.

I laughed and relayed the information to the Adams'. Greg was delighted but Jackie didn't say a word.

"Personally," I said, "I don't think you have anything to worry about. He's not destructive, just playful and wants your attention."

"How do we get him to stop moving things and making noises?" asked Greg.

"If you acknowledge his presence, he may stop doing it."

Jackie looked down but I saw her frown.

"I know it's hard to believe."

"Yes, it is," she said, moving to the counter, setting the towel down, and smoothing a wrinkle.

I remembered my earlier conversation with Greg. "Is there anything missing you haven't been able to find?" Some people needed proof.

"Jackie's necklace," Greg said. "I gave it to her for our anniversary."

"I misplaced it, is all." Jackie's voice had an edge, her expression blank.

"I knows where it is," a small voice piped up.

"Are you sure, Johnny?" I asked.

"Yup. I played wif it. Come 'ere." He trotted deeper into the house.

"May I," I asked, indicating the doorway. "He's showing me where the necklace is."

Greg grinned. Jackie sighed, shaking her head. "Go on." She wasn't happy, but she allowed it.

I hoped this wouldn't blow up in my face. The doorway led into a large, tastefully-decorated living room with a leather couch, colorful curtains, and prints of famous paintings on the walls. The Adams' followed. I didn't see Johnny but there was a hallway to the right. "Johnny? Where are you?" The first room off the hallway was a small sitting room.

"Here." Johnny jumped out of the next doorway then back in again.

I followed, stopping on the threshold.

"That's the guest bedroom," Greg said.

We entered the room.

Johnny stood in front of the closed closet door. He pointed. "In there."

I wasn't going to rummage in someone else's house. "He says it's in the closet."

"I've checked there before," Jackie said.

Greg pulled open the closet door, turning on the light. Inside, clothes hung askew or had fallen off hangers and pooled on top of shoes and boots scattered across the floor. On the overhead shelves, photos and papers slid from upended boxes.

Jackie gasped. "I cleaned and organized that closet last winter."

Johnny stood next to me, smiling from ear to ear, pleased with himself.

"Johnny." I knelt in front of him. "You can't create a mess and expect people to want to play with you."

His smile faded. "How come?"

"Jackie spent a long time making this closet neat and clean. She was proud of it. Can you imagine how she feels now after you ruined all her hard work? Do you understand?"

Johnny pushed out his lower lip. "I didn't mean to do it. It just happened."

"How about if you tell us about the necklace," I prodded.

He scowled. "It's in the brown coat."

"Thank you." I stood up.

There were two brown coats and Greg found the necklace in the second one. "Wow. Honey, she was right." He held up a gold chain with a diamond pendant.

"Yes, I see." Jackie frowned. "Now, can you make it go away?"

Uh-oh.

Johnny's eyes bugged out. "I don't wanna go. I like it here."

I felt sorry for the little guy. He wasn't doing any harm. He wanted someone to play with. But if we weren't careful, this could get ugly. "You know," I said to Jackie. "There's a ghost in my family's home. Henry's been there for a long time and he kind of watches over the place. It's possible you and Johnny can live peacefully together too. As long as Johnny promises to behave himself."

Johnny nodded his head vigorously. "I do. Cross my heart an' hope to die, stick a needle in my elbow."

I ignored his creative wording. "Johnny promises. Maybe, in return, you could say hi to him once in a while?"

Jackie lifted her chin a fraction. "I won't indulge this nonsense any longer. Thank you for finding my necklace." She marched from the room.

Greg's mouth dropped open. "I...I don't know what to say." He laughed, without humor. "Um, well, I believe you, Johnny," he said, looking around the room.

"He's here." I pointed.

Greg looked down. "I'll talk to you. And as long as you're a good boy and don't hide things anymore, I think we'll get along fine. What do you say?"

"*Yipee!*" Johnny threw his hands up in the air and hopped like a bunny.

"Are you sure?" I asked Greg.

"Jackie'll come around. She usually does."

"Johnny, this is important. You and Greg need to make a super solemn vow. Do you understand what that is?"

"No."

"It's a promise you make with everything you have in you. You can't ever break it or something bad might happen."

"Like what?"

"You would have to leave here. Do you want that?"

Johnny's eyes and mouth flew open. "No."

"Then, will you make a super solemn vow and promise not to hide Greg and Jackie's belongings or move them or make loud noises or scare Jackie?"

He sighed as only a put-upon child can. "I promise."

I asked Greg, "Do you make a super solemn vow and promise to talk to Johnny?"

Greg nodded gravely. "I promise."

Greg thanked me as we walked back through the house, Johnny skipping along behind. There was no sign of Jackie. Some people weren't ready to believe, even when the proof stared them in the face.

As I drove away, Greg and Johnny waved.

∼

IT WAS STILL MID-MORNING WHEN I RETURNED TO THE house and began sorting things in my and Nora's childhood bedroom. A box of Nora's old *Tiger Beat* magazines brought back memories. The celebrities. The clothes. The awful hairstyles. In the garbage they went.

At some point, my headache went away.

Nate and I ate our lunch outside. The tomcat showed up as we sat down. Nate pulled a piece of baloney from his sandwich and the cat devoured it. Poor thing was hungry.

"He's going to start depending on food from us now," I said.

Nate smiled. "I know, I know, but I couldn't eat with the little bugger looking at me with those big, sad eyes."

Maybe Nate identified with the cat a little.

Since we finished all the deli meat and I needed more garbage bags, I drove to Hanley's after lunch.

I was deciding between two containers of berries and glanced up. A woman trailed by two children stopped with her arm out, holding her kids back. She wheeled her cart around and ran in the opposite direction.

I turned. No one else was in the aisle and nothing was out of place or strange to cause a reaction like that.

Was she scared of me?

A cold, squirmy feeling started in my belly.

I put both cartons of blueberries in my cart, then headed over to the deli. I waited my turn, considering the salads in the case. After a bit, I turned and caught the woman in front of me and the guy behind the counter gawking at me before she took her package and left. The deli guy didn't act any different and handed over the meats and pasta salad I asked for.

Trying not to freak out, I found a quiet corner, but jumped a mile when I felt a tap on my shoulder. Behind me stood an African-American woman in medical scrubs.

"I need your help."

"Okay," I said, drawing out the word.

"I've got a ghost in my house and it has to go away. It's driving me crazy with the lights going on and off all the time and footsteps upstairs when there isn't anybody there and I'm worried it's going to hurt my kids."

Not again. But the desperate look in her sunken eyes affected me. "Who are you?" I asked. "And how do you know me?"

She looked embarrassed. "I'm sorry, my name's Sherita Mason. Everyone knows you're here to clean up your mama's home and you're a psychic, like on TV. So, I had to ask." She paused. "Can you do it?"

"Uh...well..." She had kids. "I can take a look but I'm not a professional or anything."

"You can't do it?"

"No, it means...I'll see what you have but I can't make any guarantees."

"Well, that's something. Right now, I don't have anything."

She gave me her address and I finished my shopping, wondering what I got myself into.

While bringing groceries into the house, the cat slipped in. I saw his back end, tail up, prancing into the dining room like he owned the place. Cursing under my breath, I chased after him. He scooted behind some boxes in the family room. When I checked, he must have sneaked out the other side. After searching the place, top to bottom, I gave up. I had to go to Sherita's and Heaven knew what I'd find there. I needed to calm down and get myself under control.

With images of cat poop in hidden corners preying on my mind, I left one of the dining room windows open a crack so he could get out later.

16

Driving to Sherita's house, the sun was sinking lower in the sky. I felt like hurling. What was I doing, pretending to be a ghostbuster? An image of Bill Murray covered in green slime came to mind and I smiled. "Okay. I can do this. I will do this." It couldn't be worse than my basement ghost, right? Maybe it would be more like Johnny, benign and easy to handle.

The address Sherita gave me was in a neighborhood of small, weathered houses squeezed together. Though her house had a porch and tiny strip of grass out front, Sherita, her kids, and a dog waited on the curb. Not a good sign. I felt the presence of one ghost in her house and more in nearby homes.

I parked and grabbed the grocery bag of supplies on impulse before climbing out. "Hey, what's going on?" I asked, stepping onto the sidewalk.

"Nothing new. The usual." Sherita's voice was calm, but not her eyes. "This here is Max." She held a boy about five years old on her lap. He hid his face in her chest. "My daughter, Makayla." She leaned toward the teenage girl sitting beside her, holding a shaking terrier in her arms. Animals are sensitive and this one was scared. "And the one back there who can't keep still is Jayden." The boy she pointed out was younger than the girl, and played on the sidewalk behind them. "Kids, this is Miss Tierney."

The two older children politely said hello.

"Hi. Please, call me Kenna." The fact they waited out here indicated how much the ghost disrupted their lives. Anger started to simmer and I took a deep breath to control it. "OK. I guess maybe I'll walk through the house first, see what's there. Then, I'll tell you what I find."

"Should I go in with you?" Sherita asked.

"Nope."

Sherita nodded, but her daughter's relief was obvious.

Approaching the front door, I checked on my protective white light, feeling it surround me. I went in, clutching my bag, and waited until my eyes adjusted to the dimness.

The house and furnishings had seen better days but it was neat and clean. How Sherita managed it with three kids, a dog, and a restless ghost amazed me. Most days, my apartment looked as if a tornado had ripped through it. What was unusual was the feeling of heaviness pressing down on me. She definitely had a ghost problem. I checked the downstairs, but all was quiet. Too quiet. It set my nerves jangling. Climbing the stairs to the second floor, something tickled my awareness, but I couldn't pinpoint where it came from before it stopped.

The first bedroom was empty. Walking into the

second, the pressure on my head and shoulders increased. It was here but it wasn't showing itself.

Alrighty now.

Continuing into the third bedroom, nothing presented itself as I wandered from window to bed to desk. Swiping at the sweat on my upper lip and ready to give up, I froze. It watched from the doorway. I moved to the window, hoping to lure it farther in. It didn't budge. Time to try something different.

"This is a nice house."

Nothing. Maybe a little push was required.

"I wonder if Sherita would sell it to me."

Silence.

I looked around the room. "Yup. I can see the possibilities. The bedrooms are too small, though. I bet if I knocked out a wall here and combined it with the one next door—"

"Don't you dare touch one board of this house." The ghost of an old woman appeared at the doorway, scowling.

"Really? Why?" I asked.

"This is my house and I won't have any dirty Negroes or drunk Irish living in it," she said, twitching her nose like she smelled something bad.

"Wow, what a racist thing to say." No wonder Sherita had such problems in this house.

The old woman looked down her nose, all high-and-mighty. "It makes little difference what you think. Leave now and take those others with you. Do not come back."

"Um, there's a problem. You're dead and houses are for the living."

"You are impertinent, young lady." She shook her

finger at me. "No matter. My papa built this house and he left it to me in his will. I have legal ownership to this property and you will leave now."

Huh. "I have to speak to the homeowner, anyway, so I'll be back."

"It will do you no good." She disappeared.

Not a benign ghost after all.

Outside, I pulled Sherita over to the porch. "Good news." I tried to sound cheerful, but don't think I pulled it off. "You have just one ghost."

"But..." Sherita prompted. No fooling her.

"She's going to be a problem," I said. "Her father built the house, left it to her in his will. She's old and insists the house is hers. It might take a while." I glanced at the lowering sun and checked my cell phone. "Is there somewhere all of you can stay the night?"

She raised her eyebrows. "You think it'll take that long?"

I shrugged. "I don't know. I'm new at this but I'd feel better if you were comfortable somewhere." Out of harm's way.

She thought for a moment. "Okay. How much do you think it'll cost?"

"I can't charge you. I'm not in business." And I didn't know what I was doing.

Sherita pursed her lips and looked at me for a long moment. "Alright. Let me settle the kids at a friend's house and then I'll go in with you."

"You want to be there, in the house?"

She nodded her head.

"It may not be the best idea. Things can get strange, real fast. You could get hurt."

She had a determined look on her face. "My kids have to have a safe place to live and if there's a chance to get rid of it, I want to be there."

"Okay. I'll wait for you," I said, sitting on the porch step. Sherita and her kids walked up the street.

There were some big problems with this situation. The ghost thought it her legal and moral right to be in the house. Never mind the fact dying voided any ownership rights. To top it off, she was racist and probably wouldn't listen to me. It would be an uphill battle.

I slumped over. What a day. Why was I once again at a stranger's house, pretending to know what I was doing? I wanted to get up and leave all this craziness behind. Forget the house. Go back to my normal life. I thought of Sherita and her kids and groaned. They needed help. The kind no one but me could provide. I sat up.

"Focus," I muttered. How to get the old bat out of the house? What was her Fluffy? She seemed the independent sort, but had mentioned her "papa" with affection, I thought.

"Dad? Ma?" I asked, my voice low so as not to alarm neighbors on their own porches. "Are you out there? We worked well together on the basement ghost. I need your help."

Sounds of crickets and young male laughter at the end of the street.

"Please?" I waited but still received no response.

Sherita returned and I tried to look more put together than I was. After all, I did have some pride left.

"I should explain a couple things before we go in," I told her. "You have to be ready to expect anything. You may see or hear odd things or feel strong emotions that aren't your own. In fact, try not to react, because ghosts can use your emotional energy."

"Alright."

"I've got to take a minute...to...ah...prepare." So awkward.

"You go ahead. I'll pray." she said.

Not so awkward after all.

She whispered a prayer as I did my visualization and we went in. Not knowing what to expect, but being cautious, I led Sherita from the entry to the living room. I thought I felt a light brush against my awareness but a moment later, it disappeared. Same thing in the kitchen.

On our way upstairs, I said, "The ghost's playing games. I'll feel it for a second and it goes away."

"Playing hide-and-seek is it?" she whispered.

"Yeah."

We entered the bedroom at the top of the stairs. It was quite dark now and Sherita turned on a bedside lamp.

"Well," Sherita spoke louder, hands on her hips. "I've had enough of this nonsense. You frightened my kids."

I braced for the ghost's reaction.

"This is my house," Sherita continued, "and I ain't gonna let any ghost make us leave. You go on, now. Go to Jesus, where you belong."

There was a moment of silence.

The bedside light flickered out. Sherita tried to turn it back on, but it wouldn't. I fumbled in my bag for the flashlight. The bedside and ceiling light switched on. Knocking began on the walls and ceiling, making us both jump. I laughed and patted Sherita's arm. "Cheap tricks."

The knocking turned to ferocious pounding, making the pictures on the wall skitter back and forth. The lights turned off and on, off and on. The telephone by the bed rang. "Come on, now," I said. "Are you a spoiled child or a ghost that's existed for decades? Come out and discuss this like a civilized being."

The next thing I knew, I was on the floor, gasping for breath. It felt as if fingers tightened around my throat.

Sherita screamed, but it sounded far away.

Silently, I called out to my parents, to my guide.

Somewhere down the long tunnel, Sherita began to pray. "Our Father who art in Heaven, hallowed be Thy name—"

I said it in my head with her, but it was hard to focus. Fuzziness enclosed me, like when I was a small child and Ma wrapped me in a big towel after a bath. The warmth seeped away.

A sharp slap on my face pulled me out of the haze.

"Fight it," Sherita shouted in my ear. "Don't let it win. You hear me? Kenna, fight it."

Voices faded. Darkness approached. White noise in my ears. A far away light.

"Louisa." A deep, male voice lashed out.

The grip on my throat lessened a degree. Awareness trickled back to me.

"Young lady, stop this instant." The military-sharp command broke through the fog and the pressure on my throat stopped.

Curling into a fetal position, I gasped in and coughed out. Again and again. Was barely aware of the door to the Other Side closing.

Sherita rubbed my back. "Bless the Lord, you're okay. Let's get you sitting up, honey. It'll be easier to breathe."

She hooked a hand under my elbow and helped me slowly sit up, leaning against the bed.

"There. Better?"

I nodded.

"Is it gone?" she asked.

Nodding, I wondered about my parents. I almost choked to death and they weren't here?

Sherita sighed. "Hallelujah, you did it. Kenna, thank you so much." She squeezed my arm. "I don't know what to say." She made a noise and put her hand up to her mouth.

Oh, no. She was crying.

After a minute, she wiped her eyes. "How are you feeling, now?"

"Fine," I croaked.

"I bet a cup of tea with honey would help your throat."

I shook my head. "Gotta burn sage first." My throat felt like it was on fire. "Gets rid of negative energy."

Sherita handed me my bag of supplies and helped me cleanse each room. It was a blessing her house didn't have a basement.

The herbal tea would have been awful without three big spoons of honey but it soothed my sore throat. My stomach growled and she insisted on making me scrambled eggs. I wanted to decline, but I was starving. My energy was drained from tangling with Louisa.

She put the plate of eggs and toast on the table and sat across from me. "I have to pay you. You almost died up there."

"I almost died because I was stupid, Sherita. I got

sloppy, letting you provoke a dangerous ghost without stopping you. I shouldn't have let you stay. My mistake."

"You wouldn't be here at all if I didn't beg you to. Now, I have something set aside for emergencies—"

"No," I said. "How about we argue about this another time, okay? I want to eat and go back to my motel."

"Oh, no you don't," she said. "You stay the night here and I'll feed you. It's the least I can do."

Not wanting to drive in this condition, I accepted. As I wolfed down the eggs, Sherita made up a bed for me on the couch. I liked this woman. She was good people. My last thoughts before drifting to sleep involved giving the person responsible for outing me a piece of my mind.

"WHEN'S SHE GONNA WAKE UP?"

"When she feels like it, dog breath."

I rolled over, wondering why children were playing outside my motel room so early in the morning.

"Don't call your brother names," someone said in a low voice.

I swallowed and pain in my throat woke me fully. Memories of the ghost strangling me last night. Right. I'd crashed at Sherita's. Closing my eyes again, I snuggled deeper under the blanket. Just one more minute.

Tumbled images played out in my mind. Choking. Fading. My breath hitched. I'd called out for help. Once, for my parents, but then, in a blind panic, to no one in particular. Well, not no one. I'd intended it for my spirit guide. Then the spirit of what I assumed was the ghost's father came from the Other Side to stop her from choking me. A wave of gratitude washed over me and I said a silent "thank you" into the Universe.

A rough, wet tongue licked my nose and cheek, startling me. I reached out, petting the wriggling small body. Sherita's dog yipped, trying to climb up with me.

"Oh, no, you don't." said Sherita, above me. She picked the dog up. "You leave Miss Kenna alone. She had a hard night scaring away the ghost."

"He's alright." I winced at the pain in my throat and sat up. Her children stood near the door, watching me. Probably ready to bolt as soon as something strange happened.

"You need some tea." Sherita set the dog down, heading toward the kitchen. The dog jumped up in my lap.

Her daughter, carrying the youngest, stared at me then hurried after her mom.

The dog wouldn't sit still, so I held his face, looking him in the eye. "Settle down, now," I rasped. "Or I won't let you sit with me. Okay?" I let go. He turned one circle then laid down, paws and head on my knees, and sighed. "Good boy." I pet him. Felt something wrong as my fingers moved toward his hind legs.

"You really scared away the ghost?" The oldest boy now leaned up against a nearby chair, staring at me with wide eyes.

I nodded, still focused on the dog.

He sat on the other end of the couch, bouncing a little. "How?"

I considered his question. "I can see and talk to ghosts and they can talk to me. I make them want to leave. What's your dog's name?"

"Max."

I smiled. "Good name."

"You made our ghost go away?"

With help from her father. "Yes."

"So, it's gone for good and won't come back?"

"It's gone for good."

He whooped, launching himself off the couch and up the stairs. The dog took off after him with a happy bark.

Sherita came back, mug in hand, shaking her head. "That child."

I accepted the steaming mug. "He's happy to have his home back."

She smiled. "Me too."

We ate breakfast, the children chattering. It felt comfortable, homey. Afterward, I made a point of getting ready to leave and Sherita handed me my bag of supplies. She must have gathered it all up.

"Thank you so much for your help." She gave me a hug.

"You are most welcome," I said as I stepped back. Her dog jumped up on my leg. I leaned down to pet him. "You, too."

The kids hovered close.

"Can I talk to you outside for a minute?" I asked Sherita.

"Sure." She followed me out to the curb.

I put my bag in the car and closed the door, leaning against it. "I'm a vet tech. That's my regular job."

"I didn't know that."

"How old is Max?"

She raised her eyebrows. "About eight years old."

"Does he ever limp?"

"Sometimes, but he jumps around so much I figure he just landed wrong. He's fine after a bit."

"It may be nothing, because I couldn't do an examination, but I'm a little concerned. You might want your regular vet to check him out. Explain about the periodic limp."

"I will. Thank you, Kenna. My goodness, you flush out ghosts and take care of animals, too. You are one busy lady."

Compliments didn't stop me from feeling like a slug, giving her bad news about her dog. "Let me know if you have anymore problems, with either one."

"I will."

She waved as I drove away.

Icy fear settled in my chest. Messing with ghosts was dangerous and this time, I'd been lucky.

17

After a quick shower and change of clothes at the motel, I arrived at the house at the same time as Nate. He was going to work on the garage then tinker with the lawn mower, try to get it running. If there was time, he'd mow the lawn.

The end of the long road was in sight.

"Before I forget—" He pulled something out of his backpack. "I got this for the little dude," he said, holding up a small bag of dry cat food. "Can't have him eating people food all the time."

I stared. "You're set on making him a house cat, aren't you?"

Unlocking the door, I trudged up the stairs to the kitchen, but as soon as I opened the door, my Spidey senses tingled. Setting the cat food on the counter, I examined the room but all was in order.

"Miss Kenna?" A gentle voice spoke near my ear.

I jumped, surprised. "Henry? What's wrong?"

A human shape began to form, coalescing into

Henry's tall, slim figure. "I am afraid your home has been invaded by strangers."

I rushed into the dining room. Neatly-piled boxes were knocked over, their contents strewn across the room. Stepping forward, glass crunched underfoot. "What the—"

In the living room, an easy chair and more boxes were turned over. On the wall above the couch, a black spray-painted message said, "Get Out." On top of everything else, I now had vandals and a mess to clean up. I hustled upstairs, but nothing was disturbed in the bedrooms.

Fur rubbed against my bare ankle. The tomcat. Tumblers in my brain fell into place. "And I bet I know how they got in," I said, hurrying to the dining room. The window I left open a crack for the cat to get out was now wide open.

I turned toward the kitchen and almost tripped over the cat.

Belly empty. He looked at me expectantly, shifting his weight from one front paw to the other.

"What? This mess is all your fault and now you want to be fed?" I said, hands on hips. He butted up against me. "Fine. Fine." Rummaging around in the wreckage, I found an intact bowl. Grabbing the bag of cat food, I poured a small amount into it. Before the bowl even reached the floor, he pushed his head into it.

Leaning a hip against the counter, I felt strangely contented despite discovering my house had been violated. "*The* house." I corrected, shaking my head, as if someone heard my thoughts. "You won't get fed like this for much longer, cat." The food was gone and he looked up at me, wanting more. "That's it, buddy. Time for you to go." He didn't need much coaxing.

I went back to the living room and stared at the spray-painted words. "Henry? You still here?"

"Yes, Miss Kenna." Henry said next to me.

"Did you see who did this?" I waved my arms indicating the graffiti and other destruction.

"Three young men." He looked pained. "I did not know they were here until the cat howled."

"Pitched a fit, did he?" Guess I was a little too quick in my judgment of the fur ball. "I don't suppose you could describe them? The young men?"

"They were crawling out of the window when I became aware and I am sorry I did not see their faces."

I shrugged. "Oh, well. That's more than I knew before. Thank you, Henry."

"You are most welcome, Miss Kenna." Henry dissolved into the air, as if his molecules just separated. That is, if ghosts even had molecules.

I got cleaning supplies from the kitchen and scrubbed at the black lettering till my arms felt like cooked spaghetti. No luck.

I put away the supplies and sat on the couch, glaring at the destruction. Apparently, cleaning up broken stuff, repacking boxes, and painting the wall were now on my to-do list. Instead of shrinking, that sucker was growing. I groaned and fell sideways, half laying on the cushions. I'd never get this house ready before having to go back to my job. And I wanted to drive back and forth across the state each weekend about as much as I wanted to walk on fire.

I sat up when I heard a knock at the kitchen door. "Hey, Kenna? I got the lawn mower to start."

"Nate," I called, straining. My throat was still sore. "Come here. I want you to see something."

In a moment, Nate entered from the kitchen. "You get mad or something?"

"Come in the living room." I waved him in.

He stood in the doorway and whistled. "Someone broke in?"

"Well, actually, I left a window open because the cat got in and I couldn't find him before I left last night."

He grinned. "Sneaky little bugger, ain't he?"

"Yeah, well, I'll have to be more careful about leaving windows open."

"Too bad you don't have a dog to guard the place at night."

"That'd be nice. Have one handy?"

"Nope."

"Then I guess it's just little ol' me." A thought hit me upside the head. "Hey, I could stay here instead of the motel. It'd save me money and I could keep an eye on the place."

He bobbed his head. "Or you might get bashed over the head when you surprise the next burglar. Nah, it's a good idea, but maybe turn some lights on at night."

The heaviness that settled on me after discovering the damage lifted a little. After discussing the remaining junk in the garage with Nate, I cleaned up the worst of the damage, then went back to the motel and settled up. Strangely, I looked forward to staying at the old house.

What was wrong with me?

≈

On my way back from the motel, I saw Brian's pickup truck parked at Mickey's. Time to have a little chat.

The blast of cold air as I entered the bar was welcome, but I didn't stop to enjoy it. The place was almost empty, except for a couple guys at the bar and the table where my target was holding court with his cronies.

Brian faced me, but was in the middle of telling a story. I approached the table. "Here she is." Brian beamed.

I glared at him. "What do you think you're doing, old man?"

He didn't skip a beat. "Kenna, you look upset. Come have a drink. On me." His smile grew broader. He signaled to the bartender but I shook my head.

"I don't want a drink," I said. "Everywhere I went today, people were whispering. They knew things about me I don't even tell my closest friends. I asked myself how would anyone know something like that? Well, there were two people in Hurlbutt who did."

Brian made his way around the table toward me.

"One," I said, "is too polite to ever think of telling a lady's secrets in public. And I'm looking at the other one." I poked his chest with my pointy finger. "It wasn't too hard to find you, either."

"Now, Kenna." He tried to pat my arm, but I shook him off.

He seemed surprised. "But this is a good thing. There've gotta be dozens of ghosts in this town. You could make a boatload of money gettin' rid of 'em. Like those folks on TV."

"Enough with the 'folks on TV.'" I was loud, but I didn't care. "You don't get it, Brian. I just want to clean up my parents' house, sell it, and go back home. I have a nice, quiet, life that doesn't involve," I lowered my voice, "people running away from me or pleading with me to help them with their ghost problem."

Brian's eyes lit up. His friends looked at me, expectantly.

"No." I shook my head. "No, I don't do this anymore. I helped your brother out because he was a special case and in serious trouble but I can't help everyone or I'll never leave."

"You're going to let people suffer?"

I slumped into an empty chair. "No, but I can't help everyone. It's too much for one person to handle."

"Declan can help."

I raised an eyebrow. "He's just learning how to help himself. He'd be a worse mess than when I saw him at Hanley's. "

"That's why we need you," he said, pointing at me. "You can get rid of the ghosts at the lake and a few in town, then things will get back to normal. Go home after. I won't say another thing. I promise."

My stomach spasmed. "What makes you think there's ghosts at the lake?"

"The kids down there last night said so."

"Kids lie all the time to get out of trouble."

"Sounds to me like ghosts. Never thought of it until I saw what you and Declan did the other day. I watched a couple of those shows." He nodded to his buddies.

"So, without knowing for sure, you told everyone I'd fix things? What's wrong with you?"

He grinned. "Oh, well..."

He was trying to brush it off. "Well, nothing." I stood.

"You've messed things up for me, Brian. Thanks a lot. Now, unless you want me to explain to Declan how you talk about him and his abilities to your friends," I stared at the men around the table. "You'll never speak about me in public again." They assured me they wouldn't say a word but Brian was tight-lipped. I knew the wheels were turning in his head. "Promise me, Brian."

He hemmed and hawed for a while, but finally agreed.

"Good." I stalked toward the door.

"You tell him, honey." The ghost barmaid waved.

I nodded once and kept on walking.

Returning to the house, my anger kept me scrubbing the tub and sink in the upstairs bathroom. When it started getting dark, I stopped and took a shower then made myself a sandwich, popped the top on a beer, and took it out to the back yard. It was nice to relax and listen to the sounds of a summer evening. The cat joined me. Too lazy to go back in the house for the cat food Nate gifted him, I threw out a piece of deli meat and he caught it in his mouth. Once it was full dark, he became a light-colored blob prowling the edges of the property.

Later, it was difficult to get to sleep. Upstairs in my childhood bed, even with a fan on me, it was too warm. I moved downstairs to the couch and it was cooler. Then thoughts of ghosts and the fear I wasn't good enough to cross over a whole town full of them gnawed at me. After several hours of tossing and turning, trying to find a cool spot on the pillow, I drifted off.

∼

MY HEARTBEAT POUNDED IN MY EARS. SOMETHING BRUSHED my face. I turned away, wanting to curl myself into a ball, but couldn't move. My eyes popped open to see large, green ones observing me and I flinched. The tomcat readjusted his position on my chest, then rubbed his face on my cheek, purring in a wheezy sort of way.

"*Mmrph.*" I grabbed his hindquarters and pulled him away from my face. He wasn't pleased. Digging his claws into my upper arm and chest, he leaped off the couch. I hissed and turned on my side.

The cat sat a few feet away, hind leg sticking straight up in the air, licking his butt.

"Yeah, well, good morning to you, too," I said, my voice cracking. I cleared my throat, noticing the pain wasn't as sharp today. "How did you get in here, again?" Last night I'd checked all the windows on the first floor. Then I remembered coming in from the backyard last night and not turning on lights until I reached the kitchen. "You snuck in with me in the dark, didn't you?" He sat up and licked his chest now, not deigning to even look my way. "Probably hid until I went to bed." I stretched and sat up, groaning again as something snapped in my lower back.

As I padded to the kitchen, the cat threw himself under my feet and I went shoulder-first into the door frame. "Thanks a lot, Speedy Gonzales." I poured cat food into the bowl on the linoleum as he head-butted my ankles. He attacked it, purring, while I rubbed my sore shoulder. "Ungrateful feline."

After starting the coffee maker and pouring a bowl of Frosted Flakes, I stood at the sink, crunching and staring out the window. What new insanity would the faire hamlet of Hurlbutt throw at me today?

On second thought, I didn't want to know.

The house project was winding down—huzzah!—and Nate had other jobs to do today, so I was alone, rattling around the house. Wandering into the living room, I glared at the graffiti on the wall. "Guess I'm painting today." Unfortunately, I couldn't find any left-over paint or equipment around the house or garage. Either we got rid of it or sold it.

The hardware store on Main Street was narrow and deep, with tools, plumbing, and electrical supplies on shelves lining the walls and in the middle, splitting the store into two sides. Two men talked toward the back. I soon found painting supplies but wasn't sure what to buy. My only experience had been helping a friend paint a couple rooms and we'd gotten more on ourselves than the walls.

"Can I help you with something?" A man in a blue denim apron stood behind me.

"Hi. I need to paint one wall of a living room."

"Just one?"

"Vandals broke in and spray painted."

He whistled. "That's unfortunate."

"You're lucky you weren't hurt," an old man said in a squeaky voice as he shuffled by us. "See ya later, Chris." Not waiting for an answer, he left the store.

"I wasn't there at the time," I said to the clerk. "Any-way, I need to get it ready to sell and I don't want to spend an arm and a leg. What do you recommend?"

Based on my vague description, he figured the

approximate size of the wall and set me up with primer, paint, and other supplies.

There was something off about the guy that I couldn't quite put my finger on. Maybe I was just edgy from all the ghost energy swirling in town. And tired.

I left the store with a plastic bag looped over each wrist and clutching a paint can in one hand and primer in the other. At the car, I set down one handful on the sidewalk by the trunk and reached into my shorts for my car keys. Glancing across the street, I stopped.

In front of an empty storefront that had once been a five-and-dime, stood three people. One was the guy in jeans and Army jacket I'd seen before. The ghost. He talked and gestured with his hands to two men dressed in 60s bell bottom pants. One of them shook his head. He looked up, saw me, and pointed. The others turned and stared at me. The two guys vanished but Army Jacket stood, smoking his cigarette and watching me, before fading. His eyes were the last to go, drilling into mine.

Brrr.

When I was twelve, my friends dared me to drink an Icee as fast as I could. I did it, because, duh, you had to do a dare. Afterward, my entire head felt numb.

That's how I felt when the ghost looked at me. Frozen to the pavement.

18

————

In the two weeks since Miss Tierney had helped clear his house, Declan's strength had begun to return. He was scrupulous about grounding himself and imagining the protective white light. He thought of it as God's love enveloping him. He did it every morning and every evening and sometimes during the day. One couldn't be too cautious.

With the quiet, not only could he read his beloved books again, he could also think. Which led him to Miss Tierney's door one afternoon.

"Hi," she said, opening the door. She seemed happy to see him. "How are you?" She looked over his shoulder. "Did you walk all this way?"

"Hello, Miss Tierney. It's not far. A good stretch of the legs."

She grinned. "And I told you, please call me Kenna. Is everything alright? I see the ghosts have stayed away from you."

He rubbed his hands together, over and over. It had

seemed so simple when he planned this, but now his stomach fluttered. "Kenna, then. Yes, I'm fine. I've been doing what you taught me but might we talk for a bit?"

"Of course. Come on in." She opened the door wide.

She showed him into the living room, moving a box off the couch. "Sorry about the mess."

Declan stared. The words "Get Out" were spray painted on the opposite wall.

"Yeah, somebody broke in the other night."

"My goodness." He barely noticed sitting on the couch. "You weren't hurt, were you?"

"No. I was staying at a motel." She settled into an easy chair. "So, what's up?"

"Good, good." He cleared his throat. "First, I wanted to thank you. After you taught me how to protect myself and deal with the spirits, well, I was able to have the peace and quiet. I cannot tell you what a blessing it is. Thank you so much."

Her whole face lit up. "You're very welcome."

Embarrassed, he dipped his head. "As I said, I was able to finally think and started wondering where all these ghosts came from. And why now? I told you about fishing at the lake this spring and Brian tipping our boat over?"

She nodded.

"Well, it was after that I became more and more distracted by the spirits. But it was—"

"Hold it. Where did this happen?"

"Rogers Lake."

She leaned forward. "Declan, I ran into a bunch of ghosts at Rogers Lake. And it's the same place those kids were the other night. You heard about them, right?"

A chill swept up his back. "No. What happened?"

"A bunch of kids got attacked. Claimed it was ghosts. Has something happened there lately? It would have to be big enough to light up Hurlbutt like a psychic carnival. A mass murder would do it, but I would have heard if that happened."

"I was getting there. For a while prior to our incident at the lake, I'd been hearing things, just quiet enough I couldn't make out what they were. Easy to ignore, you see. Then, after becoming so ill, I couldn't do much but lay there, so I couldn't help hearing them. Thinking it all over now, I believe I heard them before falling in the lake." He leaned forward, raising his eyebrows.

She frowned, confused.

"I thought back to the winter. There was one thing that affected everyone in town." He paused, willing her to remember.

She finally sucked in a breath. "The train."

"Good girl." He felt like a proud school teacher. "The train derailment outside of town in February. It carried crude oil from North Dakota to the refineries in New Jersey. When it derailed, one of the tankers broke open and—*kaboom*—the engineers jumped off the train. And since it was out of town in the wee hours of the morning, no one was hurt. The sound scared me out of bed, though. Scared everybody."

She nodded. "I remember. We were worried about Ma. The pictures and video on the Internet were incredible. Did they ever find out what caused it?"

"The report on it won't be released for months. I heard they took away an axle and a couple wheels, so maybe it was faulty equipment. Who knows?" He shrugged. "The point is, the explosions made a hell of a racket, pardon my French, and shook the whole town. Now, what if...it also stirred up the ghosts?"

She shrugged. "Anything's possible, I suppose."

"The timing makes sense." He slapped his hands on his thighs. "I'd like to go to the scene of the accident, but Brian will make a fuss if I ask him. Will you go with me?"

"I—but, *why* do you want to go out there?"

"Now I'm not so scared, but I am curious about all these ghosts. I want to know what's going on. Don't you? If we could figure out where they're all coming from, then maybe there's a way to stop them. Besides, I'm not getting any younger. I need answers before I run out of time."

She made a face. "Oh, you aren't going to run out of time."

He wasn't sure she'd do it. If not, then he'd have to ask Brian.

She let out a deep breath. "Okay, let's go."

He smiled. "Thank you."

The derailment site was a couple miles west of Hurlbutt. Declan directed her to park along the side of the closest road crossing the tracks.

She insisted they do grounding and visualization exercises. "No way am I going in totally unprepared again."

They started walking into the woods. Trees lined both sides of the double set of tracks. They walked about ten feet to the right of the tracks, in the shade cast by the trees. It was hushed and peaceful, with birds, crickets, and their own footsteps on gravel the only sounds. A weight seemed to lift from Declan's chest. He had always felt better when out in nature. It had been too long.

The mosquitoes found them but his long-sleeved shirt and long pants came in handy. Kenna, who wore a tank top and shorts, slapped at her bare arms and legs. He felt bad for not bringing insect spray.

As they walked, he cocked his head back and forth, trying to catch whispers, but didn't hear anything. If his theory was correct, the closer they got to the crash site, the more ghosts they should experience. Doubt settled into his chest.

They trudged on until a space in the trees on both sides of the tracks widened ahead of them. A huge area was cleared of trees, the ground disturbed and raked level.

"This is it," Declan said, looking around. "They did a good job cleaning up."

Kenna followed as he walked towards the closest edge of the woods. He placed his hand on a tree. A faint woodsmoke smell rose from the charred bark on one side of many of the trees ringing the area.

"Do you feel or, well, hear anything?"

He stood still for several moments, then sighed. "No."

"Me, neither."

He frowned. "I was so certain. It made such sense."

She snorted. "Yeah, well, I've learned the hard way that the spirit world doesn't make much sense to the living."

They headed back toward the car but didn't get far. A faint sound stopped him.

"I felt an energy blip," she said. "Did you hear anything?"

He nodded. "Whispering." He scanned the trees, waiting for it to come again. He didn't have to wait long.

Whispers. But he couldn't make out words. He turned but Kenna remained facing the other way.

"Hello?" She called out. "We know you're there. Please come and talk to us?"

They waited.

Maybe a little conversation would help. "We know something terrible happened here. Did you see it? Were you a part of it?" He closed his eyes, focusing on his hearing.

A whispered drifted from the trees across the tracks. "*Chuga-chuga-chuga-chuga-whoo-WHOO.*" Like a child imitating a train.

Excitement flashed through him.

The train noises continued getting louder, then stopped.

Declan started to cross the rails. His toe hit a track but Kenna grabbed his elbow before he could stumble.

She helped him to the other side then peered into the trees. "Please, tell us about the train."

Chugging sounds, followed by a slap, as if someone clapped their hands together. "*Crraaash!*" A child's sweet, high-pitched voice.

Kenna shifted her weight. "Did you see it happen?"

"Or did it wake you up?" Declan asked.

"We saw it," said the spirit, "but it woke up lots of others. Some even played with us."

"We?" asked Declan. She didn't answer and he glanced at Kenna.

She stared at the trees, her mouth open. "Twins. Twin girls, about seven or eight years old."

How sad. How horribly, utterly sad.

"We're nine." said one of the spirits.

How was he to keep them straight?

Kenna smiled. "I'm sorry. *Nine* years old."

The spirits whispered to each other and he strained to hear something concrete.

"So." Kenna put her hands behind her back and paced, still looking at a spot in front of the trees. "You saw the train accident here?"

The girls grew quiet. "It was very loud," one finally said.

"You were here before it happened?" Kenna paused. "They nodded 'yes,'" she said, for his benefit. "Why aren't there more ghosts here?"

Silence.

This was harder than pulling the truth out of a politician. He tried another tack. "When the train crashed, how did it effect other spirits in the area?"

The girls whispered together. "First, you have to play hide-n-seek." They giggled.

Kenna groaned. "They ran off in opposite directions."

19

Could this go any worse? "Really, right now?"

Declan grinned. "They're children."

I rolled my eyes at him. "Yeah, but I'm not." And Declan definitely wasn't.

"If we cooperate, we may get more information."

"I could be home now, in my nice, air-conditioned apartment," I said, slapping at a blood-thirsty mosquito. "Ready or not," I called, "here I come." The sound of giggling sent me through the brush to my left. After checking behind several trees, the laughter changed direction. No sooner did I run that way, the laughter came from behind me. They kept this up until I was sweaty and annoyed. I tried to be a good sport, but playing hide-n-seek with ghosts is no fun. Having had enough, I yelled, "You win. You're too good at this game. I give up," and returned to Declan, who sat on a rail, waiting.

"Had enough?" he asked.

"Enough to last the rest of my life," I grumbled plopping down next to him. "I hope a train won't be coming through here soon." I stared down the tracks and then in the opposite direction.

"I checked earlier," Declan said. "No trains are scheduled to go through this area..." He looked at his wrist watch. "For another hour, at least."

Of course he checked. I hadn't even thought of it. "Okay, girls," I called. "I played with you. Now, please come and talk to us."

The ghost girls materialized by the tree line, giggling. They were adorable little girls, with their short blond hair framing heart-shaped faces and the same pink ruffled tank tops and plaid shorts.

"About the train wreck," I began.

"It woke up the sleeping dead," said the ghost I thought was the spokesperson.

"But," Declan protested, "where are the other ghosts now?"

"They're all around." The ghost sounded exasperated. "In the houses and stores and in the cemetery."

"And more come each day," piped up her twin.

Declan raised his eyebrows. "More?"

"Where do they come from?"

"From other places," they said in unison.

Yeah, not creepy at all.

"You mean far away places?" asked Declan.

The spokesghost shrugged.

"What about the ghosts at the lake?" I asked.

A look of fear crossed the girls' faces. "They've always been here but we don't talk about them," she whispered.

The second girl shook her head.

Now we were getting somewhere. "Why not?"

"They're scary."

The second girl gasped.

"Who were they?" I asked. "And what are they now? Are they still ghosts or something worse?"

The girls huddled together, whispering again. It got heated. The second girl stamped her foot and crossed her arms. She kept shaking her head.

The spokesghost said, "Mama told us never to speak ill of the dead or they'd find a way to hurt us."

"But you are ghosts."

"Mama told us not to."

They weren't going to cross Mama. "Okay." Time to try a tactic from my childhood. "What if I ask you a question and you nod or shake your heads. You wouldn't be speaking at all."

They whispered together and then nodded their heads in the affirmative.

"Good." I grinned at Declan. "Now, are the ghosts at the lake...ghosts?"

They nodded yes.

"So they aren't like...demons or anything?"

They shook their heads.

"Good." I flicked my eyes at Declan. "They aren't demons. Did the ghosts at the lake wake up when the train crashed?"

Two "yes" nods.

I looked at Declan. "They confirmed your hunch."

"Thank you, ladies," Declan said, "for your help."

The girls giggled. It didn't take much to set them off.

He took a couple steps forward. "By the way, I'm Declan and this is Kenna. What are your names?"

I moved next to him, curious.

"I'm Katie," said the first girl, "and this is Josie."

"What is your family name?" he asked, ever the historian.

"Maines," said Katie.

The name sounded familiar.

Declan nodded, as if expecting the answer. "What are you girls doing way out here?"

"This is where we play."

"You lived near here, didn't you?"

"Our home is over there." Katie pointed into the woods.

Declan looked at me and I pointed where the ghost indicated. He had a strange look on his face. "You lived with your Mama and Grandma, correct?"

"Yes," said Katie.

He looked sad. "Have we gotten all the information we need?" he asked me.

"I think so. Why?"

"They need to go on to Heaven now."

Declan was stepping up on this one. It sounded like he knew who they were so it must feel personal for him. "Alright. Why don't you do the honors?"

He cleared his throat. "Girls, you should go on and be with your Mama and Grandma."

Their faces lit up. "You know where they are?" asked Katie. Josie clutched her arm, bouncing up on her toes.

"I believe they are in Heaven and it's high time you went there, yourselves."

"But—" Katie bit her lip. "What about the man? He said he'd hurt Mama."

"Is he here now, as a spirit?"

"We haven't seen him but he said he'd hurt Mama and Grandma. He meant it."

Declan shook his head. "He's gone and can't hurt you or anyone else."

"How do you know?" asked Josie.

"He died in prison and I imagine he went to Hell for what he did to you." Declan's voice took on a hard edge.

The girls looked relieved.

"How do we find Mama?" asked Katie.

"Look for a bright light or a doorway."

"A doorway? In the woods?" Josie asked.

Declan smiled. "God can put a doorway anywhere he wants."

Josie still looked skeptical.

"There it is." Katie pointed to the left.

"Mama," the girls squealed. They ran to the doorway and through it, their laughter echoing before it closed, cutting us off. This time, the joy and comfort stayed with me.

Declan had a huge grin on his face. "They are finally at peace," he murmured.

I returned his smile. "You okay? Not too tired or anything?" Crossing two ghosts should have affected him.

He stood straighter. "I'm feeling fine. Better than fine, in fact."

"I feel pretty good, myself. Come on." I held onto his elbow, heading for the road. "What happened to them? Their name sounded familiar."

Declan sighed. "Back in the early seventies...must

have been, oh, around 1972, I guess…the girls went missing. It was blazing hot like now but…" He looked into the distance. "It had to have been August because Brian's youngest child was born a few weeks before, in July." He blinked and focused on me. "For two weeks everyone searched for them. It was in all the papers and on TV. The state police found them in a shack deep in the woods."

It flooded back to me. A story Jim told Nora and I to scare us when we were kids. "I remember now. Some crazy guy in a shack."

He stopped and turned. "Way down there," he said, indicating an area near where the ghosts had been, but on the opposite side of the tracks. "Joseph Ogden. He wasn't right in the head. Never had been. I remember him from school. There was an incident involving a girl in his class. I was eleven, so he would have been twelve, maybe thirteen, since he was held back. Nobody talked about it, but something bad happened. The girl's family moved away and Joe didn't return to school."

I felt sick to my stomach.

"It was many years later the little girls disappeared. By then, all his family was gone. His sister ran away during high school and his father died in a farming accident not too long after. His mother died a few months before the girls went missing. She was the one who kept him in line for so long." He paused. "What he did to those little angels…"

"You don't have to explain anymore."

He took a deep breath. "The important thing is they are in a better place now."

We walked the rest of the way in silence.

When we got to my car, I was covered in sweat and itching from mosquito bites. Opening the door, a wave of heat slammed into me. I started the engine and opened the windows. Tearing off a square of the paper towel roll I kept for emergencies, I offered it to Declan but he declined. I wiped my damp face. "You got the answer you were looking for."

"Yes, but we ought to get a sense of how widespread this is. In town, I feel surrounded all the time." He paused. "I don't know how other people don't feel it."

"A medium I once knew used to say normal people were block heads. You know, made of wood, like Pinocchio? Because they couldn't sense anything beyond their own noses."

He was silent a moment. "We could drive around a bit, get a sense of where the boundaries are."

It felt like a waste of time but, if it put Declan's mind to rest, it was worth it. Besides, I didn't want to go back to the house and paint the stupid wall. "Ghost hunting it is." The AC finally kicked in. Relief, at last. I did a u-turn back to town.

Focusing on ghost energy, I felt them in the occasional house or barn. Once in town, I drove down one street after another, picking up on a lot of single entities and pockets of intense action, as if several ghosts hung out together.

Driving north, we noticed diminishing activity the farther we got. I turned around and when we got to the middle of town, turned east onto Main Street. We passed the cemetery, which wasn't as busy with ghosts as the day of Ma's burial. When the feeling decreased, I came back. We'd already been west, leaving the south, toward Rogers

Lake.

"We shouldn't go anywhere near those lake ghosts when we're this low on energy," I said. We needed fuel. It was late afternoon and neither of us had had lunch. Declan agreed. At the diner, we wolfed down Salisbury steak, mashed potatoes and gravy. Then we were ready to face ghosts. Well, Declan was ready. It amazed me how quickly he seemed to accept and move into his role as a psychic. I, on the other hand, pretended to be ready. Fake it till you make it.

As we left the diner, I noticed how dark it had become while we were inside.

Declan looked up. "Clouds rolling in."

"Maybe it'll rain."

Declan sniffed the air. "Nope. Not today."

I laughed. "You can tell just by smell?"

"Ayup."

Driving out, I felt so vulnerable with my senses open. Even before we got to the lake, my gut was flip-flopping.

Declan sucked in his breath like he'd been burned. "I feel them."

Everything looked normal, if a bit gloomy, but the feeling of wrongness oozed over me. I drove beyond the turnoff to the lake and continued on for a short distance until the feeling faded away. "There's where it stops for me. How about you?"

"I don't hear anything."

I turned the car around, steeling myself for the oppressive feeling as we passed the lake again.

"Lightning," said Declan, pointing to the left.

I slowed down to a crawl. On my left, a clearing opened and I saw snaking tongues of light flashing above the trees in the distance. "That has to mean rain, right?" I said.

"Probably just heat lightning."

Two people ran out of a farmhouse in the clearing toward a barn.

I stopped on the side of the road and opened the window. Horses screamed. My vet tech instincts kicked in. "Oh, no." I gunned it into the driveway and stomped on the brakes. Fighting with the seatbelt until it released, I jumped out, and ran. Sounds of distress from chickens and goats outside in pens. Crossing the yard, I felt ghost energy reaching for me, and I slammed down my protections. Heavy thuds came from the barn.

At the doors, I hesitated. Overhead lights lined the center with stalls on either side. Half way down the aisle, one stall stood partway open. What was I doing? I hadn't handled a horse since school. All I saw now in the office were family pets.

A slight woman held the stall door as a tall man tried to calm the horse inside. In the next stall, another horse moved back and forth, snorting, but wasn't as agitated as the first.

"Come on, boy," the man coaxed in a gentle tone of voice. "No need for all this fuss."

The horse snorted and reared up. The two people skipped back.

The woman blocking the door bumped into me and whipped around, gasping. "Who are you?" She had wide, frightened eyes.

In a calm, low voice, I said, "Can I help?"

She shrugged and gestured toward the man and horse.

Watching the agitated animal, I pitched my voice a bit louder. "Can I help?" I asked again. "I'm a vet tech."

The man didn't look away from the horse. "Who're you?" he asked, his tone controlled.

"Kenna Tierney. I drove by and heard the horses."

"They're just spooked," he said with a note of finality.

"May I?" I persisted.

"I got this."

The horse tossed his head and reared half way up on his hind legs. The man leaned aside, not willing to give up full control of the situation.

But I was already communicating with the horse on a different level. At first, he shook his head, as if trying to get rid of flies. "Hey, there. Something scared you good, didn't it?" I kept a calm, reassuring touch in his mind, while speaking aloud soothing words.

Sensations tumbled through me. Voices. Strange, burning smells. Anger. Fear. All coming from the horse but reminding me of the lake ghosts. The lake was about a half mile away.

A chill went through me and the horse reared up again. I squashed my own fears to concentrate on the horse. "Easy, now. Easy, there." I continued speaking while sending calming images of sunlit pastures and cool streams into the horse's mind. It took a long time, but he stopped stomping, tossed his head, and snorted.

I smiled. "Good boy."

He flicked his ears, listening. I got close enough to stroke his cheek. He quivered, his eyes still a little wild, but he allowed it.

"Much better. It's all over, now." I hoped. These people lived too close to Ghost Central.

After settling the horses, the young couple thanked me as we walked to my car. I no longer felt the ghosts. Declan still sat in the passenger seat, but he'd rolled down the window. He looked relieved to see me and guilt at leaving him alone shot through me. "Declan, I'm so sorry. I heard the horses and had to help."

He lifted a hand. "No harm done," he said, though he looked a little pale.

The couple mentioned the animals had been uneasy the last few weeks. They'd seen a bear lurking in the woods surrounding their property.

Declan and I shared a look. We hadn't seen a bear, but knew another kind of predator stalked this farm. "It never hurts to keep a close watch," I suggested. It seemed so inadequate but I couldn't tell them ghosts spooked the horses.

We said our goodbyes and left. "Declan? We're in big trouble here."

"There are too many of them."

"Uh-huh. More than I've ever heard of in one place before. More than I've ever...well, I thought your house was the worst I'd ever seen but Hurlbutt is the ultimate ghost town."

"It is a great deal to take in, true, but if we take it one house, one ghost at a time, we'll get to the end."

"If we're even allowed to," I said. "There are people who don't believe. We can't barge in and say, 'Sorry, but we've got to evict the ghosts in your house, whether you think they're there or not.'"

After a moment, Declan said, "One way or another, Kenna, it will work itself out."

"I hope so." Scared didn't even begin to describe the

emotion settling in my gut. Mixed up with the weird rush from talking with the twin ghosts and crossing them over, I felt shame for enjoying it after breaking away from that life, and guilt because I was pushing away the normality I wanted.

20

A fter dropping Declan back home, all I wanted was to go back to the house, curl up on the couch, and sleep for a week. My earlier high was fading and I felt a crash coming on.

I also wanted to forget what Declan and I discovered about the ghosts, but it kept nagging me. Why did this have to happen now? I was so close to finishing the clean up and getting back home. I couldn't wait to see all the fur babies at the clinic.

As I pulled into the driveway, a guy got out of a dilapidated car parked at the curb in front of the house. "Hi, Miss Tierney?" he asked from the bottom of the driveway as soon as I climbed out of my car. His scraggly beard, black glasses, and short-sleeved plaid shirt screamed wannabe hipster.

He seemed benign, so I walked toward him. "Yes?"

"I'm Brent Casey with The Bartlett Daily Chronicle, would you like to make a statement about the ghosts at

Rogers Lake and your experiences as a psychic medium for an article I'm writing? Maybe I can get a photo?"

Fear sizzled up my spine. Thinking fast, I turned up the wattage on my smile. "Hans put you up to this, didn't he?" Hans?

The reporter frowned, tilting his head.

I forced a laugh. "Oh, he did. I owe him a drink now." I patted his arm. "My friend, Hans, has a wicked sense of humor. I'm so sorry you came all the way out here for nothing, Brad."

"Brent," he said, an edge to his voice now. "And I don't know any Hans."

Pretending confusion, I said, "I don't understand then."

"I'm investigating reports of ghost activity at Rogers Lake." He looked so earnest; probably fresh out of college. "Your name kept coming up as the medium who was going to exorcise the ghosts."

This was getting way out of hand. I plastered a smile back on. "I'm sorry, but you've got some wrong information. I've heard of the ghosts. Everyone has. But the last part's totally wrong." I continued walking toward the door, praying that was the end of it.

"Then why does everyone around here say you're a psychic?" he called.

Almost there. I turned, my hand on the doorknob. "Small towns live for gossip, you know." I shrugged. "Don't believe everything you hear." Glancing up, I saw Gloria pretending not to watch as she watered flower pots by her front door. I smiled at the frustrated reporter, let myself into the house, then bolted up the kitchen stairs, trying to be quiet. At the front door, I peeked around the curtain edge, watching the reporter cross the street, talk to Gloria, then leave.

Gloria glared at my house.

After acting like my best friend, suddenly she didn't like me? I wasn't exactly bummed, but what did I do to her that justified setting reporters on me?

I noticed movement in the flowers at the far end of her house. Something low to the ground. The tomcat. He slunk through the flowers, stopped, then scratched in the dirt before moving a little farther along.

"Better be careful, cat," I mumbled. "Gloria will have your guts for garters if she catches you peeing on her prized flowers."

He repeated his actions twice more before standing still, his butt hanging down and out, straining.

I laughed. Sad to say, but it made my day.

THE NEXT MORNING WHEN I LET THE CAT IN TO EAT, I noticed the ground outside was still dry. "Guess Declan was right about no rain last night," I told the cat. He ignored me and dove into the bowl of dry food.

Later, as I opened the can of primer, attempting to paint the living room wall, my front doorbell rang.

Not again. I sighed, put the top back on the can, and went to the door.

"Hi," I said, seeing Declan's familiar figure. "Everything okay?" I eyed the two strangers behind him and Brian, who brought up the rear. This couldn't be good.

Declan looked uncomfortable. "I hope we didn't drop in at a bad time but I wonder if we might have a word?"

"Sure." I opened the door wide.

He stepped in, followed by a large, sweating man in dark suit pants and white button down shirt and a petite woman in white silk blouse and floral skirt. I hoped they weren't from the First Church.

"This is Don Houser," Declan said. "Our former mayor."

"Nice to meet you." The man's booming voice echoed in the hallway. He shook my hand, nearly crushing it in his big paw.

"This is Linda Goddard," Declan said. "A former village councilman...er...council person."

The woman smiled, a touch strained, and held out her hand. "Hello, Ms. Tierney." Her curly blond hair swung forward.

She had a decent grip. "Thank you...ah, won't you all come in?" I led them into the living room. "Sorry about the mess. I'm trying to sell the house."

They all stared at the message on the wall.

"Somebody broke in."

"Damn kids," Don said, dropping onto the couch, causing it to sag. "Bad enough they keep knocking over garbage cans. Now, they're breaking into homes."

"We need our own police department," Linda said. "State troopers don't have time for these nuisances." She moved a box off a straight-backed chair across the room before sitting.

The big man nodded, pulling a handkerchief from his pocket, wiping sweat from his face. "Too bad we can't pay for 'em."

Declan sat on the other end of the couch. Brian was the pickle in the middle.

I perched on the edge of the easy chair. "So, what's going on?" I asked.

Declan cleared his throat. "Ever since the children were hurt out at Rogers Lake, folks in town have been nervous. You know how it is. The way rumors spread."

I nodded. Yes, I was familiar with the Hurlbutt rumor mill.

"Well, you see...the thing is..."

"We need to know," broke in Don Houser, sitting forward, "what in the hell is going on here. Hurlbutt has always had its quirks, but things are getting bat shit weird. Do we have ghosts or what?"

My mouth opened, but it took a couple seconds to form words. So everyone knew my secret now? Trying to swallow past a bone-dry throat, it felt like I was standing naked on the front lawn.

"What Don means," Linda Goddard said, frowning, "is a great many unusual things have happened in Hurlbutt lately."

"That's for damn sure," Don murmured.

"I'm not normally one to believe in such nonsense." Linda smoothed her skirt. "But, let's just say, I've seen several things which have changed my mind. We heard you had a familiarity with the...unexplained...and hoped you could help us with this situation. Whatever it is."

I glared at Brian, who put his hands up, palms out. "I swear, I didn't say a word after the other day. They came to me."

Declan wouldn't look at me.

"He didn't say anything, either," said Brian. "I had to pester him to come here with us."

This sucked eggs. "I don't know what to say. I think

you've been misled about the extent of my abilities." It also scared me.

"But you do talk to ghosts?" asked Don.

"I can communicate with the spirits of those who've died," I admitted. Declan and I stared at each other for a moment and I remembered what we learned the day before. "It's not a simple or easy thing and if you're suggesting what I think you are, " I shook my head, "well, there's more ghosts than I can handle on my own. You need a professional or several."

"Do you know any?" Linda asked.

"I, well," I stammered. A couple names from my psychic fair days popped into my head. "I may, but it's been a long time. I got out of that life years ago."

"Good." Don heaved himself up. "You get ahold of your people, bring 'em here, and set 'em loose." He hiked up his pants.

I stood so fast, I almost lost my balance. "Wait." Panic gripped my chest. "That's not how it works." No way was I going to call people from my past, out of the blue, for a ghost cleansing. Besides, I hadn't been close friends with most of them. "They...they won't just drop everything to come here and they won't do it for free."

Don raised his eyebrows at Linda.

"Hurlbutt no longer has any funds at its disposal," she explained.

"You see my problem?" I said, relieved.

Linda nodded. "Go ahead and call your colleagues. See if anyone can find it in their hearts to help us without payment. Then call and let me know how it goes." She stood, handed me a business card, and walked out of the room.

"Uh." I jumped up and followed her to the door. "I'll see what I can do, but I can't guarantee anything."

"We're looking into several possible solutions," she said, shaking my hand.

"Nice to have you on the team, honey. " Don winked and crushed my hand again.

They both left and Brian slipped out with a quick good-bye.

"I am so sorry, Kenna." Declan said, like a young boy caught stealing candy. "Brian brought them to my house, wanting me to introduce you. After yesterday, I was so scared about everything, and..." he sighed. "It got muddled. I'm sorry if it made things difficult for you. I thought I was helping but it didn't work out the way I expected."

I patted his shoulder. "I know. I'm scared too."

"You aren't mad?"

"No." Frustrated, sure. "I'll make some phone calls."

Relief flooded his face. "Thank you. I honestly don't know what we'd do if you weren't here."

I closed the door behind him, feeling the weight of the situation settle right at the base of my skull. Rubbing the back of my neck, I walked to the living room. All my earlier ambition evaporated. What had I gotten myself into? Wanting to help was a little different from being recruited and depended on to lead the charge.

Looking at Ma's old TV, I wished we'd hooked up the cable. Now, all I could do was think and worry about what I had to do, what others expected me to do.

No pressure, or anything.

Who could I call? And who wouldn't be offended I'd left without a word and only called now to ask for help? I made a list. Though it was three in the afternoon, I woke up the first person and he was cranky. When I explained the situation, he roared at me for "dropping out of fucking sight" and now I needed his help, came "crawling back like a bitch in heat."

Starting out on a high note, there.

One number I called wasn't in service. At another, the person no longer lived there and left no contact info. The next one cut me short in the middle of my story. "I don't do the psychic thing anymore," she explained. "I had a real bad experience a while back."

I sympathized.

One former colleague wanted to help but she was booked ahead six months. Another quoted me an outrageous price. I hesitated over the last name on the list but cold calling had sucked everything out of me. I admit to putting very little effort into my relationships back then but after so much apathy and hostility directed at me, I had zero enthusiasm left.

I'd have to go it alone. Well, almost. I called Declan and he agreed to help. We would do it as a community service.

I tried to think and plan but besides the lousy grocery store sage and what little protective jewelry I wore, my supply list was nonexistent. That meant a trip to a certain metaphysical store in Buffalo was in order. The last place I wanted to go.

Some time in the wee hours, I laid on the couch, staring at shadow patterns on the ceiling.

A has-been and a beginner. What could go wrong?

We were doomed.

21

W hen I saw Brian at my door the next morning, I began to swing it closed.

"Wait," he said. "Before we can do anything at the lake we have to get permission."

I stopped. "From who?"

"The landowner, George Barnes."

"The Rogers family doesn't own it anymore?"

"Nah. John died and the rest moved out a few years ago."

I opened the door but leaned against the frame, not inviting him in. He brought the former mayor and councilwoman visiting yesterday and I didn't feel like playing nice.

"I told George we'd be over about ten to explain how you're gonna get rid of the ghosts."

"You what?" I straightened. "We had an agreement, remember?"

"Yes, yes, I'm not in an old folks' home, yet. Of course I remember, but Declan told me you two were doing the exorcism yourselves. I know George. He lets folks use the lake because we've all been going there for years. It's a tradition. But for an exorcism, I figured it best to get permission. Don't want him showing up with his sons and their shotguns while you're doing your woo-woo stuff, do you?"

As much as I wanted to, I couldn't fault his reasoning. "Okay, okay. I guess you're right. But, please, stop calling it an exorcism. That's when an entity possesses a human and has to be forced out. This is more of a cleansing."

"Whatever you call it, let's get a move on. George's waiting. You don't need to put makeup on or fix your hair or anything, do you? My wife is forever making me wait."

I'd been up for hours and already took a shower. Brian went on and on as I grabbed my purse and phone.

"I don't know why you women—" He looked me up and down. "That was quick. Sure you didn't forget anything?"

I raised my eyebrows. "George is waiting, remember?"

"Keep your girdle on, missy."

Brian drove. His truck was as bouncy as my car. Nearing the lake, I held very still at the twinges in my belly. Then, once we were past, I relaxed.

The Barnes family lived in a two-story farm house a couple miles beyond Rogers Lake. A barn and grain silos stood close by with equipment and various vehicles scattered around the property. Flowers bloomed near the house.

A slim woman in her forties appraised me a moment as I entered. "George is in the kitchen. Come on back."

We followed her down a straight hallway to the back

of the house. A big man with weathered features sat hunched over a coffee cup at a rustic wooden table.

Brian introduced us.

Mrs. Barnes offered us coffee, and, after pouring, proceeded to hand-wash a huge mound of breakfast dishes as we talked. They must have a big family but I didn't hear a peep in the house. Probably working on the farm.

"So, Brian, what's this about?" George had dark circles under his eyes.

"I think I've got a solution to your problem at Rogers Lake."

George took a sip of his coffee. "Do ya?"

"Yup. Kenna here's one of those psychics like you see on TV."

I winced.

George's eyes cut to me and then back to Brian, with no expression.

"She can get rid of the ghosts at the lake. If you give give her the say-so."

I stared into my coffee cup, pressing my lips together so I wouldn't scream. The man had no sense of timing or tact. I took a deep breath. "Mr. Barnes. Mrs. Barnes." I nodded toward each. "I grew up in Hurlbutt. Since I was a little girl, I've seen spirits and talked to them. Sometimes they cause problems for the living and I've had success persuading a few to leave. I've been out to the lake a couple times recently and what I experienced…" My mouth was so dry I took a sip of coffee. "There are multiple ghosts. They're angry and scaring neighboring people and animals."

George hadn't moved a muscle since I started speaking. His steady gaze made me nervous.

"Look, I can't guarantee anything, but I'd like to try to resolve this. If you allow me to."

The big man didn't say anything for a moment. He leaned back. "I haven't regretted owning the property until this year. When Tom went out this Spring, he said something spooked his dog." He shrugged. "Didn't think much of it until I was out there myself. It was the darnedest thing. The grass was blowing around but there was no wind to speak of. No crickets or birds, neither. No sound at all and the lake was still as glass. Unsettling, to say the least."

No kidding.

"'Course," George continued, "by the time I got home, I'd convinced myself my mind was playing tricks, you know? But then this stuff with the kids..." He shook his head. "I had to close the lake. Can't run the risk of someone getting hurt out there." He looked over my shoulder at his wife. "What do you think?"

I turned around.

His wife dried her hands on a towel. "It can't hurt."

I turned back.

George pursed his lips. "Alright. You've my permission."

I blinked.

Brian rapped the table with his knuckles and stood. "Thank you, George. You won't be sorry."

After shaking hands and thanking Mrs. Barnes for the coffee, Brian drove us back toward Hurlbutt. "See, that wasn't so bad, now was it?" he said.

I grunted, staring out the window. The best place to

buy the supplies I needed was in Buffalo but I'd burned bridges there. Looking at my slide-open phone, I wished I had a smart phone to connect to the Internet. Since I had a laptop at home and computers at work, I hadn't needed a better phone. Unfortunately, I didn't have my laptop with me. What I wouldn't give now to be able to do a simple search.

Once we were past the danger zone by the lake, I asked, "Do you know any place with a computer I could use? A library or something?"

"Library in Bartlett does," Brian said. "And I've got one. Well, my wife does. She shops on it and looks at pictures of the grandkids. I doubt she'd mind you using it."

We went to Brian's house and he introduced his wife, Katrina. I recognized her as one of the ladies at St. Brendan's who put on the meal after Ma's funeral and the one who helped me when I got lost. We chatted for a while. I explained the situation with Ma's house and what we'd been doing. Katrina was sympathetic and offered her help.

"What she needs," said Brian, "is a computer."

I don't know what she saw in Brian, though they say opposites attract. She insisted on feeding me lunch and then showed me to an old desktop computer and printer in the living room. As it booted up, she explained she had been an office manager for the old shirt factory but now kept in touch with her children and grandchildren on Facebook.

"I like the phone better," said Brian as he left the room.

"Don't mind him," Katrina said as she brought up her

browser. "He hates computers. Calls this 'The Beast.' You'll find pens and paper in the desk drawer. Oh, and it runs a little slow these days. Just yell if you need any help." She smiled and left me to it.

In no time, I found websites for metaphysical stores and one was new since I'd left Buffalo. I called and they set aside what I needed. Brian dropped me off at the house so I could pick up my car. Within a couple hours, I made the round trip and didn't run into anyone I knew.

I laid out my new goodies on the kitchen table. Several tied bundles of sage that looked like large cigars. A braid of sweetgrass. A bracelet of alternating black tourmaline and amethyst crystals, each crystal cut into a circular bead and polished. It wasn't much but I was watching my pennies and these few things could make a difference.

First, I smudged the whole house with sage. I didn't trust the low-quality grocery store stuff I'd used before and the house felt lighter afterward.

Then, I smudged the bracelet. Jewelry can retain the energies of previous handlers from salespeople and potential buyers to the crafter of the piece all the way down to the miners of the crystal. Smudging clears the energies. I wafted the sage smoke over the bracelet several times and put it on. The strong grounding property of the black tourmaline was intense and I sat for a long time becoming accustomed to it.

While I didn't accomplish much in cleaning or organizing the house, the time spent adding these extra layers of protection made me feel better.

~

THE SOUND OF A LAWN MOWER WOKE ME. SWIPING AT THE drool pooling in the corner of my mouth, I groaned. Crashed on the couch again. I lay there like a lazy slug, but plagued by all the crazy thoughts shuffling through my brain. Finally, I hauled myself up and checked my phone. Five twenty. Well, I hadn't been asleep long. Grabbing a Pepsi and an energy drink from the fridge, I went outside and waited until Nate saw me and stopped the mower.

"*Kennaaaaah*. How's it going?"

"Okay, I guess. Are you thirsty?" I held up the Pepsi.

"Thanks." He loped over to a pile of stuff by the garage. Returning, he held out a rolled-up newspaper. "Got something here you better see." He opened it, pointing out an article.

A photo of Rogers Lake topped it, with the headline: Local Lake Haunted.

I sucked in a breath. "Oh, no."

It described the attack on the teenagers, but also told about an incident earlier this summer and one in the spring I hadn't heard before. Near the end, I froze. It mentioned local leaders contacted a psychic medium to deal with the situation. It named me, "a hometown girl," quoting the former mayor, Don Houser. It listed my psychic fair experience, current job in Syracuse, and explained I was in Hurlbutt fixing up and selling the family home.

Holy cats, Batman.

I stared at Nate, my mouth open, trying to form words, but couldn't.

"I never talked to no one about nothing," he said.

"I know you wouldn't," I assured him. "Yesterday, a

reporter came to the house but I pretended not to know what he was talking about. Pretty stupid, considering what he already knew about me."

"A guy was in the diner asking questions but none of us said a word."

"It looks like the ex-mayor did."

He made a face. "Sorry to bring you bad news, but I figured it was better than hearing it from someone else."

"Thank you. I appreciate it."

"No *problemo*." He hesitated. "Do you know about Pastor Graves?"

I shook my head. "No. Never heard of him."

"He's the head honcho at the Church of Love and Peace."

"Ah. What about him?"

"Some of his people were in the diner this morning. Guess they saw the paper, too, 'cause they were talking about what was happening at the lake and doing something about it. If Pastor Graves gets in the middle of it, you need to be careful. He's bad news."

"I thought they were just a bunch of hippies?"

"Not anymore. When he took over, things changed. Instead of keeping to themselves, they started knocking on doors and talking to people."

I nodded. "We had a couple of them at our garage sale trying to 'spread the word.'"

"Yeah. They have a lot more people in the church these days and Graves has clout. A few years ago, he didn't like Cam Martin selling girly magazines at his news stand and got him shut down."

Mr. Martin had been a fixture in town, selling newspapers and magazines from his tiny shop since I was a kid. It was well-known he kept porn magazines behind the counter in plain, brown wrappers so as not to offend anyone. "Some people can't mind their own business."

He shrugged. "We all thought Graves was a crack pot until then. He and the church started butting into more stuff. 'Course things haven't been booming around here in some time, so they've been kinda quiet. But, if he gets involved in the lake stuff, it could get messy for you."

"I had no idea but thanks for letting me know."

After he left, I felt unsettled. It took me a while to realize it was a very different Nate I'd just talked to. This Pastor Graves guy really bothered him, which blew me away. I thought Nate got along with everyone.

I read through the article two more times. Going to the grocery store and gas station were bad enough lately. I considered calling the newspaper and complaining, but what was the point? The damage was done.

What if the story spread farther, all the way to Syracuse? "Stop being so paranoid," I said out loud. The Bartlett Daily Chronicle was a small newspaper. It probably didn't have a big circulation.

Still, I'd have the local reaction to deal with which was bad enough. I wallowed, opening a bag of candy bars I'd been saving for an emergency. Enjoying the chocolaty goodness, I admired how the light hit the alternating black and purple stones of my new bracelet. Tourmaline for protection against negative energies and amethyst to increase intuition and psychic powers as well as protect against psychic attacks. The combination of stones felt right and strong to me. As soon as I'd tried it on in the store, it calmed me.

I turned events of the last few weeks over in my mind.

Declan and Brian stopped by. I pointed to the newspaper Declan carried. "Already saw that."

"I'm sorry, Kenna." Declan patted my arm.

"Me too." I said cheerfully, showing them into the living room. The chocolate had hit my system, making me feel a little wired.

"Don always did have a big mouth," Brian said.

"Well, if it wasn't him, it would've been someone else. So," I turned to Declan, "what else did you have on your mind?"

He glanced at Brian. "We thought it best to get going on this cleansing before the whole town is riled up. Can you do it tonight?"

My gut twinged. "Why tonight?"

"'Cause Pastor Dick," Brian emphasized on the last word, "is whipping everyone into a tizzy."

"We're afraid if we wait," Declan said, "he'll bring his influence to bear and block us."

"He can do that?"

"Damn right he can," said Brian. "I heard he has the county legislator in his hip pocket."

"And," added Declan, "the sheriff's wife is part of his congregation."

"Yeah, but not the sheriff." Brian pointed at Declan. "I heard he's had trouble with her since she joined that bunch. He'd probably enjoy arresting them."

As they bantered, my mind raced. Could I do this on such short notice? I had my supplies, but I didn't feel ready. I shouldn't have agreed to it.

A whistle brought me back to the conversation.

"There she is," Brian said. "You was off in La La Land for a minute."

I frowned at Brian, then looked to Declan. "Do we have a choice?"

"We could wait," he said, "though it gives Pastor Graves a chance to organize his people."

"Believe me," Brian said, "don't give him the chance."

I sighed. "Fine. I'll do it." Actually, I didn't want to. My stomach growled. "But Declan and I should eat before facing the ghosts."

They tried to convince me to come back to Brian's house, but I'd already eaten there today. I didn't want to wear out my welcome with Katrina. After they left, a look in the refrigerator proved uninspiring. My stomach was in the mood for pizza, so, braving the stares and whispers, I went to Alonzo's. They had the best pizza in town, though now they were the only pizza place in town.

Walking in the sweltering shop with its baking bread and tomato sauce smells reminded me of the one summer I'd worked here. Teenage laughter drifted in from the adjoining dining room. I ordered a large pizza at the window, but it was disappointing to see no familiar faces in the kitchen.

While waiting, I looked at the old photos hung on the walls in the entry way. The oldest ones featured a large man with a mustache, Alonzo. Since then, three generations had run the place.

The outside door opened. I stepped closer to the wall, giving them room to get by me and recognized Greg Adams. "Hi, Greg."

Startled, he said, "Hello." He attempted to smile, but it didn't work.

"Is everything okay?"

He wiped sweat from his brow. "Whew, it's hot in

here. Actually, no. We're selling the house." He shrugged. "Jackie couldn't cope."

"I'm so sorry. Not everyone's able to," I looked around, lowering my voice, "live with a ghost. Even one as friendly as Johnny."

He sighed, nodding his head. "Johnny behaved himself but Jackie wasn't comfortable knowing he was there. She's staying with her sister in Rochester while a couple friends and I pack up the house. "

I felt horrible but wished him luck in his new home. He paid for his waiting food and left, his distress and worry evident in his bent form.

Uh-oh. Did Johnny understand? I made a mental note to check on him tomorrow.

22

After inhaling most of the pizza, I made a final check of my supplies, then sat cross-legged on the couch. Doing my breathing and visualization exercises helped take the edge off my nerves. This time, I was prepared.

A shiver ran through me.

I could do this. I'd been doing it, first with our basement ghost, then with Sherita's. The lake ghosts were the same. There were just more of them.

I winced. Who was I kidding? I needed help.

"Henry?" I called out. "Are you there?"

Henry solidified in front of me. "Yes, Miss Kenna?" His glasses reflected no light.

"Do you know anything about the other ghosts in town?"

"Others come and go."

"Like the old man in the basement?"

He nodded. "Though usually they go on their way."

"How about the ghosts at Rodgers' Lake? Know anything about them?"

For a long moment, Henry said nothing, unmoving. I thought he wouldn't answer.

"I feel them." He cut his eyes in the general direction of the lake. "Like a storm, making its way closer."

He sort of winked out and came back. I'd never seen him do that before. Was it the ghost equivalent to a shiver? "Are you afraid of them?"

"They are very angry."

That was putting it mildly. "Er, right. Do you know where they came from? Why they are here?"

"They...are."

I waited for a beat. "They are what?"

"They exist."

"Who were they, then?"

"They lived long, long ago."

No kidding. "Can you narrow it down?"

"I am sorry but I cannot."

I sighed. "It's okay. Thank you for your help, Henry."

"You are most welcome, Miss Kenna." He disappeared.

It was worth a shot and another confirmation the lake ghosts weren't something worse. "Dad? How about you? Are you around?" I waited. Nothing, again. I started pacing, realized what I was doing, then sat on the couch and grounded myself until my body felt loose.

Dad appeared beside me.

"About time."

"Aw, darling,'" he said, in a mock hurt tone of voice. "I'm not a mutt to come whenever you call, you know."

"Excuse me? This is serious stuff I'm dealing with here."

"Of course it is. What was I thinking?" He used the same tone of voice when Ma was unreasonable.

It stung but also poked a hole in my anger. "I'm sorry. I'm wound up tight and I'm scared."

"I know," he said. "But I'm always near and I'll do whatever I can to keep you from harm's way."

I almost lost it. "Thanks, Dad," I said, my throat tight.

Brian and Declan arrived after seven. I felt better, though still on edge. The sun was more than half way down in the western sky. Time was slipping away. Squashed between the two of them in the pickup, my bag of supplies on my lap, I looked at Declan. "You prepared yourself?"

"I believe so."

"Okay. Follow my lead and send them to the other side, just as we practiced."

"I'll do my best," he replied. He didn't sound too sure of himself, though.

We all sat in silence until the oily ghost emotions began to build up layers on my skin. "They seem to have spread farther," I said. We reached the turn-off but several vehicles were parked along the side of the road. "No," I whispered. "No, no, no."

"What did you expect?" Brian said. "Haven't had this much fuss in town since Ann Carlton chased her husband down Main Street with a kitchen knife. 'Course that was only 'cause he was running around with her best friend." He swerved over to the left, pulling up to a silver SUV.

Linda Goddard sat in the passenger seat and lowered the window.

Don Houser leaned over to see us from the driver's seat. "Howdy," he boomed. "Are you ready, little lady?"

Little lady? "What's with the newspaper article?" I countered.

"Word spread and folks were scared." He shrugged. "We had to let them know we were doing something about it." His teeth caught the lowering sun, gleaming in the shadowed interior.

Politicians.

"I can't do this with a bunch of people gawking." I pointed my chin at the rest of the cars. It was hard enough following this conversation with the ghosts' emotions already smacking into me.

"Why not?" asked Linda.

"I'm not a performing seal. I need to focus and it could be dangerous. Remember what happened to the teenagers?"

"What if only Don and I watched?"

They weren't going to give up. "Fine, whatever. But don't get in my way. I can't guarantee your safety."

"We understand." Linda's tone dripped with superiority.

I wasn't sure they did, but I'd warned them. They were on their own. "Come on," I said to Brian. "Let's do this."

"Good luck," Don called.

I didn't feel very lucky.

As we drove past, people cheered and honked. Some stared. I recognized the couple from the Church of Love and Peace who had come to our yard sale. I hoped Pastor Graves wasn't here.

Brian turned into the driveway. He stopped in front of a chain strung across between two trees.

"That's new," I said.

"George did it to keep people out. He gave me a key." He unlocked the chain, pulled the pickup ahead enough so Don could get in too, relocked the chain, and we continued forward.

The oppressiveness increased. Declan tensed up next to me. I gave his hand a squeeze. "We can do this." I was trying to convince myself, too.

He squeezed back.

The closer we got, the darker it seemed, the raw emotions lapping over us. Declan sucked in his breath with a hiss.

"Those aren't your emotions," I assured him. "Let them wash over you, but not touch you."

Brian parked by the lake edge, turning off the engine. It was darker now, the sun low in the sky behind the trees. And silent. No sound of birds or insects or air. Not even water lapping at the edge of the lake. I shivered.

Overlaying the calm, though, was an emotional storm.

We got out of the truck. Don's SUV stopped at the tree line but they didn't get out.

"I don't feel a thing," said Brian. "You sure they're here?"

"Yes."

I looked at Declan, who leaned against the truck, his head bowed. He was already effected. I touched his arm. "Declan?"

"Something bad happened here," he said.

"Where's your rosary?"

He fumbled in his pocket and pulled out the string of beads. "In the name of the Father and of the Son and of the Holy Spirit," he said as he made the sign of the cross. "I believe..."

I shouldn't have involved him. He wasn't strong enough yet.

Brian came around the front of the truck. "What happened?"

"They're very strong. Watch him," I said.

Brian nodded. "Damn right I will."

I visualized the white light surrounding me to stretch and include Declan and Brian. So far, so good. Digging through the grocery bag I carried, I found a sage bundle and lighter by feel. I lit the dried herbs, my hand shaking, then blew out the fire. Smoke rose, leaving an acrid scent. "You must leave this place," I said, my mouth drier than a lint ball. I swallowed. "You don't belong here," I said, with more force. "This is a place for the living. You need to cross over, be with your family, your loved ones."

I shivered, feeling tension build inside me, wanting to hurt someone.

～

MY PROTECTIVE JEWELRY GREW WARM. "DAD, YOU HERE?"

"I'm here, my Kenna."

"Good." I could still feel the alien emotions but they didn't force their way into my mind like before. This was more of a knocking at the door. Annoying and distracting, but better than the alternative. "You, the people who once lived here. Your bodies have died," I said, pleased that I almost sounded normal. "This place is for the living. You need to go. Go to your loved ones. Go to the light. You can't stay here and scare people."

Without any human shape, like blobs of energy, they swirled around me. I flinched as one got too close.

Dad materialized in front of me. "Oh, no you don't, laddie."

The blob moved back. So did a few of the others. I smiled, but it didn't last long. They moved close again.

To put some space between them and me, I began to move as I spoke. But the ghosts weren't listening. They followed me, crowding close. This must be what Declan felt when I first met him.

A muffled sound made me turn. Declan had collapsed in Brian's arms. I rushed over and opened the truck door.

"He can't take this anymore," Brian said, hoisting Declan into the seat with a groan of effort. "I'm taking him home. You coming?" He tucked Declan's arm and leg in.

The swirl of energy and emotions continued behind me. I shook my head. "I've got to finish this."

"Suit yourself. Don can take you home. I'll tell him on the way out." He started the truck and turned it around, spitting dirt and gravel. He stopped next to Don's SUV for a moment and left.

The SUV started up and moved to block the entrance to the lake where the trees ended.

The sage had stopped smoking. I lit it again, blew it out, and walked around the lake. Water gives spirits power and they were concentrated here. Losing track of time, all my focus was on coaxing the ghosts to leave. It was a battle of wills. They didn't lose strength but wouldn't cross over, either. They swirled about me, sometimes making it hard to see where I walked, but Dad kept my feet on the safe path.

My throat grew scratchy from the pungent smoke. Half way across, I felt a weakness in my legs. "Dad, I can't keep this up much longer. They're zapping my strength."

"As much as it pains me, dear," Dad said. "You may need to cut and run. Live to fight another day."

I nodded. Trying to conserve my strength, I trudged along, keeping up my protections but stopped engaging the ghosts. The headlights of Don's SUV were my beacon.

Wiping sweat from my forehead, I realized my jewelry was getting hot. I rolled the bracelet farther up my arm and pulled the necklaces out from beneath the neck of my T-shirt. At least now there was a layer of material between them and my skin. I longed to fall in a heap on the ground. "Have to keep going," I mumbled.

Closer.

Closer.

As I neared the gravel drive, I tossed the still-smoking sage bundle in the lake. Relief flooded through me. "Thanks, Dad."

"You're welcome, my—oh, for crying out loud—what have we got here?"

Almost full dark now, I stared for a moment before noticing a darker shadow about ten feet away in the tall grass. I felt no ghost energy, so it had to be living.

It sprang up. Because I hesitated, it gained on me before I sprinted toward the SUV. The sounds of heavy breathing and snarls dumped more adrenalin in my system but my strength was at its limit.

The SUV started moving, the lights bouncing, but wouldn't reach me in time.

I went down hard, my legs pinned by whatever was chasing me.

23

With every ounce of energy I had left, I bucked until one of my legs was free, then kicked at my attacker. It shrieked and loosened its grip. I scrambled away as the SUV stopped. Linda hurried over and helped me up.

"Whoa, there, son," Don said as he grabbed a skinny teenage boy by the collar of his t-shirt. "What are you doing here? This lake's closed."

The kid held one arm close to his body, protected by the other. "You broke it," he raged. He fought to get away, still partly effected by the ghosts. Don held him by the shoulders.

The ghosts were feeding on all this high emotion. "We need to get out of here, now," I said, feeling them close in.

"We'll take this young fella with us." Don steered him toward the SUV. "You're Jesse Winter's boy, aren't you?"

"He dropped something back there," Linda said, opening the SUV door for me.

"Can you get it?" I asked, sliding into the back seat. "It may be important." She didn't seem effected by the ghosts and I couldn't walk through them again, tired and vulnerable as I was.

"I'll try."

The door on the other side of me opened, but as he was about to get in, the teenager turned on Don. He tried to knock him over, but Don didn't budge. "Why you little —" Don grabbed his ear and pulled.

The kid snarled, then cried out. "Hey, man!"

Don hoisted him in by the seat of his pants. The kid fell into me and howled in pain. I tried to help him, but Don grabbed his other arm and set him up straight, then pulled the seatbelt out and over to me. I snapped it in and the door closed.

I tensed, expecting the kid to lash out, but he shoved his back into the door and looked at me like I was the bad guy. "Jeez Louise," I said, feeling a twinge of guilt. "I'm not going to hurt you. You probably don't remember this because of the ghosts but you chased me and tackled me. I was defending myself."

The kid looked confused for a moment before Don and Linda got in and the overhead light shut off.

"It's a video camera," Linda said, holding up something square-shaped.

Don turned the SUV around and headed toward the road.

"Trying to record what I was doing at the lake, huh?" I should have known. Closing the lake amid rumors of ghosts was like catnip to a cat.

"I was tr...trying," the kid spoke, with effort, "to g...get something good for my channel."

"What do you mean, 'your channel?'" asked Linda.

"YouTube, right?" I said.

The kid nodded.

"Christ Almighty," said Don. "Just what we need now. All this splashed across the Internet."

At the road, the number of cars had increased. Groups of people gathered in the glare of the headlights. "Wonderful," I muttered.

Don stopped and relocked the chain across the driveway. We drove in silence for a while before I realized the kid was crying. I sighed. "What's your name?"

He didn't speak for a long moment, then croaked, "Andy."

"Hi, Andy. I'm Kenna. Your arm still hurts?" I asked.

"Yeah."

"Don," I said. "I think Andy needs to go to the ER."

"There's an after-hours clinic in Bartlett," said Linda. "I'll call his parents and we can meet them there."

"See," I told the kid. "It'll be okay."

He didn't say anything and I couldn't see his expression in the dark. It was a silent trip, other than Linda talking to Andy's mother.

At the clinic, Don explained Andy's "accident" to the nurse at the desk, while I sat in the waiting room next to the kid, who huddled in on himself. "Everything will be alright," I assured him, not really believing it myself.

How did I keep getting myself into these bizarre situations? My life was going down the toilet, for sure.

Then, the newspaper reporter who talked to me at the house and wrote the article walked in and snapped a photo of Andy and me. I leaped up. "Hey!"

Don and Linda got involved, and the desk nurse. After a lot of shouting, the reporter was kicked out.

"Don't worry," Don said. "I know the owner of the newspaper. The photo won't get printed."

Then Andy's dad arrived and chaos erupted.

I stayed on the periphery of it until Andy's dad pointed at me, saying, "It's because of scammers like her that decent people get screwed. If my kid's hurt, I'm suing you all 'til your eyes bleed."

"Now, Jesse," Don said. "Let's be reasonable..."

The two men continued arguing even when Andy went for an x-ray. I sat down, feeling disconnected. Indirectly, I was responsible for Andy getting hurt. If I hadn't quit the psychic life, things may have been different but dabbling in ghost hunting when I wasn't strong enough was stupid. This sloppiness hit my pride.

A loud, piercing whistle stopped the argument. We all turned to see a young woman in a white lab coat with a police whistle in her hand. The doctor? Andy stood next to her, his arm in a sling, wincing.

"Much better," said the doctor, with a grim smile. "This boy has a sprained wrist, he's exhausted, in pain, and needs to go home. Now, we will get the paperwork straightened out with a minimum of noise or I will call the police. In which case, I'll personally escort Andy home and you all can fight it out until dawn at the police station. Understood?"

I didn't know if she had the power to do that but within fifteen minutes Don and Andy's father came to an arrangement, the paperwork completed, and we were on our way back to Hurlbutt.

~

THE NEXT MORNING, I FELT BATTERED AND BRUISED AS I rolled off the couch. Stumbling into the bathroom, I swallowed three ibuprofen. In my mind, I kept playing out scenes from the night before, feeling the mixed-up emotions of the ghosts again. Then getting tackled by Andy.

I let the cat in, pet him, and fed him, noticing it was almost noon. Not surprising.

An image of Declan pinged in my mind. Elderly and bent over, but holding on in the midst of the emotional storm. It was like a stab to the chest. Guilt set in. "I should check on him," I told the cat, ruffling his fur.

After last night, I knew I couldn't handle this ghost situation alone. There was one last person I could call for help. Cell phone in hand, thumb hovering over the number, I almost did it. But stopped. Again. And threw the phone on the couch. "Coward."

The cat wound around my legs. *Hello.*

I picked him up and wandered to the kitchen, looking out the back window but not seeing the view. What did we accomplish? Did the spirits get stronger feeding off us? Did they expand their reach? Did we make things worse?

"Henry?" I asked. "Are you here?"

"As always, Miss Kenna," a soft voice said behind me.

I turned. "You said before you could feel other ghosts, those in town and those at Rogers Lake?"

"Yes, Miss."

"What about today? Do they feel different from yesterday?"

"Today and yesterday have no relevancy, but the storm grows." He glanced in the direction of Rogers Lake. "The others know it as well. Many are agitated. Some have left. Others want to leave, but are bound here and cannot. I cannot."

"Do you wish to go?"

He shook his head. "No, Miss. I don't."

Relief flooded over me. "I'm glad. This old house would be lonely without you, Henry."

The cat squirmed in my arms and I let him down. He padded to the door and sat, looking over his shoulder at me.

"I get the hint." I let him out, then was at a loss for what to do next. Scratching an itch on my neck, I noticed I didn't have my necklaces on, so searched for the shorts I'd worn to the lake. Pulling a wad of jewelry from the pocket of the shorts, I carried it to the kitchen counter. Separating the pieces, they felt off, almost dull. Heavy, but not in a physical sense. They were sucking in all the light around them. My tools needed some care.

I smudged them with sage smoke and then held up the gold chain and crucifix. They still didn't feel right. "Weird." The stainless steel chain with the onyx ring and the bracelet weren't fully cleansed of negative energy, either. Holding each piece under the running water of a faucet seemed to help but didn't clean them completely. For good measure, I smudged them again. That did the trick. Relieved, I put on my jewelry, feeling the protective energies once more.

Crisis now averted, Declan sprang to mind. I grabbed my purse and keys and left the house. Unlocking my car door, I heard laughter. The type of sneering female laughter that used to catch between my shoulder blades when I was young. Gloria and two other women stood in her driveway watching me.

So, word got around about last night. What a surprise.

I opened the door and was about to get in, when I heard a yip and then a screech. Gloria's Pomeranian, Ralph, trotted across the road, and up my driveway, trailing his leash. Luckily, no cars drove by. He threw himself at me and I picked up his wiggling body, receiving a slobber bath. "You, my friend, have lousy timing."

Gloria and her posse had already marched across the street. I met them at the bottom of the driveway, forcing a smile. "You should keep better track of this little guy. Never know when he's going to see something he likes and runs away." I handed him to Gloria, who held him so tight, he began to squirm.

"Yes, well, you better watch yourself," she said, her friends nodding in unison. "People around here won't stand for weird things happening like they do in the city. I'm keeping an eye on you." She stalked away.

I laughed. First, I was in a teen slasher movie, now it was like the horrible dialogue from an old B-movie. Backing the car out, I saw they'd clustered in Gloria's driveway, giving me the evil eye. I waved and smiled.

High school never ends for some people.

～

DECLAN SAT ON BRIAN'S COUCH, LOOKING TIRED, BUT otherwise okay.

Katrina wasn't happy. "What's the matter with you

two?" Hands on hips and eyes blazing, she was every inch the fiery Irish mama. "Declan isn't robust to begin with and certainly can't take the kind of activity you all were up to last night."

"Now, love..."

"Don't you 'now, love' me, Brian Kelly Quinn. This chasing after ghosts nonsense will have to stop." If looks could kill, Brian would've been skewered like a kabob. "Bad enough you go off, getting into trouble, and dragging poor Declan into it. Then Maida Maglennon asks me why the men in my family 'are encouraging the delusions of a troubled young woman,' as she put it." She looked at me. "I'm sorry, Kenna, but you should know what's being said in town."

I raised my eyebrows. "I've heard worse." And expected nothing less from Mrs. Maglennon though, to be honest, I'd forgotten about her.

Katrina contemplated a yawning Brian, then threw her hands up. "I don't know why I bother," she said, marching into the kitchen.

Declan patted the couch next to him and I sat. Brian pulled a chair up close.

"We've been talking," Brian said, his voice low.

Declan's eyes sparkled. "For there to be so many ghosts in one place, something bad must have happened. Correct?"

"Yes. But..." I looked at them both. "Don't you care about what she said? She's worried about you two and Mrs. Maglennon is, well, scary."

Brian laughed. "My wife worries enough for any ten people. Maida Maglennon is an old battle ax who thinks she runs things around here but she doesn't. Go on, Declan."

They'd lived in Hurlbutt longer than me so they should know.

Declan patted my knee. "Don't worry about me," he said, looking me in the eye. "This is what I want to do, what I need to do, and I won't let anyone stop me. Understand?"

"Okay." I still felt guilty involving him, but if this is what he wanted to do, then, darn it, no one had the right to keep him from it.

He looked at Brian. "We have to find out if anything significant ever happened at Rogers Lake in the past."

"Nothing while we've been alive," said Brian.

"We must go back farther," Declan said. "I—"

The doorbell rang.

Brian stood. "This place is busier than a whore house on nickle night." He went to answer it. We heard voices and then Don Houser and Linda Goddard walked in the room.

"Hello, Declan," Don's voice thundered in the enclosed space. "Feeling better today?"

"Yes, thank you."

"Good." Don rubbed his hands together. "Well, Kenna, quite the to-do last night."

An understatement, for sure. "Er, yes, it was."

"Unfortunately, it didn't solve our little ghost problem."

"We were very disappointed," Linda said.

I stood up, incensed. "I never gave you any guarantees. What's at the lake is big and mean, and you're lucky I even tried."

Linda's eyebrows rose half way up her forehead.

Don smiled like a wolf. "Sometimes you have to do something even if it's wrong. Okay, little lady. What do you think? You've seen it. Sniffed at it. Is there anything we can do about it? I got people, scared to death, banging on my door at all hours. If it's not ghosts, it's the poor economy or bears getting into the garbage."

Declan gasped. "All this time it was a bear?"

"Someone should shoot it," said Brian.

I rounded on him. "No. It should be tranquilized and set free where it belongs."

"Let's get back on the same page here," Don said. "This ghost-thing is getting out of hand. Our residents are worried. They got children and the elderly depending on 'em. We have to help 'em. Now, what do you need? I can get you supplies and manpower. Say the word."

I turned to Declan. "Is he for real?" Still mad at Brian's stupid remarks made it come out more hostile than intended.

He sighed. "It won't be that easy, Don. These ghosts aren't a physical object you can move from place to place."

"Any suggestions?" asked Linda.

"I think it would be a good idea to talk to Jane Coleridge," Declan said. "Discovering the history of the property will help us understand what we're dealing with."

"The former town historian? Sounds reasonable. But we can't let this go on for much longer without making a public plea for help. As much as I loath such an idea, it may be the way to get some so-called 'professionals' in here to help."

"More likely," I said, "you'll get a bunch of frauds taking advantage of free publicity." I sighed. "It may be a long-shot, but I can try one more person."

Linda brightened up. "Good. I want a report by this evening so we know where we stand. Time is of the essence." She stood.

Don wiped his face with a handkerchief. "Yeah. Call us tonight. We gotta have answers yesterday, you know?"

As they left, a few choice words came to mind but I couldn't make my mouth say them.

Declan turned to me. "Last night, during the...at the lake...what did you see?"

"Actually, not much," I said. "I felt emotions."

"Ah." Declan's expression was bleak.

"Did you hear anything?"

He frowned. "Screams. Cries. Women and children."

"Oh," I breathed, my stomach feeling hallow.

Declan nodded. "It had to be something big which included families. During the French and Indian War, Indians raided isolated settlements. Then again, it could be disease or a natural disaster of some sort."

"Brush fire, maybe." Brian added.

"I'll call Jane," Declan said, scooching himself to the edge of the couch and carefully standing up. "If she doesn't know, she may be able to point me in the right direction." He exited the room, taking his time.

Brian and I stared at each other. "What can I do?" Brian asked.

"Don't talk to anybody," I said.

He scowled "*Ach.* Just like my wife. Nag. Nag. Nag."

Only one thing left to do. I pulled my cell phone out of my pocket, flipping through my contacts. My thumb hovered over the name "Raeanne Guyon." She was what they called a root worker from New Orleans.

She also made my bowels turn inside out.

Wanting privacy for this particular conversation, I slipped the phone back in my pocket and headed back to the house.

24

Before picking the town historian's mind, Declan needed to speak to one other person.

Katrina was in the kitchen, talking to herself as she washed dishes in the sink, every movement sharp and angry. She rinsed a dish and clanked it against another in the drainer.

Declan stood behind and to her right. "Please, don't break dishes on my account."

Hands still in the sink, she turned her head. "If I want to break dishes, I'll do it over my husband's thick skull."

He smiled, moving closer. "And most of the time, he would deserve it, but not now."

She wiped her hands on a dishtowel. "You two are going to be the death of me." She led him to the kitchen table. "This is so unlike you. What's going on?"

Katrina could ruin everything if she didn't understand. He sat in the chair. "Long ago, when I was young, when I first heard the spirit voices, I thought God was punishing me."

"God wouldn't do that."

"I was convinced he did. After the voices finally stopped, it was like I'd been given a second chance. I worked hard to be the perfect son and brother and student I could be. But it never went any further." He stared at the yellowing leaves of the maple tree standing sentinel in the backyard. "There was always this barrier I couldn't get past. I didn't feel I was good enough talking to people and making friends or putting myself forward in my job at the plant. I just couldn't take the extra step. I wasted many, many years when I could have been doing something." He thumped the table with his fist.

Katrina's kind eyes revealed pity. "Oh, Declan. I'm so sorry."

He swatted at the unwanted sentiment like a fly. "Don't be. For a while, I thought I would die with regret eating at me. Then the ghosts returned and this time I couldn't pray them away. I'm improving, though, because of Kenna. Helping her gives me the opportunity to help people, to do something after all."

"There are other ways, better ways to help people." Her eyes lit up. "I could—"

"No. That's not for me." He trudged on, despite her shocked look. "You've got to understand. I'm uniquely equipped. I have to learn how to use this ability. It's something I need to do, Katrina."

She looked at him for a long time, a slight crease between her eyes. He honestly didn't know if he'd gotten through to her. He hoped revealing his fears wasn't for naught.

"Well, then," she sighed, looking troubled. "I guess you better get to it."

25

A young girl answered my call. She then yelled Rae's name so loud and long, she must have been all the way down the street. A screen door slammed and then Rae's distinctive drawl filled my ear. "*Bonjour?*"

"Raeanne Guyon? This is Kenna Tierney. I don't know if you remember me from about seven years ago doing the psychic fairs here in the north? I was a medium?"

Silence on the other end.

"Oh, yeah, yeah, yeah. You the one who got all pie-eyed with that English *couyon?*"

I didn't know what a *couyon* was, but at one point back then I was crazy in love with a guy from England. "Wow. That was a long time ago. How are you?"

"Can't complain. And you?"

"I'm fine, but I have a situation I could use some advice about."

"Go ahead, shoot."

I took a deep breath. "I'm in this place called Hurl-butt, New York."

"Some name."

"Uh, right, anyway, we've got ghosts here. A lot more than I've ever seen in one place before. The largest concentration is by a small lake and they're strong."

"Near water, eh?"

"Yes. They're angry and causing problems, scaring people and animals, and they're spreading. At first, I only felt them around the lake. Then, it was at a neighboring farm. This is way stronger than I can handle on my own. Can you or someone else you know help me?"

"You kept your hand in?"

"Excuse me?"

"You got out of doing the fairs, but did you get out of the life?"

"I haven't done readings or anything for years but crossed a couple ghosts recently."

Rae breathed in and out before answering. "What's your sun sign?"

"Cancer."

"Water, again. Emotional. Okay, I'm gonna cut the deck, then we'll see what's what."

"Alright." What she suggested was a standard, quick method of divination. After shuffling a deck of tarot cards, she would cut the deck three times. The first card would represent my past, the second, my present, and the last card, my future. I heard her shuffle, then a moment of silence.

"The first is the Three of Swords. Do you remember what it means?"

"Uh...I'm a little rusty."

"Right. Well, it shows three swords piercing a heart. Now, this ain't a pleasant card. It's associated with pain and suffering. With things like rejection, betrayal, and grief. But the Swords are about character and principles. This one teaches pain is sometimes necessary. Without it, there'd be nothing to overcome and life would be meaningless. Since this is your past card, you must have learned from your mistakes and grew stronger."

As she spoke, I thought of the fights with my family when I was a teenager. The loneliness of knowing those closest to me didn't believe a word coming out of my mouth. Then, how far I'd come since then. "I hope so."

"The next card is the Ace of Wands," she said. "You got a cloud with a hand coming out of it, holding a wand, and behind that, a river and a castle on a hill. It tells you it's time to start something new, particularly if you need to get a jump on it and be bold. Wands are associated with energy and inspiration and planning. If there's something you want to do, but are afraid, grab hold of the fear and do it anyway. Be careful, though, 'cause this Ace is one of those cards with a double meaning. It's unpredictable and can't be controlled. It can help, but sometimes it's like a raging forest fire, out of control. Just be alert."

Neither good nor bad.

Another silence. "Uh, huh," Rae finally said. "You're future card is the Moon, which also happens to be your planet. With the Moon, you know, things all nice an' friendly during the day can seem dangerous at night. We have a wolf and a dog, two of the same family but one's wild and the other's domesticated, and they're both howling at the Moon. So, no matter your place in society, you can still be swayed by illusion and deception. Now, there's ties between the Moon and fertility, but the Moon of the Tarot tends to be about fertility of the mind rather than the body. A crayfish coming up out of the water is a sign of the subconscious rising up and influencing your conscious mind. Now, for those with closed minds, they can't tell what's real and what's their fears talking."

"*Mmm*," I said.

"The challenge of the Moon," Rae continued, "is a journey that has to be made alone, in the dark, and without a map. You got to rely on your own inner GPS. Pay attention. You can lose your way and flail around in the dark. But if you wait until the sun rises, the road may have changed and your chance lost. The Moon's a card of intuition and psychic forces. You may be rusty but I don't think you've forgotten everything, so just...let go. Let your intuition guide you. Stop throwing up roadblocks. Your way forward'll be revealed and you'll learn something about yourself you'll need later on."

I'd forgotten how this stuff made me feel naked, exposed.

"So," said Rae. "All in all, this ain't a bad spread. You've learned from your past. Now's the time to start something new, as long as you keep a tight hold on the energy. And things'll go okay in the future if you let your-self be guided by your intuition. You can beat what's going on in that town of yours."

"I'm not so sure."

There was an awkward moment of silence.

"I'm going to say something," Rae said, slowly. "You may not like it, but you need to hear it. You ready?"

Great. I was already shaking in my sneakers as it was. "Yeah."

"You've gotten away from your true self. I suspect you

ran into problems and threw yourself in the exact opposite direction. Am I right?"

"Well..." Who was I kidding? "Yeah."

"You can't tear yourself in two. You got to be whole for what's coming."

"But—"

"This is a part of you, whether you want it or not. Make peace with it before something bad happens. Trust yourself. Trust your gut. It'll guide you home."

I put a shaky hand up to wipe my forehead. I was sweating again. "Thank you. You've given me a lot to think about." Too much, maybe.

"Take care, now, you hear? Let me know how it all goes, okay?"

"I will. Thank you."

"*De rien*. It's nothing. *Au revoir,* Kenna. And *bon chance!* Good luck."

I needed it.

It was a lot to take in. On one hand, it made me feel better. At least I was going in the right direction. On the other hand, the immediate future terrified me. So, I did what I do best when faced with impossible choices—procrastinated—by sorting more stuff in the bedrooms. The living room wall still taunted me, but I didn't feel up to it yet.

I lost track of time until the doorbell rang.

~

SHERITA AND HER KIDS STOOD ON THE FRONT STEPS. SHE held a casserole dish covered with aluminum foil. "Hello. I brought you dinner," she said.

My mouth fell open. "You didn't have to do that."

Sherita smiled. "I know, but I figured you'd had a bad couple days here and you'd probably get a pizza or something else unhealthy."

"You're right. Come on in."

Before anyone could cross the threshold, though, the tomcat pushed his way through the forest of feet and scampered in ahead of them. "Well, hello to you, too, cat." I said.

Sherita's older son, Jayden, laughed. "He's fast."

"Yes, he is," I said. "Probably hungry, too."

We all marched up the kitchen stairs.

"What's his name?" Jayden asked.

"He doesn't have one yet," I said. "He's a stray and I'm looking for a good home for him. Do you know anyone who wants a cat?"

He thought for a moment. "No."

"I'll ask around," Sherita said, waiting for her youngest son to climb the stairs. He was still young enough to use his hands to help himself up.

I smiled, watching his slow, determined progress. As soon as he reached the top, Sherita's daughter, Makayla, scooped him up.

Sherita placed her casserole dish on the counter next to the smaller containers her older children had set down already. "There's macaroni and cheese, fresh green beans, and cupcakes."

I opened my eyes wide in surprise. "This is a feast. Can you all join me?"

"Ours is at home," piped up Jayden, with a grin. He hopped from one foot to the other, unable to stand still.

Sherita ruffled his hair. "We made a big batch of

everything so you enjoy this and we'll go home and eat ours."

"I helped," said her son.

"Helped make a mess," Makayla grumbled, shifting the toddler from one hip to the other.

I chuckled. "I don't know what to say." This little kindness overwhelmed me and I hugged Sherita. "Thank you so much." I hugged the kids too. "You guys are fantastic."

"You're very welcome," Sherita said. "Our house feels like it's ours and we have you to thank for it. If there's anything you need, you let me know." She touched my arm. "I mean it, now."

My throat tightened. All I could do was cover her hand with mine and nod.

"Can we go now?" Jayden asked. "I'm hungry."

"Absolutely," I spluttered, blinking to clear my eyes.

As they left, Sherita turned on the stairs. "I almost forgot," she said. "We took Max to the vet. He said he's in the early stages of arthritis so I'm giving him daily supplements and we're keeping an eye on it now."

"Good. I'm glad you followed up on it." One less worry on my mind.

After they left, the cat made a nuisance of himself, so I refilled his bowl. Watching him eat, emotions crowded in my throat. I swallowed but they wouldn't settle. Good people like Sherita and her kids didn't deserve the danger caused by the lake ghosts. I felt ashamed that for so long I'd acted like a coward, wanting to cut and run. Thankfully I called Rae. Talking to her made me feel better. And this meal, out of nowhere, was the cherry on top.

I spooned up some mac and cheese. Smooth, creamy, and tangy. Heaven. I hadn't eaten anything so good since before I left home. One thing I did miss about Ma when I left was her cooking. I didn't realize how hungry I was until I started eating.

Mmm-mmm.

It didn't take long for my thoughts to circle back to the problems squeezing me on all sides. I wanted to make this town safe for people like Sherita and her family but what could I do? Since coming back here, my life was a mess. I missed feeling competent and in control. I needed to get some of my mojo back.

Without realizing it, I polished off half the mac and cheese, all the beans, and one of two chocolate, chocolate chip cupcakes. I put what remained in the fridge.

I wasn't an actual coward. I'd completely changed my life not too long ago. As Rae said, I knew what to do. I was just a little rusty. Maybe a little scared. Okay, a lot scared. But, I'd also been terrified to quit the psychic life and become a vet tech and it turned out better than I imagined.

One solitary beer remained in the almost-empty refrigerator. I snatched it and went outside, collapsing into a lawn chair in the back yard. The cat wandered over and jumped into my lap.

"Aren't you getting friendly," I murmured, scratching his head. I took a swig of my beer as he leaned into my hand, purring. "I'll figure out a way to kick out the lake ghosts and then I'll go home and everything will be normal again." The cat didn't care about anything but the attention I gave him.

The neighborhood was quiet, with only the sounds of crickets and a neighbor's TV and the cat's purring. The sun was low behind the trees, the backyard in shadow. I set the can on the ground beside me and closed my eyes, hand resting on the cat's back. The quiet was so nice.

I jerked awake.

It was now fully dark. Neighborhood dogs barked. The cat growled low in his throat.

Something moved in the bushes on the edge of the yard. Fear sizzled through me before a twinge in my gut changed my mind about bolting into the house.

The cat hissed and tried to jump down, but I held onto him and stood up. The yard was dark. Street lights didn't penetrate this deep and the neighbors' had their back lights off. Bushes and trees around the property border created dark shadows. The crickets and cicadas were silent.

Opening my mind, I felt curiosity. It was an animal.

Holy moly, it was a bear.

26

The cat hissed and clawed at me. I opened my arms and he sprang away. I couldn't tell how big the bear was and didn't feel any fear or anger coming from it. No indication it was about to charge. Moving closer, I went deeper into its mind. It was a young male and overriding everything was an intense need to see and smell and experience new places and things.

Interesting. I'd noticed something similar in puppies and kittens; young animals wanted to explore their world. But this was more intense than it should have been. Usually, when a bear wandered into human territory, it was driven by hunger. Which would explain the overturned garbage cans around town.

A complicated bear, then.

It snuffled and moved away from the shadows. On all fours, it was almost as tall as me. Granted, I was short but it was a big animal. If not able to sense its benign intentions, I would have been paralyzed with fear. Or running for my life. "Hello, Mr. Bear. What are you doing here?"

The bear stopped and sat, as if considering my question.

Pictures flashed across my mind. Fields and lakes and streams and foxes and birds and dogs and mountains and forests and people and cows and horses and houses and fences and more, faster than I could grasp onto them.

The bear had moved closer during the slide show. My nose wrinkled at the smell of garbage and wet dog. How he found water in this drought, I couldn't imagine.

Then, the images slowed and showed a mother bear and cub. Watching the cub charge toward me, I looked down and saw the paws of another cub and realized this must be from the bear's point of view, when he was young. This was his family. I got a sense of contentment and affection.

Fascinated, I didn't interrupt, though I had lots of questions.

The cubs grew, learning to hunt for vegetation, berries, and insects. Yet the bear felt a strong pull away from its mother and sibling. The scene switched and the bear was on its own, walking down out of the mountains, maybe the Adirondacks, and into human territory. He'd come a long way and been very lucky.

"You're in danger here." I formed images of hunters with guns and sent them to the bear. "People want to hunt you, either kill you or put you to sleep and move you somewhere else. You can't stay here."

The bear moved closer. He was curious and sniffed me. I stood still and allowed it yet turned my head away from his pungent odor. I'm sure no other human ever communicated with him like I did.

A hiss came from the ground near my feet. The tom

was scared, but defending me from a dangerous intruder. Or what he thought was a dangerous intruder.

This amused the bear. He sniffed me one more time, then turned, and lumbered back into the bushes.

The cat followed him at a safe distance. "Hey, come back here, cat." I could barely make out a light-colored rear end disappearing into the bushes and sighed.

The neighborhood dogs went nuts for a while, then settled down.

I looked up at the stars, savoring the quiet before stumbling into the house and collapsing on the couch, fully-dressed.

Next thing I knew, something sharp dug into my chest, then my face.

Wake up.

When I opened my eyes, it was dark. "Wha—" I sat up. Something fell on the floor. Oh. The cat. Of course.

A scraping sound in the kitchen made me stop and listen. Mice, maybe?

"Miss Kenna," Henry said softly near my right ear.

I gasped. "Don't do that," I whispered, hand on my chest.

"I am sorry. However, there are intruders in the house."

～

NOT AGAIN.

I stood up, wobbling, holding onto the couch for support. I needed a weapon. But what? I remembered Jim's twisted metal table lamp.

Switching directions, I felt for the side table, and

walked right into it. Grabbing for the lamp before it fell, I stood still, listening, but whoever was in the kitchen hadn't heard the elephant in the living room. Calling myself all kinds of names in my head and trying to calm my breathing, I unscrewed the top, lifting the shade off. Gently pulling on the cord, it separated from the wall socket and I wrapped it around the base.

Cupboard doors opened and closed and then the fridge. Talking. Male voices. They sounded young. Probably teenagers. What if these were the same ones who broke in before? "Came back to the scene of the crime did you, boys?" I murmured.

It's impossible to move quietly across the wood floors. Staying to the perimeter of the room, I hoped it would minimize the creaking. I froze after every little noise but the intruders were oblivious.

Glass smashed on a hard surface. Giggling.

Anger swept through me. "What's going on?" I called. I slapped on the dining room light behind me. "Who's in there?" Squinting, I saw figures piling out of the kitchen door. A streak of white ran after them. Remembering the broken glass and reversing, I tripped over my own feet and fell backward with an *"oof,"* the lamp digging into my chest.

Thuds on the stairs turned to cries and moans and one feline screech.

"Good kitty." I hoped he wasn't crushed.

My shoes were by the kitchen door, on the other side of the room. I scrambled up and grabbed a handful of clothes from a box. Throwing them on the kitchen floor, I stepped on them, scooting over to my shoes. I had an inspiration.

"Henry," I called. "Don't let them leave the house." Shoving my feet into sneakers, I flew down the stairs, tripping on the last step. I grabbed the railing, the lamp tumbling out of my hands, and heard the tinkling of the bulb breaking. I turned the side door handle. Closed and locked. They didn't leave. I flipped on the light, looking for the lamp.

Scraping sounds in the basement then an unearthly roar and high-pitched boy screams. "Yay, Henry," I whispered, snatching up the lamp.

"Go, go, go," urged a cracking voice.

I raced down the basement stairs, cradling the lamp in my arms, and almost tripped on the trailing cord.

Across the room, one boy was outside a broken window high up on the wall, pulling another one through. The next kid scrambled up the precarious pile of stuff in front of the window. Nobody helped him and he couldn't reach high enough to pull himself through.

I dropped the lamp and grabbed the seat of his long shorts, hauling him back from the window. "No, you don't," I said, pulling so hard the elastic waistband stretched, revealing his tighty whities. He screamed. I let go and they snapped back.

He yelped, pulling his pants up as he fell back against the wall. "I'm sorry. I'm sorry. Please, don't hurt me. I don't want to die."

"I'm not going to hurt you," I said, hands on my hips. "I want to know what you're doing here."

The cat butted into me, hard. *Look at what I did.*

"Yes, yes." I squatted to pet him, never taking my eyes off the kid. "You did a good job."

"What?" the kid shrieked.

"I'm talking to the cat. Relax."

"There...there's something down here." He trembled, his eyes sweeping the basement. About thirteen or fourteen, he was thin and gangling, with long, stringy brown hair.

"Just you and me and the cat." I set the lamp on the concrete floor and picked up the tom. He rubbed against my face, purring.

"There's something else here." The kid's voice quivered. "I saw it. It had these teeth and glowing eyes and—"

I tried not to smile. Henry had done a jump scare on the kids. Who knew he had it in him? "Oh, you mean the ghost haunting this house? Yeah, he kind of guards the place." Might as well start a rumor to discourage any more visitors.

"A ghost? You aren't scared?"

"No. This is my family's house. I belong here. Now, what were you kids doing?" I asked, sternly.

Tears welled up in his eyes. "Nothing. I swear. They said no one was here."

"What's your name?"

He mumbled, glancing away.

"What did you say? I couldn't hear you."

He sighed. "Billy Campbell."

There had been Campbells older and younger than me in school. I guessed the younger one. "Is your father Ken?"

He nodded, looking like he wanted the floor to open up and swallow him whole. For once, being in a small town worked to my advantage.

"Why did you and your friends break in?"

"I di—" he squeaked and cleared his throat. "I didn't. I

just," he shrugged his thin shoulders, "came in with them."

"I see. Are they older?"

"Yes." He snuffled and wiped his nose on his shoulder.

"And you didn't see my car in the driveway?"

He looked down, hiding his face behind his hair. "No. We came in from the other direction."

"Did you help mess up the kitchen?"

He shrugged.

"Billy, look at me." I tried to mimic Ma's intimidation techniques.

He glanced up, then hid his face again.

"I expect an answer from you. Were you involved with making the mess in my kitchen?"

He nodded. "But I didn't want to. He made me drop the dish. Said I was a sissy if I didn't."

Bullies were always so original.

"I see." Goosebumps broke out on my arms. My righteous indignation had drained away, and the basement was chilly. "Alright, mister. Upstairs, so you can clean up your mess." I turned, waving him by.

Billy sighed, preceding me up the stairs to the kitchen, all the while, his head swiveling, watching for Henry to jump out at him.

The cat squirmed out of my arms at the top of the stairs, heading straight for his dish.

My jaw fell open at the damage in the kitchen. Earlier, I hadn't noticed the black spray paint on the cabinets and counters. It was even on the floor, though smudged from all the activity earlier. The few towels and napkins I kept in drawers were tossed on counters and the floor. One even hung from the light fixture. Ketchup pooled like blood in front of the fridge. And my mother's favorite platter, on which many a Tierney roast had rested, was in pieces on the linoleum. It was one of the few things I'd meant to keep. Hurt and anger flooded through me. I took a big breath and let it out, controlling the worst of the feeling. I've had long practice with the technique, and in this very house, too.

Billy hung his head, not looking at the damage. I kinda felt sorry for the kid. My gut feeling was he was telling the truth. He followed along and got caught. I remembered trying to hang out with kids in school, doing stupid stuff to get them to like me. My anger transferred to the two older boys who let their friend get caught so they could escape.

Cowards.

I handed Billy a broom, dustpan, and the garbage can. He picked up big pieces first.

"What are the names of the two boys with you?" I asked.

He shook his head, not wanting to be a snitch.

"How old are you?" I leaned my hip against a cabinet, crossing my arms over my chest.

He sighed. "Thirteen."

"Enjoying your summer so far?"

He began to sweep. "I guess."

"What do you do for fun?"

"Hang out 'n stuff."

Typical. "What's your favorite class in school?"

"I don't know."

Apparently not a fan of school. "Do you work with your hands? Make things? Fix stuff?"

"Sometimes."

After the broken platter, he moved onto picking linens and papers off the floor and cleaning up the spilled ketchup. When he was done, he hesitated.

"That'll do," I said. "Now, Mr. Campbell, since you won't tell me who your buddies are, you will be responsible for continuing to clean up this mess. Tomorrow, I expect to see you here to start working on the spray paint. If you don't show up, I'll have a talk with your father. Do you understand me?"

He nodded. "You'll keep the ghost away from me?"

"Yes, I will." I ushered him toward the stairs. "Now go straight home."

"Yes, ma'am."

I unlocked the side door and he shot out of the house, disappearing into the dark.

Closing and locking the door, I trudged back up the stairs. Maybe I'd have him finish the living room wall too.

Henry appeared. "Did I do it right, Miss Kenna?"

I laughed. "You put a good scare in them and we got one, so yeah. Great job."

He wavered for a moment, then smiled. "My grandfather used to say 'many hands make light work.' I'm glad to be of help." He paused. "It has been a long time." Then, he disintegrated.

Who knew a spirit wanted to feel needed?

I shook my head at the graffiti on the floor. Hopefully, it would clean up. I tilted my head. Ignoring the smudges, it looked like some kind of symbol. I walked around it until I realized what I was looking at.

A crude but clear picture of male anatomy.

Little perverts.

27

The next morning I went out to the backyard, coffee cup in hand. Was the bear still around? Opening my senses, I felt ghosts, pets, birds, squirrels and other small animals in the neighborhood, but no bear. Good. After closing off, I took a sip of coffee, enjoying the roasted taste.

"Kenna." Nate strolled up and handed me the latest newspaper. He wasn't his usual perky self.

"Do I really want to read it?"

He shrugged. "Thought you might. Some folks agree with it, some don't. Some need to take a chill pill, you know?"

I laughed. He reminded me of better times. Wait. How could I think high school was better times?

He pointed to an article and the title made me cringe: Exorcism at Local Lake a Bust. It rehashed everything going on, described our impromptu meeting on the road with Don Houser and Linda Goddard, going into the woods together, and leaving "in a hurry" about an hour later.

It felt longer than that.

The article quoted Don Houser. "We tried something and it didn't work. But don't go getting discouraged. We have other things up our sleeves. You watch. Folks in Hurlbutt have nothing to fear. This will all be cleared up soon."

"He's got balls," I whispered.

"The ex-mayor?" Nate's smile turned ironic. "Yeah, saw him this morning, shaking hands and smoothing things over. Hey, do you need help? I don't know about busting ghosts, but I swing a mean shovel."

I grinned. "Thanks for the offer. I may take you up on it." I went back to reading.

In the article, Pastor Graves had added his two cents: "Modern-day hauntings are no more than demonic spirits pretending to be deceased humans to lead us away from our Christian faith. We must resist these spirits and send them to Hell where they belong."

At least it didn't mention Andy or the clinic. "C'mon, I want to show you something." I led him up the back stairs.

As soon as he walked in and saw the graffiti in the kitchen, he said, "Not again? *Kennaaaaah*, they really opened a can of whoop-ass on your house."

"Yup, but this time I saw who did it. Three teenagers. They broke in last night through a basement window. I was able to grab one and convinced him to fix the damage or I'd tell his parents."

He laughed. "Blackmail. I like it."

Not long after Nate left to help an old lady put up shelves in her living room, Billy arrived, apologizing and thanking me again for not telling his parents. I set him to scrubbing the cabinets and floor. We tried a couple different cleaners, but nothing worked 100%. "I have an idea," I said and showed him the graffiti on the living room wall. "I bought paint to cover up this." I watched his reaction.

He turned pink and looked away.

Gotcha. "I think I bought enough to use on the cabinets, too. How are you with a paintbrush?"

"P...pretty good," he stammered. "I helped my dad paint the house last year."

"Excellent, let's get started."

We removed the cabinet doors, taking them outside. In the garage, I found sandpaper in a box of stuff to donate and he started sanding.

Then, I remembered the broken basement window. Hoping every critter in the neighborhood wasn't already camped out in my basement, I looked up local contractors in an old phone book I'd rescued from the garbage. It took a couple tries until I found one who could be out the next day.

I'd be so happy when I didn't have to fix one more thing on this house.

I checked on Billy, inspecting the one door he had worked on. Smooth job, even around the corners. Most of the spray paint came off when he sanded. Cool. "Very nice. Keep going."

He smiled shyly at the praise and continued sanding.

I was struck by the thought of how simple his life

must be. What would it be like to have normal childhood memories?

Soon after, the auction company truck arrived.

Hallelujah!

But when it came right down to it, I kept the bed and dresser in my parents' old bedroom, the dining room table and chairs, the couch, and one easy chair. What can I say? It felt right. Besides, I wasn't leaving yet and couldn't exactly sit on the floor. I'd figure out what to do with it all later.

I gave the go ahead on all the other furniture and dozens of boxes of furnishings, craft supplies, toys, and knick-knacks. I'd be lying if I said I didn't get a bit of a twinge seeing the furniture go. A lot of memories were attached to these pieces of my childhood. I almost understood why Ma kept it all. Almost.

After the auction guys left, I drifted from room to room, memories coming in waves.

There was the corner in the living room where Dad set up the gaudy 60s-style aluminum Christmas tree each year. We never had an abundance of gifts like some kids, but we always had a couple nice ones and stockings filled with candy and small items.

The dining room where many a holiday meal was served, usually with a friend or two in attendance. And plenty of alcohol afterward, which always put Dad in a nostalgic mood. I loved listening to his stories of the old days, particularly of growing up in New York City. He ran with a tough crowd back then, getting into trouble that his quick-thinking got him out of.

The stairway where once, when we were real young,

Jim had the brilliant idea to slide down the stairs on Ma's silver serving tray from Great-Grandma. Years later, carpeting covered up the scratches, but Ma had still muttered every time she climbed those stairs.

Despite the problems I had growing up, there were good memories in this house.

Now, it felt different and it made me a little sad.

My phone buzzed in my pocket. It was Declan, excited by his research with the historian. I let him ramble for a while about Colonial settlements in the area, but then he started droning on about different Native American tribes during the Neolithic age.

"Wait a minute, now," I said. "What about any big events at the lake?"

He hesitated. "We couldn't find any."

"So we're still in the dark?"

"I'm afraid so but I haven't tried the library in Bartlett. I'll have Brian take me over."

Declan was doing his best but I hated not knowing what we were dealing with. At least researching was keeping him busy and out of harm's way. Between my weird emotions about the house and the ghost problem hanging heavy over my head, the rest of my day sucked rotten eggs.

THE CONTRACTOR WOKE ME UP THE NEXT MORNING BY banging on the front door. After I showed him the broken window in the basement, Billy arrived. Yesterday, he had sanded and primed the cabinet doors and primed the living room wall. Today, he began painting.

I collapsed on the couch, still not mentally together. Checking my cell phone, I saw it was 10:00 a.m. and I had missed calls. One was from Nora, then Pat at the animal clinic, and finally, from Doc.

My stomach did a little flip. What was today? I clicked over to the calendar. When was I supposed to be back to work? I had forgotten to enter it. I listened to my messages. Nora wanted a report on the progress with the house. I'd deal with her later. Next, Pat gave me her condolences and said they needed me back to work as soon as possible. Oh, no.

The last one played.

"Kenna. This is Doc." His voice was clipped. "Um, you were supposed to be back two days ago. I'm sorry about your mother, but we're in a tight spot. I hired a temp this morning. I had no choice." He paused. "Call me."

"Son of a biscuit," I whispered. My hands shook as I called the clinic.

Pat answered and filled me in on the new temp. "He's gorgeous," she gushed. "I mean it. All the women are in love with him. And he knows his stuff. Doc's impressed with his work and Susan's taken a shine to him. You'd better get back here if you want to keep your job."

I sighed. "Thanks, Pat. Can I talk to Doc?"

He was in between patients and I didn't have to wait long before he picked up the line. "Kenna. Thanks for calling back."

"Doc, I'm so sorry but we had a break-in at the house and everything's been a mess and I apologize for leaving you short-handed."

"A call would have been helpful."

"You're right. This whole thing has me out of my mind

and I'm sorry for all the inconvenience I've caused you and everybody at the clinic." I cringed, not wanting to say the rest. "But I'm stuck here for a few more days."

The line went silent and the tension screeched in my head.

"I see," Doc said at last, sounding tired. "Well, please be back by next Monday or I'll have to believe you don't want to work here anymore."

"Absolutely," I exhaled. "I'll be there on Monday. No problem."

Getting off the phone, I entered it in my calendar and set up three notifications to remind me. "There. Can't forget it now." I'd come way too close to losing my dream job.

I wandered around the house, avoiding Billy and the contractor, but not able to settle anywhere. For two years I worked crazy hours while attending college, always keeping my eyes on the prize. Then, I landed the clinic job and everything was going so well. Now, after only a few weeks, all my discipline was gone? How did that happen?

Upstairs in my old bedroom, I stared out the window.

Everything I'd worked so hard to accomplish was collapsing and all I felt was, what? A soul-sucking tiredness? What was wrong with me? And what would I do now? I felt responsible for helping with the lake ghosts, but what about my own life? At what point do I say, "Enough?"

"Kenna?" Billy called up the stairs. "The guy in the basement says he's done."

Somehow, I summoned up the energy to show appreciation for the contractor's window job. As I wrote him a check, though, I noticed my dwindling funds.

Things kept getting better and better.

Needing to get away from the house for a while, I loaded up my car with bags of clothing to donate to the Vietnam Vet's Donation Center. Even at midday, Hurlbutt was almost deserted. Only two cars were parked on Main Street and those were in front of the diner. The lunch crowd.

I parked in front of the donation center. Studying the storefront, I remembered it had once been a shoe store. A memory of Ma marching us kids in to buy shoes flashed through my mind.

While wrestling a garbage bag of clothing out of the car, my phone rang. I set the bag on the sidewalk, pulled out my phone, and groaned.

"Hi, Nora," I answered.

"Kenna. Why didn't you call me back?" Her Texas twang had returned. "Anyway, I had a little chat with the Realtor."

"Okay." What now?

"She says you aren't moving forward on the house. Honestly, I should have known not to leave you in charge of finishing things. The minute I left, it all fell apart. So what have you been doing instead of working?"

Gritting my teeth so hard my jaw hurt, I then took a deep breath and counted to five, leaning against the car. "We had a break-in. Two, actually, and I had to fix the damage."

"But there's nothing of value in the house. What damage?"

"Spray paint on the walls, floors, and kitchen cabinets."

She sighed, heavily. "Vandalism. The Realtor didn't mention it."

I rolled my eyes. "That's because I didn't tell her about it."

"So you have a little painting to do. It shouldn't take long. And what about this ghost nonsense at Rogers Lake, for God's sake? I was shocked she believed in that sort of thing."

"Hurlbutt isn't exactly the armpit of America, you know. It's just had some bad luck over the years."

She snorted. "I'd say it's more than bad luck."

Not interested in continuing this old argument, I opened my mouth to cut her off but heard children shrieking on her end.

"Kenna, I've got to go. Do wrap things up there quickly. I won't pay for delays."

I ground my teeth. "I didn't ask you to Nora."

"Good." She hung up.

I kicked the tire on my car. Unfortunately, I wore flip-flops. A big, baby blue car crawled down the street toward me. Tears gathered in the corners of my eyes. Miss Maglennon glared at me as she rolled by, paralyzing me until she turned the corner. "Old bat," I gasped, rubbing my big toe.

After the fourth trip lugging stuff into the center, Brian pulled into the parking spot ahead of me.

"Were've you been?" he bellowed, climbing out of his pickup. "Don's breathing down my neck and Declan has me taking him over hill and dale to libraries." He screwed up his face. "Mind you, it's better than Katrina's To-Do

List but I'd rather go somewhere a might bit more inter-esting. Most of those librarians are two days older than dirt and just as pretty. Or they're men." He shook his head.

Swiping back hairs stuck to my sweaty forehead, I said, "I've been busy with the house. Can't drop every-thing, you know."

"Well, why not? You..." Brian trailed off, looking at something over my shoulder.

I turned. Two men and two women stepped out of a maroon car and into the diner. They wore suits and dresses. "From the Church of Peace and Love?" I asked.

Brian grinned like a wolf. "That," he said, "is Pastor Dick, himself. Looks like he has his hip boots on today."

Nobody in the group wore boots. "What boots?" I asked.

"He wouldn't want to ruin his nice suit walking amongst us sinners, now would he?"

I groaned at his lousy joke.

He started down the sidewalk toward the diner. "C'mon, it's show time."

Wanting to see this pastor for myself, I followed him, curious.

∽

WHEN WE WALKED IN, PASTOR GRAVES AND HIS PEOPLE stood in the middle of the restaurant, their backs to the door. Brian and I slipped into two empty stools at the counter, almost even with the group. "Which one is he?" I whispered.

"The short one," said Brian.

I studied Graves. His profile was strong with even features and dark brown hair. He appeared fit, maybe in his forties. In the suit, he looked like a lawyer. Until he opened his mouth.

"Brothers and sisters, we have an infestation of demons." He had a deep, warm voice that caught people's attention and drew them in. "Yes, right here in Hurlbutt." He nodded. "These so-called ghosts at Rogers Lake are nothing more than Satan's creatures in disguise. TV and movies try to convince us these are friendly spirits, spirits of family members, who want to help us, or need our help. But the Bible tells us Satan disguises himself as an 'angel of light.'"

The man and women standing next to Graves nodded at each statement he made.

The older waitress, Bonny, stalked up to Pastor Graves. "You can't do that here. This is a diner, not a church."

Graves glanced at the other man in the group.

Taller and more solid than his leader, the man gently moved the waitress to the side. "Please, the Pastor is speaking."

Brian chuckled. "They've gone and done it now."

Bonny pulled away, glaring at the man, then turned on her heel.

As soon as she moved aside, Pastor Graves began talking again. "Satan and his creatures know all the details of our deceased loved ones."

He stared at me.

"He can use that information to draw us away from God, using signs and visions to get us to experiment with Ouija boards and fortune telling."

My skin crawled until he broke eye contact and then I noticed people staring at me.

"This opens us up to influence by dark forces, brothers and sisters. We must resist. Resist the temptation of those around you. Resist those," he said, pointing right at me, "who stumble around in darkness. We must cast out these unclean spirits."

"Hey." The shout came from the kitchen door at the end of the counter. A middle-aged guy in an apron hurried into the dining room, wiping his hands on a towel. "What are you doing?"

Brian leaned closer. "That's Frank, the owner."

Frank had been muscular once but his arms looked a little soft, and his dirty white apron spread over a small paunch. "This is my diner and you're bothering my customers. Go on. Get out of here."

Pastor Graves drew himself up. "Sir, as a local proprietor, you must be concerned by the strange occurrences going on in this town and at Rogers Lake?"

"I'm concerned by a religious nut spouting off in my establishment." Frank walked closer to the group. "Now, turn around and walk out of here while you still can or I'm gonna throw you out, starting with him." He pointed at the other man, who whispered something in Graves' ear.

Graves smiled, unconcerned. "I see our message is lost here. May you and your customers enjoy the fruits of your doubt and iniquity." He turned and left the restaurant, followed by his supporters.

Frank watched until they were out the door, then turned. "Sorry, folks," he announced. "Some people just gotta shoot their mouths off. Please, go back to your meals." He returned to the kitchen.

Brian elbowed me. "That was more fun than a five-dollar whore in church."

28

Driving back to the house, I worked myself into a fury. How dare the arrogant jerk point fingers at me like this was all my fault? I didn't open a door and let all the ghosts in. I was trying to help.

When I pulled in the driveway, the kitchen cabinet doors set up on boxes reminded me Billy was still here. I had to sit in my car for a while to chill out. Inspecting the doors, I was pleased with the results and found Billy in the living room putting the finishing touches on the wall. I was impressed. No drips on the wall or the floor.

"This is excellent work, Billy. I'll keep you in mind if I need anything more done. Paying work."

His eyes lit up at the praise. "Thank you," he said, from behind his curtain of hair.

After he left, Declan called and asked if I'd come over to his house to discuss his research. Once there, he was bursting with an enthusiasm he seemed to save for historical facts. "Come in, come in," he said. "I've just read some fascinating tidbits about..." He continued to talk as he walked away.

I closed the door. "Hello to you, too," I said under my breath, following him to the kitchen. I didn't want to get caught up in another of his lectures.

Several books were open across his kitchen table surrounding a paper tablet with hand-written notes. Obviously, he'd been hard at work. "By the mid 1600s," he began, "the French had expanded from Montreal and around Lake Ontario to the north. Pushing further, they ran into problems with the Iroquois Indians. You see, the French were allied with the Hurons, their enemies."

He'd gone down the rabbit hole. "What about Rogers Lake?" I asked. "Anything in particular happen there?"

He consulted the tablet on the table, paging through it. "Well, I searched Gibson County and Hurlbutt records as far back as I could find, right up to the present, and, while nothing large-scale seems to have happened at the lake, there's a history of tragedies in the area—fires, car accidents, murders, that sort of thing."

"Nothing supernatural about those," I said.

Declan smiled. "There is if it occurs every thirty years and always results in at least one death."

"What?"

Declan picked up the pad and flipped pages. "Obviously, taken together, all the different occurrences over time appear random." He showed me a list of events with corresponding dates starting in the 1800s. "But I noticed a pattern with the dates. There are more occurring in August than any other month and, of those, there's a cluster of several every thirty years.

I stared at him. "No way."

Declan's eyes drilled into mine. "Yes." He looked at his notes. "I don't know what the significance of the thirty years means. The last time something happened in August was in 1972, when those two little angels were kidnapped and died."

"The twin ghosts at the derailment site?"

He nodded.

"Jeez Louise." I paused. "That was, what? Over forty years ago? Why didn't something bad happen at the thirty year mark?"

"I don't know. My research suggests over time, the hauntings in a particular place can decrease. It's as if the ghosts lose their power or energy or whatever. Perhaps the lake ghosts were starting to fade when the train derailment woke them up."

"Maybe."

"There's something else. The occurrences usually happen between the tenth and the twentieth of August. Today is the nineteenth."

"It is? " I tried to add up the days in my head, but everything was a jumbled mess. "If the dates are off, like you say, it could mean nothing."

"True. What bothers me is each cluster in previous years included a death. We haven't had one. Yet."

I groaned.

He nodded. "We also don't know anything about the ghosts, who they were, why they died, and under what circumstances."

"That bothers me, too."

"I've been researching ghosts and methods of releasing them and I think we could deal with them better if we knew more about them. I went as far back as I could find in the records, but before the Europeans arrived, before we had records, different groups of Indians roamed all over this area. Eventually, the Iroquois chased out the others or, in the case of the Neutral Nation, utterly destroyed them. It is possible these ghosts come from that time."

"But we don't know for sure?"

He raised his hands, palm up, then dropped them. "True, and who's to say the records we have are complete? Some may have been lost to fires, floods, what have you. It is so frustrating not to be able to have a definitive answer to this."

Beyond frustrating, actually, but Declan had worked hard to get this little bit of information. "No kidding. You did your best, though, and it's more than we knew before."

Back at the house, my thoughts returned to the diner and Pastor Graves and I got mad all over again. I threw myself into scrubbing the walls and floors of the upstairs bedrooms. By the third bedroom, my energy and some of the anger had faded and the doubts crept in. Half the town probably wanted me to leave and the other half expected me to make all the ghosts disappear. I'd tried and failed. Things were spiraling out of control.

"Dad? Ma? Can you hear me?" I hated the pleading sound of my voice.

No answer.

"Don't you think I'm more important than a vacation? I thought you said you were always there for me."

Silence, except for the neighborhood sounds drifting through the open windows.

Maybe I should ask my spirit guide? No. I'd done nothing but mess things up.

The floor blurred and then a white hot rage filled me, blotting everything else out. I tossed the scrub brush into the bucket, splashing dirty water on the clean floor. I was pathetic.

I was scared.

For so long, I'd put the past out of my mind. Recent events brought it near the surface over and over and I couldn't ignore it any longer. Sliding down the wall, I sat on the floor, arms wrapped tight around my knees.

~

Seven years wasn't long ago, but it had been a different life.

I was arrogant, a professional psychic medium with private clients. I'd just broken up with my boyfriend and slammed out of our apartment. I needed a place to stay and my friend, Gail, came to the rescue. Old places with history often have a ghost or two lingering so I usually check out apartments before moving in. This time, I was desperate and didn't inspect the location first.

The minute I walked into her building, I felt a ghost squatting like a toad, watching me.

I had little experience with strong or malevolent spirits but expected to cross this one without a problem. Boy, was I wrong. After two weeks of little sleep, constant disruption, and frightening incidents, I exhausted my knowledge and abilities. The ghost was still entrenched and Gail asked me to leave. It was like getting pushed out of a plane without a parachute.

You'd think I'd get used to the feeling, as many times as it's happened to me, but I thought this time was different. I had thought Gail was different.

We'd worked together at a factory when I first moved to Buffalo and had stayed friends as I pursued the psychic biz. In fact, she'd encouraged me, was my cheerleader. For some people, ghosts are cool in theory or when everything is fun, but they can't handle the reality if things go sideways.

Feeling crushed because Gail threw me out, I pretended it didn't bother me. Pros don't let that stuff affect them. So I found a temporary place to stay and focused on a way to banish the ghost. The darn thing had anticipated all my tactics. A psychic friend who had helped me in the past gave me a pep talk, pulling me out of my funk with a couple ideas. I was fired up and ready to do battle.

"I told you," Gail said, when I called her. "I can't live with all the chaos. The ghost or whatever is quiet now and that's the way I like it."

She sounded drained and it fueled my need to get rid of the destructive ghost. For her. Or at least that's what I told myself. "It may be quiet now, but it's going to suck you dry, slowly, without you even being aware of it. Are you okay?"

"I'm fine."

"You sound tired," I persisted. "Are you sleeping good? This can't be a healthy situation for you. Come on, give me one more chance. I don't want you to suffer for something I failed to do."

For a long moment she was silent. "Alright," she sighed. "But this is the last time."

I fist-pumped the air.

"If this doesn't work, though," she added, "you have to promise you'll drop it."

"I promise."

"And even if you do take care of it, I can't let you move back in. Too much has happened, so please give me back the key."

I'd forgotten I still had it and felt a moment of hurt, but brushed it aside, looking forward to taking on the ghost. "Sure. I'll be right over."

"Okay," she said, reluctance in her tone.

Half an hour later, I hesitated at the apartment door, key chain in hand. Shoving it in my jacket pocket, I knocked. Reaching out with my senses, I didn't feel the presence of the ghost and smiled. "Hiding, are we?" I whispered.

Gail didn't answer the door.

I knocked a little louder and waited. Put my ear to the door. No sound inside. My gut screamed at me and I fumbled the key in the lock. Inside, the apartment was dark. Flipping the switch by the door, light flooded the living room. Takeout boxes were piled on the coffee table. Dirty dishes and glasses crowded the side table and TV credenza. Something smelled funky. Following my nose, I discovered an overflowing kitchen garbage can. More dishes in the sink, food crusted on. Gail wasn't a neat freak but this level of messiness surprised me.

"Gail? Where are you?" Starting to worry, I rushed to the hallway in back. Not in the bathroom. Opening her bedroom door, a metallic smell hit me. Gagging, I groped for the bedside lamp and snapped it on.

Gail sat up in bed, one hand in her lap, the one

closest to me rested beside her, a red bloom spreading outward on her blue fitted sheet. Her face looked so white. Her lips bluish. And her eyes were open, unblinking.

"Oh, God."

The room was oddly empty. No ghost energy, hers or the other.

Fumbling for my cell phone, almost dropping it, I tried to dial 9-1-1, got it wrong, and tried again.

"9-1-1, what is your emergency?"

"My roommate—" My mind went blank.

"Has something happened to your roommate?"

My brain restarted. "Yes. Yes. She's bleeding. She cut her wrists."

"What is your address?"

The rest of the call was a blur. I started crying so bad I could barely speak to the operator. When the police and paramedics arrived, I answered questions. I made no mention of the ghost, explaining the arrangement with Gail to return my key, how she hadn't answered the door, and so I entered and found her. Apparently, I was convincing enough and the evidence backed me up, so her death was ruled a suicide.

But I knew better.

Somehow, the ghost made her do it or made her life unbearable to the point killing herself was her only escape. I'll never know for sure, except that I was responsible. I shouldn't have forced the ghost issue.

I was a horrible human being.

My life fell apart. Nothing went right with my business. I used to think I was giving my clients closure, hope.

Now, I realized it was a crutch keeping them from living and I was done toying with their lives.

I sold my tarot and crystals and everything else and got a job waitressing. Later, I helped one of my customers with his dog and he suggested I should be a veterinarian. The idea grew until I enrolled in college and the rest is history.

The pain of Gail's death was an open wound for a long time but I learned to live with it and promised myself I'd never hold someone's life in my hands again. After ignoring the ghosts and refusing to acknowledge them, they gradually stopped affecting me.

Some days I even felt normal.

~

STUCK BETWEEN A ROCK AND A HARD PLACE.

If I wasn't able to evict one strong ghost at the height of my abilities, using them daily, what chance did I have of driving out a horde of them after all these years?

I wiped my eyes and nose with the back of my hands.

Didn't matter. I had to do something. Anything. People depended on me. Declan and Katrina. Sherita and her kids. The couple on the farm by Rogers Lake. All the other innocent people in town I didn't know. Even Brian, as much of a pain as he was.

What happened to Gail wouldn't happen to anyone else. A spark of anger grew until I jumped up. "Nope," I said to the empty room. "I won't run away this time."

After a moment of feeling pretty good, the enormity hit me.

Now what?

Slumping back down to the floor, I held my head in my hands.

Just breathe.

Rae had said I needed to be whole to face what was coming. To make peace with my psychic side before something really bad happened.

She was right. I'd been going through the motions, talking to ghosts, crossing them over, always trying to keep myself separate from what I was doing. I wasn't all in and that had to change or I was going to fail, miserably and spectacularly, bringing everyone else with me.

As much as I wanted to be normal, I wasn't. Never had been. And when I gave up my psychic side, the part dealing with ghosts anyway, I lost a big part of me. My heart broke thinking about giving up my fur babies. But I'd been living half a life. I was so tired of being lonely. As much as I hated the lack of privacy in a small town, the people had become a part of me. They were my friends. For the first time since leaving the psychic life, I felt connected to a community.

Emotion tightened my throat.

Maybe there was a way to have both. I didn't know how but I'd figure it out later. Right now, I needed to get myself together. I took a deep breath and smoothed my hair back behind my ear. "So, how do we get rid of these *frakking* lake ghosts?"

Despite Rae's little "you can do it" speech, the ghosts were so strong, anything short of several mediums working together wouldn't force them out. Since I'd struck out on that idea, what were the alternatives?

What resources did we have besides Declan and I? Not much. Hurlbutt was a small town and half the population had moved out. All it had was land, a bunch of run-down buildings, and Rogers Lake. Like Rae said, the ghosts no doubt used the lake itself as an energy source. Even so, the ghosts were angry and that's a strong emotion.

Knowing why they were angry would be helpful. Planning without knowing the enemy sucked eggs. The only thing I could think of was that we needed larger numbers to overwhelm the lake ghosts.

Hold the phone.

Hurlbutt had ghosts. It had so many we were tripping over them. Ghosts could fight each other, right? Except Henry said the town ghosts were afraid of those at the lake. I called out to Henry and his lanky figure soon appeared by my side. "When you told me the old man ghost 'bound' you, what did you mean?"

Henry frowned. "He attacked me, without provocation, then attached himself to me, siphoning off my vitality to make himself stronger."

"What did he do with your vitality?" I almost smiled at the old-fashioned word.

"Overwhelmed others who came near, becoming stronger still."

"So it was kind of an energy transfer?" This might be the advantage we needed.

"I am sorry, Miss. I do not understand such things."

"Do you know how he did it?"

"No, I'm afraid not."

Henry must have died before electricity became a normal part of life. "What did it feel like?" I might be able to reverse engineer it.

Henry's expression was bleak. "Terrible. I prefer not to dwell on the incident."

Obviously, it had been a traumatic experience for him, a violation, and I felt awful pushing the subject. "I'm sorry, Henry. I ask because I'm trying to figure out a way to send the lake ghosts on. They've gotten so strong and I'm worried."

"As am I and many others."

"I don't know much about what's possible with ghosts. I suspect the way to overcome them is with a stronger force, but I'm not sure how. Maybe the ghosts in town could band together?" I'd been crossing over ghosts for weeks. All those following Declan around and living in his house would have come in handy now.

"Some ghosts, such as myself," said Henry, "are attached to houses or land and cannot move elsewhere. Others do not appear to be aware."

"Okay." I chewed my lower lip, wondering how many were free to move around. If the twin ghosts at the train tracks were right, there should be plenty arriving in town each day. I wouldn't know unless I tried. "Well, I guess it's time to find me some ghosts."

Oh, the irony.

"Do be careful, please."

"Believe me, I plan on it." Now, where would I find ghosts? The best places to start—away from the public—were the abandoned buildings all over town, particularly the warehouses along the railroad. Once, they held shipments of sugar, coal, and steel coming into Hurlbutt and shipments of wheat, corn, farm equipment, and clothing going out. Now, they were in various states of disrepair. The perfect ghost hang-out.

Driving slowly along the service road running behind the warehouses on the south side, I prayed my tires wouldn't pick up a nail. I didn't want to explain to a nosy tow truck driver what I was doing here. Probably think I was scoring drugs.

I parked in the dark alley between two buildings and pulled my mini flashlight from the glove box. The first two I checked had boarded-up doors and windows or were padlocked. The next was a crumbling brick building with loose boards over a window opening about six feet up. Old pallets and wooden boxes conveniently placed beneath the window made me suspect others had discovered this access point too.

Climbing the precarious pile, I windmilled my arms for balance, then grabbed the wooden window sill, its glass long since gone. Hauling myself up, my arm muscles strained. It had definitely been a while since high school PE class. Thankfully, no one was watching. I got one leg over, but my other foot hit the sill and I dropped like a rock, falling on top of another pile of pallets.

I lay there for a moment, dazed, then slowly stood up. "This stuff never happened to Veronica Mars," I muttered, climbing off the pallets, dusting myself off, and examining a scraped knee and splinters in my palms.

The heavy blanket feeling hit me a moment before the ghosts filled the room.

29

Dozens of ghosts watched me and they didn't look happy. In fact, most of them looked angry, even disgusted. Suddenly, the room felt very small.

"Hello." I tried to sound friendly, but my racing heart and dry mouth made me squeak instead. I cleared my throat. "My name is Kenna and I'm looking for a few good ghosts." I waited but the joke fell flat. Duh, ghosts didn't watch movies.

"Why?" asked a short ghost, once a body-builder by the looks of him, arms barely contained in his short-sleeved button-down shirt.

In my mind, I named him Muscles.

"So," he continued, "you can force us to leave like the others? Well, we won't go."

Several ghosts near Muscles nodded their heads in agreement.

"No. I, we," I stuttered. "The whole town of Hurlbutt needs your help."

"They need our help?" asked someone from the middle of the crowd.

A low buzz of conversation started. This could get ugly, fast.

"Do you know about the ghosts at Rogers Lake?" I asked.

Some of them looked frightened.

"What about 'em?" asked Muscles, crossing his arms.

"They're effecting the whole area, scaring people and animals and they're spreading. Soon, they'll reach town and be a huge problem for humans and ghosts. Something's got to be done now, before they get any worse."

"She's right," said a female ghost with long red hair in ponytails.

"And," I continued, "as far as I know, I'm the only one around here who can communicate with them. Well, there's Declan, but he's a beginner. I'm a little out of practice, but I'm it. Anyway, I wondered what all the ghosts in town thought about the situation. Maybe we could work together to get rid of them?"

"Yeah," said Muscles, "and then you'll get rid of us, right?"

"Not unless you're a problem for the living."

That caused a few raised voices.

"Yes, some of the ghosts I crossed over were destructive and needed to go. The others, well, I'm sorry. I didn't know we were headed for a ghost apocalypse." As soon as the words left my mouth, I knew they were the wrong thing to say. I began to panic. "You know there's way more ghosts in Hurlbutt than usual."

"What business is it of yours?" asked Muscles.

I tried not to show fear, though I was quaking in my Skechers. "Normally, I don't care, but when people came to me, scared out of their minds, they expected me to do something. So I did."

Muscles sneered. "Just like a human."

Another ghost piped up. "She doesn't know a damn thing."

"She's a ghost-killer," shouted someone.

"She refused to send on one ghost," said a deep, commanding voice from the back of the room.

All talk ceased.

I craned my neck to see. "Witch on a stick," I whispered.

Army Jacket leaned on a doorway.

I didn't think I could get more scared than I already was, but I was wrong. Fear shot through me but I clutched his words like a drowning victim. "That's right. Johnny, the little boy ghost, wanted people to know he was there. I saw no reason to cross him over. I explained to the people in the house how to treat him kindly."

"That's just one," said Muscles, though without his previous animosity.

"True." The military ghost straightened up and started walking toward me. The others moved out of his way. "But, she's the only one who can talk to us and to people. She's valuable as a liaison."

No ghost spoke. Not even Muscles.

Who was this guy? He walked toward me at a lazy stroll, but I got the feeling he was putting on a show. For the ghosts or me? Should I stand my ground or run like the scaredy cat I was?

He stopped when he reached the front of the crowd. "What did you have in mind?" he asked.

I blanked.

"You came here to talk to us, right?"

I nodded. The name on his jacket said Laird. I licked my dry lips. "A couple ideas, maybe. Were you in the service, Mr. Laird?"

"Yes, ma'am. And call me Mitch. Mr. Laird was my father."

"Okay. Good," I said, relieved. "We need someone who knows tactics and planning. We need a ghost army, Mitch."

He snorted, taking a pack of cigarettes out of his jacket pocket and shaking one up. "You don't think small."

"I've faced the lake ghosts," I said. "I know what I'm talking about."

He lit the cigarette and blew out smoke I couldn't smell. "You got your army."

IN EXCHANGE FOR FIGHTING THE LAKE GHOSTS, THE TOWN ghosts had terms, some of which were outrageous. Buildings left vacant for exclusive ghost use? No improvements made on properties without permission from the resident ghosts?

I wanted to pull out my hair.

And Mitch lounged against the doorway. Fat lot of help he was. He didn't use his influence to contribute to the discussion in any meaningful way.

Finally, I couldn't stand it anymore. "You all are dreaming if you think people will agree to this."

"How bad you want the lake ghosts gone?" Muscles crossed his arms again.

"We don't even have a plan for getting rid of the lake ghosts yet." I glanced down, blowing out a breath. "Look, they're getting freaky strong while we stand here arguing and I haven't even brought this to the town yet." I was sure Don and the others could spend a week arguing terms. "We have to keep it simple. Very, very basic. What is the one thing you all want the most?"

They argued for a while. Surprise, surprise. In the end, they decided it was most important that nobody, not townspeople, mediums, or outside forces of any kind, should compel the ghosts to cross over if they didn't want to, now or in the future, within the limits of the community calling itself Hurlbutt, NY.

"Now that sounds reasonable. Thank you," I said, smiling. "Next, let's work on the plan to fight the lake ghosts. I have an idea. One of the ghosts I crossed over was in my basement. He forced some kind of a bond on several ghosts, siphoning their energy for his own use and was very strong."

"I remember him," said the red-haired ghost. "He caught my best friend but I got away." She looked ready to cry. "I stayed far away from him and the house after that."

"I'm sorry," I said. "My parents and I convinced him to cross. It released all the ghosts he bonded with."

"It did?" The ghost beamed, then her happiness dimmed. "But, then, where is she? I haven't seen her."

I shrugged. "I don't know. The ghosts left as soon as

they were released, except for Henry. He's always lived in my house. He stayed."

"Oh," she said, clearly disappointed.

Possibly, her friend had been so traumatized by the experience she crossed over on her own. I kept the thought to myself, though, since this discussion was balanced on a thin edge as it was. "Anyway," I said, steering the conversation back on topic. "I thought we could use bonding to increase your strength." I raised my hands, encompassing the group. "All the town ghosts' strength. So you could fight the lake ghosts." I let my hands drop to my sides. "But Henry didn't know how the bonding process worked. I thought maybe one of you might know."

Muscles looked at the ghosts on either side, then behind him. Everyone looked confused.

"Nobody knows about this?" My excitement plummeted. "Then I guess we need to face them head-on. What do you think?" I asked Mitch. "Is it possible?"

Mitch looked over the crowd. "Alright, you dogs," he shouted, scaring the bejesus out of me. "If we're to defeat the enemy, we need overwhelming forces. Time to recruit. Every last one of you needs to get out there and find two or three more to add to our ranks and don't come back until you do. Do I make myself clear?" He waited a moment. "Dis-missed."

Mitch had surprised me but from the ghosts' shocked expressions, apparently, Mitch hadn't gone full sergeant on them before.

"I don't remember joining up," Muscles grumbled to the ghost next to him before they disappeared.

Eventually, Mitch was the only ghost remaining.

"Meet you back here," he said, "after you talk to the town fathers. This is HQ."

"Okay, but—"

Mitch disappeared.

"Wonderful," I said. "No 'thanks' or 'see you later.' Just gone."

30

When I called Don Houser, it took a while to explain the plan and convince him, but he promised to get some people together.

"You know," he said. "There's been two accidents out there today."

"Car accidents? Was anyone hurt?"

"A-yup," Don said. "One banged up enough to go to the hospital in an ambulance but he's going to be okay. So, I finagled the state police into closing the road."

"Good idea."

"I didn't want to take any chances. If your ghosts can kick out those other ones, it'll save our bacon."

"They're not my ghosts. They're as much a part of Hurlbutt as the living."

"Right. I'll make a few calls and we'll come around to your place around seven thirty."

After hanging up, I remembered the lack of furniture in the house and shrugged. I paced, planning what I'd say. Nibbling on my fingernail, I worried I'd be outnumbered. What I needed was people who'd be on my side, who'd witnessed ghosts first-hand and be able to explain what it was like. I called Declan and Sherita and they both wanted to attend.

At the appointed time, Don arrived looking more comfortable in casual slacks and a golf shirt than his usual suit. He was followed by Sherita, Declan, Brian and Katrina, Linda, and three other former muckety-mucks of Hurlbutt. They congregated in the living room. I had added the dining room chairs, lawn chairs from outside, and a three-step ladder.

"You did a nice job on the wall," Declan pointed to where the graffiti used to be.

"Actually," I said. "Billy Campbell did it."

The group settled down but it didn't last long. Before I even had a chance to outline my plan, they were squabbling. When it devolved into a shouting match between Brian and the former police chief, Carl Ingham, I intervened.

"This is getting us nowhere," I said, standing up. "We have a threat at the lake. A large, very powerful group of ghosts. Whether or not you believe it, they're there. You've seen the damage. The kids getting hurt, the car accident today. I've personally been attacked twice. And their influence is spreading to nearby properties. If we don't do something soon, I'm afraid they'll get stronger and reach into town, causing more problems." I sat down.

"For Christ's sake," said Carl, a short man with graying hair and a mustache, radiating pent-up energy. "Who's ever heard of ghosts taking over a town?"

"You'd believe," Sherita said, "if you had one in your house scaring your kids. This young woman," she pointed at me, "who didn't know me at all, came to my house and sent the ghost packing. She almost died. Now, my kids aren't afraid to sleep in their beds anymore. And I'm not afraid to leave them when I go to work. Kenna gave me back my peace of mind."

"And Kenna helped me," said Declan, "with my houseful of ghosts. Believe you me, those ghosts at Rogers Lake are worse than anything I experienced before."

"How did this happen?" asked Linda. "Where are all these ghosts coming from?"

I glanced at Declan. "We believe the train accident last winter sort of woke them up and those are attracting more from other places."

"What?" Linda's jaw dropped.

"Oh, my God," said Katrina.

They all started talking at once and I waited for the shock and outrage to die down. "The biggest threat right now is the lake ghosts. I've tried, but nothing I did worked. The best resource we have are the ghosts here in town. They're threatened just as much as we are. They've agreed to fight, and in return, asked the human community of Hurlbutt to promise that no one, not townspeople, mediums, or outside forces of any kind, will try to remove a ghost or force it to cross over, now or in the future, within the community limits."

Carl snorted. "I thought the point was to get rid of all the damn ghosts."

"What if they make our lives miserable?" asked Linda.

"Couldn't they," said Carl, "cause the same kind of problems these lake ghosts are doing?"

I sighed. "Honestly, most of the time, people aren't

even aware ghosts exist. I've lived with them since I was a kid. Saw several of them here in town and they never caused any harm. Now, we simply have more of them. Sure, people asked me to deal with ghosts in their houses and I crossed those over or gave them advice on how to live with the ghost. But the ones causing serious problems are the lake ghosts. What else can we do? I've run out of ideas."

Carl didn't look happy. "How do we even know these town ghosts can get rid of the lake ghosts?"

"We don't," I said. "But they're willing to put their existence on the line to save the town. What are you willing to do?"

They debated it for ages, while I yawned, wishing I was anywhere else. Finally, they agreed that if the town ghosts removed the lake ghosts, they could stay without being forced away or crossed over, as long as they behaved themselves and didn't cause more problems.

"God help us if anyone finds out about this," Carl muttered.

"Let's make something clear," Don said, looking each person in the eye. "It's in everyone's best interest not to talk about this. It'd just cause a panic and we need to keep everyone safe. Later on, though, it may not look that way to folks. Do I have your word that you won't speak of this agreement with the ghosts, or anything else discussed here tonight to anyone not a part of this informal town council?"

"You can be damn sure I won't," said Carl.

"I agree," Linda said.

Each person, including me, promised not to speak of it.

To be honest, I was surprised they consented to the agreement but chalked it up to the pressure of time and circumstance making everyone focus on survival and covering their butts.

Then, they ruined it all.

"Kenna?" Don asked. "I want to say 'thank you' for what you've done on behalf of the town. If you hadn't been here, we'd be in deep shit right about now."

Sherita humphed. "About time somebody said it."

"The fact is," Don continued, "when you're done selling your mother's house and leave, we lose our connection to the ghosts. Things could go to hell in a hand-basket."

"Then," asked Linda, "who will speak to the ghosts for us and let us know what they want?"

I raised my eyebrows at Declan. After a moment, he nodded. "Declan should be able to."

Next to him, Katrina looked ready to strangle me.

"I can work with him on it," I added.

"Pardon me for stating the obvious," Carl said, "but Declan ain't exactly a spring chicken."

"Neither are you, Carl," said Brian.

"That's right," Carl pointed at him. "So I know what I'm talking about."

"We'd feel better," Don boomed, drowning out the two men, "if you would take care of things when problems come up."

Not what I expected to hear. Besides, I still wasn't certain about my future plans. "I appreciate your belief in my abilities, but I've never made it a secret I was only in town temporarily." They all stared at me. "Maybe I can find another medium willing to move to Hurlbutt." Yeah, right. Who'd want to move to a place too small for a McDonald's? "I could come back and visit if you needed my help but you can't depend on me on a regular basis."

"We'd have to have final say, of course," Don said. "Got to make sure we can all get along."

"I'll figure out something. I won't leave you or Hurlbutt hanging."

They seemed satisfied. On the other hand, I felt like a cement truck had flattened me.

Declan, Brian, and Katrina stayed after the others left. "Loads of fun, huh?" I said, my sarcasm getting the better of me.

"I've had fun before," Brian said. "And that wasn't it."

"As committee meetings go," Katrina said, "it went pretty well."

Before she had a chance to scold me, I turned to Declan. "I know we never talked about what would happen after I went back home. With the ghosts. I'm sorry if I put you on the spot."

Declan smiled. "Not at all. It's not as if there's an instruction manual for this sort of thing."

"We're kind of making it up as we go along."

He patted my arm. "Don't worry yourself, Kenna. I'll do what I can, though, perhaps, further instruction would be helpful."

"Of course. Do you want to get together and practice tomorrow?"

"Sounds good to me."

I yawned. "Sorry. I'd better go talk to the ghosts."

"Can't you snap your fingers and they appear?" Brian asked.

I screwed up my face. "No. It's...they have a headquarters in an abandoned building and I promised to meet them there."

"Oh, yeah? Where?"

"I can't tell you."

Katrina pulled Brian's arm. "Come on. I'm tired and I want to go home."

Brian ignored her. "One of the buildings on Main Street?"

Katrina pulled harder. "Brian."

"Oh, alright, woman." He steered them toward the front door but turned back. "You coming, Declan?"

Declan looked at me.

"I'll call you tonight and let you know how it goes."

He smiled. "Good luck."

I grabbed my keys and followed them out. It was dark now but the streetlight illuminated the way to our cars. Curtains moved in a lighted window across the street. "Neighborhood Watch is on duty."

As I drove, I thought about what Brian said. As much as it annoyed me, he was correct about one thing. It would have been much easier if I called the ghosts and they came to me instead of meeting at the warehouse. I'd definitely mention it to Mitch.

When I got there, though, the ghosts were gone. I called and called and finally, Mitch showed up.

After I told him the town representatives agreed to the ghosts' terms, he nodded. "Good." Then he disappeared again.

"But—" I stared at the spot where he'd been. "Arrogant jerk."

I hoped he heard me.

~

THE NEXT DAY, I ARRIVED AT DECLAN'S, YAWNING. AFTER getting to bed late last night, my gut had been bothering me so much, I tossed and turned. Now, I was on edge.

Declan poured us iced tea and led me to a back porch with cushioned lawn chairs set up. I placed the drink tray on a small wooden table between the chairs. A warm breeze blew through, though it was well on its way to humid and sticky.

"It's very comfortable here in the evening. A touch sunny right now." He settled into a chair with a little grunt. "I wish it would rain. The lawn could use it." He pointed to the patches of brown grass.

"Right." I took a sip of tea. It was deliciously cold. "I noticed the other night you had your rosary. Have you been using it for protection every day?"

Declan nodded, reaching into his pants pocket and drawing out a rosary of wooden beads, holding it loosely in his hand for me to see. "My mother brought it with her from Ireland."

I didn't have a chance to examine it before and leaned forward. Each bead was carved in a subtle flower bud pattern. "It's lovely, Declan. And it means more with the family connection, too."

"I feel her presence, though she never speaks to me," he said. "I've also taken to wearing her crucifix and I strung my St. Christopher medal on it, too." He pulled the gold chain out from under his shirt.

"Excellent. Does it help?"

He tucked the chain back under his collar. "Yes. I believe so. The ghosts go away much quicker, though I don't know if it's because of these or the fact I'm more confident."

I smiled. "Maybe both."

Declan practiced grounding and opening himself to the spirit world. There were still a few ghosts Mitch and his army hadn't recruited. We didn't want to cross them over, in case Mitch needed them, so Declan sent them away from him and his house.

"I'm impressed. You're becoming a real pro at this and in such a short time, too."

Declan blushed, though he sat straighter in his chair.

I was tired. Lack of sleep and the days of physical, mental, and spiritual heavy-lifting were wearing on me. Everyone looked to me for answers and guidance but I wasn't any kind of expert. I was the rope in a tug-of-war, pulled in two directions. And whenever I thought of the lake ghosts, the stress clobbered me. I wasn't very good at meditation, but I needed something to calm me down. Thinking Declan may be feeling out-of-sorts too, I taught him the basics of meditation.

"It sounds a bit like saying the rosary," he said.

I thought about it for a second. "I guess so, but you allow your mind to drift instead of filling it with words."

He had a lot of questions, which I answered, trying to hold down my growing frustration. Eventually, he stopped talking and relaxed into it.

I closed my eyes, breathed deeply, but couldn't stop the thoughts and worries tumbling around. As soon as I brushed one aside, another replaced it. After a while, my body finally took over. Loosened up. Surrendering my need to think, to do.

The sounds of birds and children playing in back yards faded.

Deeper.

The dark of my closed eyelids and sound of my own breathing.

Time no longer existed.

Body felt lighter.

Calm.

Drifting.

Letting go.

Letting

go.

Let

go.

Let

go.

Floating.

I came aware with a gasp, an intense lightness in my chest, knowing I had to do something. "Let go," I whispered.

"What's the matter?" Declan asked, from far away. "Are you alright?"

I sat up straight, hands pressing my chest to relieve the empty feeling, yet my heart beat like an 80's hair band drum solo. The words "let go" echoed in my head.

A door slammed in the house and someone called out.

I couldn't move. I tried to grab onto the thoughts.

"On the porch," Declan responded.

What was I supposed to let go of?

Movement near me.

The more I tried to hold on, the faster it flew away.

The meaning was gone. I slammed my fist on the chair arm.

"Kenna, what's wrong?"

Declan stood next to me. I saw his striped, button down shirt and khakis in my peripheral vision but I didn't look up. Didn't want to see his concerned expression. "I'm okay. I just...I'm fine." My hand shook as I reached for the glass. Clutching with both hands, I raised it to my mouth and gulped what was left.

"There you are." Brian's shout startled me and I held tighter to the glass.

The kitchen door slammed shut.

I set the glass back on the table. More steady now. Took a deep breath.

"Bad news," Brian said, but his tone was almost gleeful. "Pastor Dick and his flock are down at the lake, doing some dumb-ass ritual."

"It's a blessing, dude."

At the familiar voice, my attention snapped to the side. Nate stood in the doorway.

"He's gonna start a riot with those ghosts," Brian continued.

"We heard it at the diner," said Nate.

"Ol' Joe Latham couldn't wait to spread the news." Brian grinned. "Hates Dick ever since his wife started going to that church. She divorced him, you know. Took him for every cent he owned. Poor bastard. Probably hopes the ghosts knock Dicky-boy around a bit."

What a mess. I stood up. "We have to go out there. Convince Dick—" I frowned. "Pastor Graves and his people to leave."

"I bet George Barnes wouldn't take too kindly to them

trespassing," Brian said. "Particularly since he gave you permission to deal with the ghosts, not them."

"Someone saw a couple TV news trucks, too," Nate said. "A bunch of people went to see what's happening."

Shooting pain developed behind my eyes. "Wonderful. I'll tell the town ghosts their fight has been moved up, then I'll meet you at the lake."

"It's a plan." Brian rubbed his hands together, grinning. Confronting Pastor Graves no doubt appealed to him.

"Are you sure about this?" I asked Declan.

Declan nodded gravely. "Yes, I am."

I was encouraged by his firm tone of voice. "You'll be on your own."

"I have my bodyguard," he said, glancing at his brother.

"Quit wasting time." Brian transformed back into his curmudgeonly self again. "Let's get this show on the road."

"You remember what you have to do?" I asked Declan.

"Yes, Mary Poppins," Brian growled. "He knows what he has to do. You two have been at it for hours."

As I opened my mouth to tell him off, Declan touched my arm. "I'll be fine. We'll all be fine."

I wasn't as certain but nodded and entered the kitchen door.

Nate touched my shoulder. "You can do this, Kenna."

"Thanks, but I feel like I have to barf."

He quirked the corner of his mouth. "You've been ninja fighting ghosts all summer."

"A ghost or two at a time. This is way bigger. I'm not ready yet."

"*Kennaaaaah*," he drawled, smiling. "Sure you are. And though me and Brian can't, like, help with things ghostly, we'll take care of you and Declan. Don't you worry."

I attempted a smile, but could only stretch my lips. "I'll try not to."

31

I drove home and grabbed my bag of supplies. Time was not on my side and I felt behind every step of the way. As I left the house, I caught a glimpse of Gloria's disapproving face in her front window.

Like I cared.

Driving to the warehouse, I felt minimal ghost presence in town. When I climbed through the window, it felt empty. "Hello? Mitch? Anybody here?"

Silence.

"They're all gone."

Turning, I saw the Adams' ghost boy, sucking his thumb. "Johnny." Guilt washed over me. I'd forgotten to check on him.

"They lefted already," he said, around his thumb. "Jus' like my new fambly did. Will you stay wif me?" A spark of hope flared in his eyes.

I squatted in front of him. "I'm sorry I forgot to visit you. So much has been happening lately."

Johnny took his thumb out of his mouth. "My new

friends went to fight big, bad meanies by the lake and make 'em go 'way so we're all safe. They're scary."

"Yes they are." I wanted to hug him. "In fact, I came here to tell your friends it was time to fight. But they need my help. I have to find them. Can you stay here by yourself for a little bit longer?"

"Can't I go wif you?"

"It's safer for you to stay here. I promise I'll be back."

The hope died in his expression. "Oh, a'right."

～

As I drove to Roger's Lake, dark, angry-looking clouds rolled in from the west. "Not good." I tore the wrapper off a granola bar with my teeth and took a huge bite.

Had the lake ghosts attacked Pastor Graves' group? Were the town ghosts at the lake? Did it start already? Were people injured? Would I miss it?

I sent out a silent plea. *Please, help me.* I didn't know what good it would do but it couldn't hurt.

Pushing the accelerator down, my poor car shuddered at the increased speed. Something felt off. After a moment, I realized it was because I didn't feel the lake ghosts. What did that mean?

Cars lined the road beside the entrance to Rogers Lake. I turned into the driveway, tires spitting gravel. Jouncing over potholes, people on foot waved as I drove past. Emerging from the woods, I stopped behind Brian's pickup. "I can do this," I muttered. Now the heaviness settled on my head and shoulders. Each step was like slogging through mud.

Three teenage girls ran past me, talking and laughing as if they were at a carnival.

The strong voice of Pastor Graves reached me. Whether praying or preaching, all I heard was the steady, measured tone, not the actual words.

As the emotions hit me, I bowed my head and stopped to strengthen my protections and to catch my breath.

About forty people stood in small knots. Some talked and laughed while others listened to Pastor Graves. He stood with his back to the lake, holding a bible to his chest with one hand. He faced two cameramen, his congregation arrayed on either side of him.

"Damn fool," said someone.

"Does he actually think this'll work?" asked someone else.

"Who knows? But it's the best show in town."

Laughter.

Walking closer, I heard the pastor's words.

"...as it was in Jesus' day, my friends, we have demons in our midst." Pastor Graves made a sweeping gesture with his arm towards the lake. "Right here, in these modern times and what are we going to do about it?" He paused. "Are we going to stay in our homes and cower in fear like dogs?"

His congregation shook their collective heads.

"No," he thundered. "Are we going to run and tell our congressman, like tattling school children?"

His people joined him in shouting, "No."

"My friends, we will face this abomination head on. Hurlbutt is a spiritual battle-ground and we are modern-day crusaders. Called upon by Jesus..."

I shifted my attention to the crowd. Not too far from me was the reporter for The Daily Chronicle. I crossed behind him, hoping he wouldn't see me. I saw Don and Linda on the other side, watching the crowd. I moved toward them but felt a touch on my shoulder.

"There you are." Nate grinned. Declan and Brian stood behind him.

"Pastor Dick's in full swing now," Brian said, loudly.

Two men near us snickered.

"So far, so good," I said. "But I don't think it'll last."

Declan was pale. "I hear them," he said.

"Are you okay?" I asked, holding his elbow. Nate moved to his other side.

A slight smile. "I just need a minute."

I nodded. "Strengthen your protections. Use your rosary."

We stood quietly. Pastor Graves was now emphasizing his words with a raised fist. Three boys ran past and I grabbed the shirt of the last one. "Billy?"

His eyes opened wide. "Oh, hey."

I was about to speak but the breeze shifted and I shivered. The feel of the crowd changed. The laughter stopped. I clutched Billy's arm. "Go home, now. Something bad's about to happen."

He stared at me with an open mouth.

"Please."

He ran off. I didn't know if he'd listen, but at least I gave him the warning.

Brian grunted and I snapped around. His face flushed pink and his eyes narrowed.

I shook him. "Brian, snap out of it. The emotions you're feeling aren't your own. It's the ghosts. Fight it."

He looked at me, startled, then nodded.

I glanced at Nate. "You, too. Try to stay calm." I looked back and forth between them. "Don't let the feelings pull you under."

"No *problemo*."

"No ghost is gonna take over my mind," Brian announced.

"Good. Because Declan and I need to be able to depend on you two."

"Hey, Pastor Dick," someone shouted, to much snickering. "Why don't you go back to your church and leave us alone."

"We don't want you here."

"You tell him."

Pastor Graves continued on without a pause. His people, however, nervously watched the crowd.

Something was building. "Declan, are you ready?"

"Yes."

Rumbling in the distance made me turn but I dismissed it as a big truck on the highway.

Declan sniffed. "Smells like rain."

"About time," Brian said.

The next rumble was closer. The clouds had gotten thicker, darker. "Yeah, but I don't think this is normal." I said.

I saw a flicker in the distance.

"Lightning," said Declan.

"I hope not," said Brian. "It's been a dry summer and with all these fields? Lightning could start a brush fire."

In all the time I'd been in Hurlbutt, it hadn't rained.

We turned at the sound of shouts nearby. Teenage boys wrestled on the ground. Next to them, Billy watched, his mouth open in shock. Were those his friends? Two men pulled them apart. One boy twisted and hit the man behind him. The other boy shoved back on the man who held him, both stumbling to the ground. It was Andy, the boy who tried to film me during the failed cleansing and sprained his wrist.

Shouts. Crying. Fist-fights. I lost Billy and Andy in the crowd.

The news cameras turned around, continuing to film.

Pastor Graves was startled but kept on talking. "We do not know what happened on this land, but we know a place can be defiled by the evil deeds of its inhabitants. I speak love and peace here in the name of our Lord Jesus. I invite you to come, Holy—"

"Is it love and peace," a familiar voice shouted. "When you steal money from your congregation?"

Nate no longer stood next to Declan.

The cameras swung toward Nate as he walked through the crowd.

"Is it love and peace," he called out. "When you convince them to hand over their life savings to you?"

"That's right," said someone in the crowd.

"You tell him."

"Is it love and peace," continued Nate, "when you keep asking for more? Until they can't buy the food and medication they need? Or pay their bills and lose their house?"

I'd never heard him so angry before. It was so totally not his usual, laid-back self. I fought the crowd to get to him. "Please, Nate." I clutched his arm. "You don't want to do this. You aren't yourself."

He didn't look at me. "I need to do this."

"Somebody, please help that man," Pastor Graves said. Two of his followers walked forward, but the crowd held them back.

"Let him speak," someone demanded.

"Yeah," said another. "It's still a free country, last I looked."

Nate gently pulled my hand away, focused on Graves. "My mother died of cancer," he shouted. "She didn't have insurance and couldn't afford treatment 'cause she gave all her money to your church. And when she came to you for help, what did you do? You prayed for her. Convinced her God would cure her." His voice broke and he had to clear his throat before he went on. "Well, my mother died full of cancer and in debt. Is that what you think is love and peace, Pastor Graves? I don't. You're a fraud, man."

The crowd broke into wild applause.

Pastor Graves smoothed his tie. "It appears divine intervention isn't wanted here. You would rather live with demons in your midst than follow the path of righteousness." He punctuated with his upraised fist.

In the field to my left, lightning hit with a crack so loud I jumped a foot in the air.

32

I crouched, closing my eyes and covering my ears. After a moment, I peeked and stood up. "Too close," I said, but could barely hear myself. My ears felt plugged with cotton.

"God has spoken!" Pastor Graves' words sounded like they came from a tunnel. "Witness the destruction God visits upon unbelievers!"

"What a blow-hard." Brian and Declan had caught up to us.

Don shoved his way through the crowd. "Alright, folks. Time for everyone to get on home, now. We don't want things getting out of hand or anyone getting hurt."

A great gust of wind blew through the crowd, sending someone's baseball hat flying and knocking Pastor Graves on his butt. His people scrambled to help him up as he bellowed.

Nate ran toward them. I shoved my bag of supplies at Declan and ran after him. Grabbing the back of Nate's shirt, I pulled, then scrambled in front of him, attempting to hold him back.

"Nate, please don't do this," I said, losing ground. "If you hurt him, you'll get arrested. Then you'll be the bad guy. It won't bring back your mother and it won't change him."

Nate didn't look at me, but something in his expression softened.

Don came up beside Nate, grabbing his arm. "Hey, there, son. Time to go. It ain't safe here."

"Fight it, Nate," I said. "Let go of the anger. It's not real. It's the ghosts. Don't let them win."

He stood still, sweat running down his face.

"Nate! Your mother wouldn't want you to hurt anyone, would she?"

After a long moment, he shook himself, looking dazed. He focused on me. "Kenna. We gonna kick some ghost butt, or what?"

Relieved, I hugged him.

Pastor Graves still shouted, though his people attempted to calm him.

Lightning didn't strike near us again but thunder boomed close. Still no rain. But a ribbon of smoke danced on the breeze in the field hit by lightning.

"Fire!" someone yelled, and others took up the cry.

It was a stampede. We struggled to the side, out of the way of the crowd rushing for their cars. Some yelled into cell phones. Don and Linda tried to calm people, but it was impossible.

One camera guy continued filming Pastor Graves fighting his own people as they dragged him away while the other filmed the brush fire.

From over the fields to the northeast, an incredible amount of concentrated energy rushed toward us.

The wind picked up.

In the air around and above us, the lake spirits showed themselves as vaguely human-shaped blobs of white energy. They knew what approached and were pumped up.

"The cavalry has arrived!" Declan declared.

Looking up, I moved our group away from a ghost blob hovering above us.

The town ghosts crossed the fields, Mitch in the lead. With yells and screams, they clashed with the lake ghosts.

It was like the psychic equivalent of bombs going off. One after another. I winced, fought to remain standing.

Declan stumbled. Brian and Nate caught him before he hit the ground. "I'm alright. I'm alright," Declan said, straightening his back. "It surprised me, is all."

"What did?" asked Brian.

"The town ghosts attacked the lake ghosts," I explained.

Though the bulk of the crowd was gone, there were still people in the field. Some had fallen to the ground during the mad rush and others assisted them.

Something pulled hard at me. I resisted. Declan and I looked at each other.

Nate's eyes opened wide.

Brian scowled, bracing his legs. "What the hell was that?"

I blinked. "The ghosts siphoned energy from us."

Over the fields, the battle raged, though not with the

ferocity of the first wave. Every once in a while, a pocket of energy winked out.

I grinned at Declan and was about to whoop in triumph, then stopped.

"Oh, dear," said Declan, his smile faltering.

The town ghosts weren't the ones winning.

From the south came another buildup of energy. If this was the end of the town ghosts, then I'd bear witness.

The energy drew closer and closer.

"What are you looking at?" Brian asked.

The energy rushed directly over us. At the front of the mass was Muscles, howling like a madman. He and the others smashed into the lake ghosts.

I braced for the blow. When it passed, I tried to pick out individual ghosts in the battle, but it was impossible.

"Ah, Kenna?" said Nate. "We gotta book."

The wind had shifted again, pushing the fire in our direction.

"Closer to the lake," Brian commanded.

We hurried away from the fire, settling on the far side of the lake. "Did anyone call 9-1-1?" I asked.

"I saw Don on the phone earlier," said Brian. "He's probably called out everyone including the National Guard."

"I wonder where they are then?" said Nate, searching the wooded entry to the lake.

"That's what we get for consolidating with the county," said Brian.

Our first day in town, my brother, Jim, mentioned the same thing about longer response times for rescue services.

Declan touched my arm. "Something is wrong."

Focusing on the ghost battle, I felt a hallow in my chest. Things weren't going well for Mitch and his army. Despite better tactics early on, fewer of them now remained. They were getting clobbered.

~

"WHAT CAN WE DO?" I ASKED DECLAN. "ANY IDEAS?"

He shook his head.

"Kenna."

I turned to see Dad and Ma behind me. "Where have you two been?" At Declan's questioning look, I explained, "It's my parents."

"No shit," said Brian. "Hey, Big Jim, how about you tell these ghosts where they can go, huh?"

Dad smiled tightly at Brian, then focused on me. "It's time, Kenna."

"For what?"

"To do what you need to do," Ma said.

I sighed. "If I knew what to do, I'd have done it already." My mind was a complete blank. Frozen.

Ma moved closer. "You know what to do. You always have. I'm the one who didn't want to know. Do what you do best, Kenna. Talk to the ghosts."

My head hurt. "Talk to them? Sure. But what do I say? I don't know who they are or what they want." I glanced at Declan, remembering his research. "They could be people who existed hundreds of years ago. How would they even understand my language?"

"It'll come to you," said Dad, winking. "Those others have softened them up for you."

"It may work," Declan said.

Let go.

The words from my earlier meditation came to mind. My gut twinged and I put a hand over it, nodding, though the idea scared me. I took a deep breath. It was either the bravest thing I'd ever done or the dumbest. Either way, there was no backing out now. Not if I wanted to live with myself later. "Yeah, I just wish I didn't have to pee right now."

Declan laughed, like I'd hoped he would.

Brian snorted. "Suck it up, buttercup."

Acting more confident than I felt, I walked toward the battlefield. Nervous energy coursed through me but panic lodged in my throat.

The ghosts skirmished all over the area, on the ground and in the air. Near me, I watched an energy form fight the ghost of a middle-aged man. They whirled around each other and clashed together. Over and over. Eventually, the town ghost seemed to slow down. Then, the other one pounced on it and the man *blooped* out of existence. Before I lost courage, I ran to the energy form.

"Who are you?" I yelled at it.

The lake ghost didn't move. Another form joined it, then another. The first one left and the remaining two moved closer.

"Hey, you big meanies. You leave her alone."

Johnny glided in front of me and stood his ground, pudgy fists on hips. I gawked at him then felt Dad and Ma's presence behind me. "Johnny," I said, moving in front of him and keeping my eyes on the lake ghosts. "You were supposed to stay at the warehouse, where it's safe."

"I was bored." His voice came from beside me. "Who're they?"

I assumed he meant my parents. "My protectors. And we have everything under control so you can go back now."

"*Nah-uhn*. I'm helpin' you." His arms were crossed over his chest and his lower lip stuck out.

I'd seen that look a lot as a kid when Nora refused to help me with something. "Well, keep out of the fighting. I don't want you to get hurt." After a moment of silence, I risked another look. "Okay, Johnny?" I said in a firmer tone.

He scowled. "Oh, alright."

"Thank you." Returning my gaze to the lake ghosts, I braced for the worst.

The two forms morphed into people. Native American men. One looked very old, stooped, with pure white hair and a wrinkled face. The other looked middle-aged, fit, and stern. Both wore clothing of tanned animal hide with feather and seed decorations. The younger one held a bow with a knocked arrow, pointed down, but watching me.

"Wow, real *Injuns*," Johnny whooped.

The two men shifted their eyes toward Johnny, and the warrior tensed.

"Hush, now," I told him.

The old man murmured to his companion and the warrior relaxed slightly.

"Who...who are you? What do you want from us?" I hoped they understood me.

They conversed again, but neither stopped glaring at me.

Sweat beaded on my upper lip.

A series of images flashed through my mind: women

gathered roots and leaves in a forest, children playing a short distance away; two men, stalked a deer, bows ready; people gathered in the dark around a campfire, listening to another speak; a naked couple whispered together as others slept nearby.

All seemed to be Native Americans.

Next, a peaceful night scene: moonless, fires banked, everyone asleep. Then, utter chaos. People startled awake. Men grabbed weapons. Women gathered children and ran into the forest. Longhouses burned. Naked men fought clothed men, who were also Native Americans, with knives, spears, sticks of firewood, whatever was handy. Women and children were dragged from the forest, screaming.

"Jesus, Mary, and Joseph," I said, closing my eyes, trying to look away, but it was in my brain. I saw limbs hacked off, women pulled by their hair and throats slit, babies smashed to the ground. Scenes of horror worse than anything I could imagine played out before me. The cries and screams pierced to my soul.

I fell to my knees, gagging.

"What's wrong?" Brian said.

"How can I help?" Nate asked.

Wiping my mouth, I gasped. "The ghosts. Native Americans. Declan, can you hear them?"

"No, but I heard someone say they were Indians." Declan's excited voice spoke near. "Can you see them?"

Apparently, the vision was mine alone. "Yes." I gagged again. I didn't see the empty fields around the lake. I saw hacked up bodies and blood everywhere. The village was a ruin, utterly still, except for smoke and birds picking at the bodies. The intruders had melted away with the sunrise. "They were attacked by other Native Americans."

My heart raced. My shock at the violence I witnessed changed to grief, humiliation. I wanted to hurt someone.

A drum beat in cadence. *Ba-DUM-dum-dum. Ba-DUM-dum-dum.*

The scene changed. Native American men prepared for war. Sharpened knives. Made arrows. Painted their bodies. One began to dance, followed by others. A group of old men started chanting.

The vision faded but I shivered, feeling the buildup of shame and the need to vent my rage. Wanting to draw blood.

33

I stood up, ready to tear something or someone apart.

"Hey! You tolded *me* not to fight."

Voices echoed down a tunnel. Vision blurred. I hesitated. Shook my head at the muzzy feeling. My vision cleared. People stared at me with concerned expressions. Familiar people.

Recognition flashed through me. These were my friends and this was not my fight. The lake ghosts had messed with my head again. Had to separate my emotions from theirs. I took a few deep breaths, forcing myself to calm down. Think. Don't just react. Wiping sweat from my forehead, I realized how warm I was. Heat radiated from my necklaces. I took a shuddering breath, sharpening my attention on the here and now.

So. A native-on-native massacre. Who knew how long ago? Probably before the Europeans showed up. I licked my lips, focusing on the two lake ghosts who watched me. "But...but that happened hundreds of years ago. The people you've attacked now had nothing to do with your death. They're innocent."

The men's expressions didn't change. Maybe they didn't understand after all.

"The revenge you want is pointless. These aren't the people who massacred you. They aren't even their descendants. What happened to you was horrific." I shuddered, remembering the butchered bodies, and convulsively swallowed bile. "But this isn't the way to fix the wrong done to you. It just keeps the cycle going."

Another vision began. This time, I saw Native Americans weeping and falling to the ground next to the laid-out body of a dead man. They scratched themselves and tore their clothing, crying out. Then, it switched to two groups of people meeting in an open field. One group sang. The second group wept, obviously the family and friends of the dead person. When the first group stopped singing, several spoke and I understood them. They announced the good qualities of the deceased, such as strength like an oak tree, loyalty to his tribe and family, and skills as a hunter and protector. When they were done with the speeches, they did a curious thing. The first group wiped the faces of the second group. It was almost as if they dried the mourner's tears.

The scene switched, this time to a procession, followed by burial of the deceased, sitting up, with his possessions around him. Then they went back to the village for a feast.

That seemed obvious enough. "You want a funeral?" I asked.

The old man nodded.

My jewelry was now so uncomfortably hot, I had to

take the pieces off and shove them in my pocket, giving me time to think. Inaccurate and probably insulting words from old western movies came to mind until I settled on the simplest. "If we put on a funeral for you, will you stop fighting with us and leave this place? Go on to be with your ancestors?"

The old man nodded.

Hard to believe it could be that simple but I wasn't about to question it. "I promise we'll conduct a funeral. Um, there aren't any bodies to bury but we can leave you gifts by the lake."

The old man nodded for a third time.

"It's a deal, then," I said.

The warrior whooped, jumped up and waved his arms.

Surprised at his reaction, I stumbled backward before catching myself.

He ran into the middle of the fighting ghosts, yelling. Others took up his cry and the battle which had continued during our little conference stopped.

But the old Indian remained, watching me. "My people were destroyed," he said, his voice thin, but firm, "by those who wanted us to leave this place."

So they *could* speak.

"I did not expect," he said, "to see any of our descendants among the people of this village. However, I see none of our race, either. What has become of us?"

Oh, Lordy. How to explain the atrocities white settlers committed on Native Americans or the history of devastating government policies and treaties? I was ashamed, even though my ancestors didn't come over from Ireland until later.

Mitch suddenly stood next to me. "What's going on?"

I flinched.

He appeared ragged and worn. The fighting had taken its toll.

The old Indian watched, his face emotionless but his eyes showed deep pain.

"I negotiated a cease-fire," I said to Mitch.

"What are the terms?"

I shook my head, frustrated. "Give me a minute here to wrap things up, then I'll explain."

I turned back to the old man. "It's true. Very few of your race still live here, though many live in other places." I wondered if he understood what I was reluctant to explain. Technically, they'd been around long enough to see the changes in the world. Whether they noticed was another thing.

He nodded. "We will await the mourning rituals." He faded away.

"What are the terms?" Mitch repeated.

"What did you promise them?" asked Brian. "I hope you didn't give away the farm or anything."

"What's going on, here?" Don's booming voice preceded him and Linda.

"The lake ghosts are Native Americans," I spoke up, so I wouldn't have to repeat myself. "They promised to stop attacking everyone and cross over if we had a funeral for them."

"A funeral?" Linda asked.

"Their entire village was ambushed by other Native Americans and everyone killed. Men, women, and children. There was no one left to mourn them or give them a proper funeral or burial. Their bodies were left to the animals."

"No wonder they've been such a damn nuisance," said Don.

"Obviously, they're angry," I said.

Declan touched my arm. "Was there anything in particular they wanted for the ceremony?"

"They showed me." I explained what I had seen.

Declan's eyes lit up. "That's similar to what I learned in my research. Of course, rituals may change over time. Oh, how I wish I could see them." He rubbed his hands together.

"They're actually pretty scary." I frowned, looking up.

All the ghosts had assembled in the open field, the two groups glaring at each other.

"Seems like appeasing the enemy." Mitch scratched his chin. "War is war. Bad things happen on both sides."

"They need this ceremony to move on," I said. "Besides, when it comes to ghosts, I don't think it's about obliterating the enemy but about making things right." If only I'd realized it seven years ago.

"Possibly," he growled, then disappeared.

I sighed, hoping he wouldn't do anything to mess up my negotiations.

34

Declan could barely contain his excitement. Indian spirits? He'd been fascinated by the successive groups of Native Americans in this area since he was a boy. First things first, though. "Who is it you're talking to now?" he asked Kenna.

She seemed annoyed. "His name's Mitch. He was in the Vietnam War and set up the town ghost army."

Brian snorted. "Should have got someone from WWII. Those boys knew how to get the job done."

Declan couldn't let that go. "They kept the lake ghosts busy while Kenna worked things out."

Brian mumbled. Typical. He admired a great many things about his brother but his desire for the last word was an infuriating habit.

Sirens blared close.

He looked up, noticing his surroundings. It was still cloudy and dark but the lightning and thunder had subsided. The fields on the other side of the lake, though, were in flames. The acrid smell filled him with a sense of urgency. "We must do the death rituals quickly and leave."

"What do you need?" asked Don.

He thought for a moment. "They would have had a feast. So, food."

"We don't have time to go to the grocery store," Linda said.

"Maybe we can borrow from nearby farms?" Kenna said.

"What do we tell them it's for?"

Kenna shrugged. "Make something up."

Linda nodded, frowning, and walked away.

"Hey, I'll help forage," Nate volunteered, running after her.

The sirens drew closer.

Declan asked Brian, "Do you have your pocket knife on you? Grave goods would have included weapons."

"Yes." Brian's lip twisted. "But I ain't giving it to a bunch of heathen ghosts."

Don dug into his pocket. "Come on, Brian," he yelled over the sirens. "Man-up." He handed Declan a pearl-handled pocket knife.

The sirens cut out as two fire trucks roared to the lake. Fire fighters jumped out of the truck and threw big, black hoses into the water.

Kenna searched the ground. "Where's my bag of supplies?"

"Here." Declan had looped the handles over his arm. He handed it to her.

"Okay, let's start a pile." She dug through the contents of the bag, pulled out a sage bundle, sweetgrass braid, and lighter and placed them in the trampled-down weeds at the lake's edge. Pulling a jumble of jewelry from her pocket, she extracted a purple and black bracelet and silver chain, tossing them on the pile. She slipped the other things back in her pocket. "What else do we have?" Her voice sounded thick with emotion.

Declan didn't think twice. He pulled Mama's crucifix and his St. Christopher medal from around his neck and added them and Don's pocket knife to the pile. He nodded and glanced at his brother.

Brian scowled. "This is bullshit. Putting on a phony funeral for a bunch of savages who would have killed us as soon as look at us if they were alive and standing here today. You know what? Let's get a priest out here to do a proper exorcism and send these bastards to Hell where they belong."

Kenna shot to her feet. "Since day one, you've been nothing but a pain in my butt. First, you didn't believe I talked to ghosts and then, when I proved it, you blabbed it all over town because you figured out a way to use me. And now we need your help and you can't be bothered? Too damn bad, old man. We're all giving up something here today and that includes you. Now, cough it up."

Declan smiled but covered it with his fingertips. He didn't remember Kenna ever swearing before. Of course, Brian deserved it.

Nobody said a word. The crackle of fire, shouts of the firemen, and clank of equipment seemed loud.

Brian dug into his pocket and pulled out the pocket knife. He stared at it in the palm of his hand, then threw it on the small pile of gifts.

"Thank you," Kenna said.

He stalked away, mumbling.

She watched him, frowning and breathing hard as if she'd run a marathon.

Declan patted her arm. "You were correct and he'll get over it."

She tried to smile. "Thanks."

Don added some change to the pile and a fancy metal pen from his suit pocket.

As one group of fire fighters sprayed water onto the fire, others were checking on the few injured people remaining in the field. More sirens blared in the distance.

Linda and Nate hurried up, carrying grocery bags. "You went to the store?" Kenna asked.

"The store came to us," Nate said. He moved aside.

An African American woman stood behind him, wearing nurse's scrubs. "I heard about Reverend Graves in the store parking lot," she said, putting down bags and hugging Kenna. "I knew there'd be trouble and rushed over to help."

"Thank you so much, Sherita." Kenna said.

"We met her on the road," Linda said. "I explained what happened and saw the groceries in her back seat. She offered."

"You're welcome," the woman said. "Now, I'm going to go help those injured people. See you later, Kenna." She hurried off.

One firefighter walked toward them. "We'd better finish this soon," Declan said, eying the firefighter.

"Leave him to me," said Don. He hurried to intercept.

Kenna gazed at the open field.

He wondered what she saw. Perhaps the ghosts were getting restless? "Should we proceed with the ceremony?"

"Yes," Kenna said. "Nate, you're with me. We're the

mourners. We have to cry and carry on like our entire family just died." She pointed to Declan and Linda. "While you two stand in front of me and sing."

"Sing?" Linda asked. "I don't know any Indian songs."

"What about hymns?" Declan suggested.

"Excellent idea," Kenna said. "Go for it."

Linda moved close. "What about In the Garden?" she whispered.

He shook his head. "I don't know it but how about Amazing Grace?"

"Perfect."

"Would you mind starting? My voice isn't what it used to be."

Linda smiled and started singing in a clear soprano:

"Amazing Grace, how sweet the sound..."

Declan added his wavering high tenor for the next line.

Kenna fell on her knees, moaning.

Nate copied her. "All gone," he cried, clutching his head. "How will I live without them?" He was quite impressive.

Kenna tore at her hair. Scratched her arms.

This continued until they finished the hymn.

"What next?" Linda asked.

"Speeches?" Declan prompted.

"Yes."

"May I?" Declan asked.

Kenna nodded.

Declan almost smiled at the prospect before remembering this was serious business. He cleared his throat. "We honor the dead today. The brave men, women, and children who were brutally murdered in the dark of night by cowards who wouldn't face them in proper battle. The people who lived by this lake were proud warriors who did not deserve such an ignoble fate. May their spirits soon find peace."

Don had finished speaking to the firefighter and stood off to the side, watching.

Declan continued on for a while longer, throwing in everything he could think of to flatter the Indians. At the end, during a moment of quiet, he heard hushed conversation near them. He hoped the spirits had liked his impromptu speech.

Linda spoke next. "The women of this tribe worked hard to care for their families. They searched the forest for roots and berries, they cooked the meat the men brought home from hunting. They made clothing, bore children, cared for those children, and taught them. They worked hard from sun-up to sun-down every day. They deserved better than what they got."

Don even stepped in. "Ladies and gentlemen, we're here to acknowledge a great tragedy and right a terrible injustice." He continued on for a good five minutes.

As Don droned on, Declan fought the exhaustion creeping over him.

Brian returned and stood on the periphery. Declan inched over. When Don finished, Declan elbowed Brian.

"Eh?" Brian said. "No. I'm not making a speech."

Declan elbowed him and gave him a look. Brian's jaw clenched but Declan stared him down.

Brian cleared his throat. "What happened here a long time ago was wrong."

They waited for more.

"That's all I got," he said.

Declan stepped in front of Kenna and she stood. He wiped the tears from her face with his dry fingertips. Linda did the same for Nate.

There was an uncomfortable pause. Everyone looked at Kenna.

She faced the ghosts, pointing toward the offerings. "I hope the ceremony and these gifts will help you...brave people who once lived, loved, and died here to heal and leave this place of...horrific memory and...take the next step on your journey."

Silence.

"Anyone know any good jokes?" Brian muttered.

Declan shushed him.

Kenna licked her lips. "You're weary. The time for battle is over. Your ancestors look for you. It's time to leave this place of pain. Do you accept our gifts?"

The spirits whispered, then their voices grew louder. Angrier. "Oh, no," breathed Declan.

"What's the matter?" asked Brian. "Didn't they like it? That's what we get for trying to reason with ghosts."

Declan turned to Kenna. "Is there anything else we can do?"

She shook her head. "I don't know. We did the best we could with what we had."

One voice rose amongst the spirits. A female, demanding quiet. The spirits stopped talking. Another female voice spoke, this one old. Very old. A clan mother. Declan could only catch a word or two. Something about a dream of a snake and a dog. Other female voices agreed with her. He didn't understand what it all meant, but the tone of voice was clear enough.

"Declan, do you know what they're talking about?"

"I don't think the clan mothers liked the way we did the rituals."

"Well, then," said Linda, holding her bedraggled hair out of her eyes. "Why didn't they do it themselves and save us all this trouble?"

"Because they all died," Declan replied, head cocked to catch the ghosts' conversation. "There was no one left to play the part of the consoler."

After more argument, one of the clan mothers said, "She is a witch. Why do you listen to her?" All the spirits started talking.

Kenna's eyes flashed. "What did she say?"

"She called you a witch." Declan shook his head. This was getting out of hand.

Brian laughed.

"Well, I'll be damned," Don said, staring at the tree line by the highway.

A big bear waddled toward them.

35

I groaned. Reaching out, I felt the curious, alien mind from a few nights ago in my back yard.

"Anybody have a shotgun?" Brian asked.

I rounded on him. "Don't you dare. That bear wouldn't hurt anyone."

"Wild animals are unpredictable, missy, no matter if they've been eating out of garbage cans all summer."

"This one isn't."

"How do you know?"

"I'm a vet tech," I snarled. "And I know animals."

"Maybe not this animal," he muttered.

The bear continued on, oblivious to the attention he got from us, the firefighters, and the few spectators still here.

"Kenna?" Declan tugged on my arm. "They're quiet now."

I glanced back at the lake ghosts. Silently, they watched. Walking toward the bear, I felt exposed. Again.

My other secret ability would be revealed for public inspection.

A firefighter with an ax ran toward the bear.

I walked faster.

The bear plopped down about ten feet away from me, as if ready for a little chat.

The firefighter slowed but he was only about fifty feet away. I thrust out my open hand but he didn't stop.

"You shouldn't be here," I told the bear, slipping into his mind. Once again, there was an intense interest, a burning need to know what was going on, why all these people were here. And happiness to find me again. "Thanks," I said. "I like you too, but you're in danger. See the guy over there with the ax?"

He turned his head. The firefighter was close enough to hear me talking.

"As much as I want to talk to you some more, you have to leave. I'm afraid something bad will happen." I hated to do it, but I formed a video in my mind of the firefighter attacking the bear with the ax.

The bear made a sound, kind of a whiny grunt. He got up, ambling toward me.

The firefighter picked up speed.

"No," I shouted at him.

The bear angled a little to the side, detoured around me, and went right under the area the town ghosts and lake ghosts were gathered.

The firefighter watched the bear make his way across the field. He looked at me a moment, then ran back toward his men, talking into a walkie talkie.

Hopefully, the bear would get away before they caught him. Or killed him. I shuddered.

"You're a regular Dr. Doolittle, ain't you?" said Brian.

Ignoring him and switching mental gears again, I returned to the ghosts. "What more do we have to do to satisfy you?" I tried not to sound impatient or pleading but it was way past time to wrap this up.

The elders huddled. The clan mother who spoke against me needed to be convinced but, after a while, they all nodded, coming to an agreement.

My heart hammered in my chest.

The old man stepped forward while the others remained behind, faces impassive. "You speak to Brother Bear and he trusts you," he said, so slow and deliberate I wanted to shake the verdict out of him. "We trust Brother Bear. The lust for revenge has been quenched. You, who are not of our people, have made an acceptable effort to honor our memory and sacrifice. We are ready to go to the next world."

Just like that, the door to the Other Side opened.

Declan sighed as the joy and peace spread from the doorway.

This time, it overwhelmed me. Clamping a hand over my mouth, I muffled a cry.

"What is it?" Linda asked. "What's wrong? Are they attacking again?"

I shook my head, unable to control the tears filling my eyes. Through a watery blur, the Native American ghosts walked off the field and through the doorway large enough for four of them to walk side by side.

"It's alright," Declan said, reverence in his voice. "They are leaving now."

"Oh, thank God," said Linda.

When the last of the lake ghosts passed through the

doorway, it closed. The loss of the light, happy feeling dug into my soul with sharp talons.

Mitch appeared in front of me. "I guess it worked after all."

"Did we lose many?" I whispered.

"A fair number but we all knew what we were getting into." He drew himself up straight, saluting me. "Catch you on the flip side, Miss Kenna." He marched back to the ragtag group of town ghosts and they faded away.

The strength left my legs and I collapsed on the ground. Everyone talked above me but I couldn't stop crying like an idiot. What was wrong with me?

An arm circled my shoulders. "Kenna," Nate said, urgency in his voice. "We got to go."

I nodded, rubbing my eyes. Felt hands on both arms helping me up. I took a shuddering breath. "I'm okay."

A firefighter shouted, "You people, get out of here. The wind's shifted and the fire's headed this way."

Leaving the lake edge, I noticed Brian hung back. Looking around, he picked his knife out of the pile beside the lake. He saw me watching. "What? They're gone now, right?"

I shook my head, too tired to protest.

The spectators, including Sherita, were gone. One firetruck moved from the lake to the other side of the fire. When it stopped, men swarmed it, pulling out hoses.

As we walked to our vehicles, it started to rain.

Don looked up. "About damn time."

A dark green pickup roared up the gravel drive and halted beside us. "What's going on?" George Barnes' ruddy face peered out of the open window. Two young men sat next to him, probably his sons. "We saw smoke coming from this direction."

"George." Don put on his good ol' boy persona. "We had a little bru-ha-ha up here but it's over now."

"Lightening caused a brush fire," said Nate.

"And you won't have anymore problems with ghosts," Brian said.

George's sons looked uncomfortable but he said, "That right?" He nodded at me. "Thank you. Well, we better see what the damage is." He drove closer to the lake where they met the firefighter in charge.

"A man of few words," said Linda.

"A good man," said Brian.

Nate helped me to my car and insisted on driving. I didn't have much choice. I was a mess. On the way back to town, I wolfed down several smoked meat sticks until I regained some strength. At the house, I assured him I was strong enough to drive him home. He wouldn't listen and, honestly, I was too tired to argue with him. He walked home. Wherever that was.

Yawning, I dropped onto the couch, grounded, and did my visualization. "Thank you," I whispered and fell asleep, wrapped in love and protection.

THE NEXT MORNING, RAIN SPLATTERED AGAINST WINDOWS and washed down gutters.

After showering, I let in the cat. He was dry, except for his paws. "Found a place to hide out, huh?" I stretched, feeling stiff, but, overall, pretty darn good. Not even the gray day could bring down my mood as I puttered around, feeding the cat and making coffee.

"Henry?" I called.

After a moment, he materialized beside me. "Yes, Miss?"

"How are you, Henry?"

His brow furrowed. "The same as always, Miss. And you?"

"Fabulous." I couldn't help but smile. "Did you notice the absence of doom and gloom toward Rogers Lake?"

Henry faced that direction. "They are truly gone?"

"Yes. Hurlbutt is now safe."

"Congratulations, and thank you, Miss."

"You're welcome, but it was a group effort."

"A victory for all, then."

"Yeah." I remembered something Mitch had said. "We lost some of the town ghosts, though."

"That is unfortunate but I am sure their sacrifice was not in vain."

"It wasn't."

Loud pounding on my side door revealed Nate and Brian. I hurried Nate in, but put my arm up against Brian. "Not so fast there, mister. For you, there's a magic password."

He frowned, water streaming off his hood. "It's a little wet out here."

"I noticed."

He blew out a breath. "Okay. I guess I got kind of carried away yesterday."

"Yes, you did."

He shifted to come in, but I didn't move my arm. He

stopped, mild surprise on his face, then scowled. "I said some stuff I shouldn't have."

"That's true." I didn't budge.

He narrowed his eyes. "Have you always been like this or trying extra hard today?"

"The magic words, please, Brian," I said, sweetly.

For a moment, I thought he'd storm off. Then he winked. "I'm sorry I stomped on your sandcastle yesterday. How's that?"

I rolled my eyes and stepped aside. "I guess that's as good as it gets from you."

"Pretty much," he agreed.

They hung up their rain coats on nails in the stairway and we went up to the kitchen. I was still annoyed with Brian but at least he apologized. "How's Declan?" I asked.

"Happy as a dog cornering a bitch in heat."

I groaned. "Is he okay, physically? He didn't overdo it yesterday, did he?"

Brian scowled. "He's fine. Go ask him if you don't believe me."

"I will."

Once they had steaming cups of coffee in their hands, Nate gave me a soggy, rolled-up Chronicle. "How bad is it?" I asked, scanning the front page.

"About what you'd expect from those idiots," Brian said.

Nate grinned. "They spelled my name right."

I winced.

"You never know," said Brian. "Maybe getting his name in the paper will help drum up business."

Nate shrugged. "It called me a local handyman, so maybe."

They filled me in on all the latest town gossip, including the rumor Pastor Graves currently resided on the psychiatric floor of the hospital in Bartlett.

"I doubt we could get that lucky, though," said Brian, draining his cup.

"Anything new on the ghost-front?" I asked, trying to sound unconcerned.

"You'd know more about it than us."

"Well, I haven't been out yet, and was wondering..."

"If anyone's run screaming from their home?" asked Brian. "Seen or heard anything weird? Crashed a car because a non-existent dog ran in front of it?" He looked at Nate. "I haven't heard anything."

Nate shook his head. "Me neither."

I breathed easier, not realizing how anxious I'd been until they said it. "What about the bear?"

"No one's seen it," Nate said. "Must have got away."

"Good." I hoped the bear had many years to roam, satisfying his curiosity.

Brian stood up. "Yeah, well. Promised my wife I'd fix her shelves today. Still got to stop at the hardware store."

Nate finished the last swallow in his cup and stood up. "Gotta bounce. Later, *Kennaaaaah.*"

After they left I did housekeeping, of the psychic variety. I grounded and protected myself then smudged my jewelry.

Later in the day, after it stopped raining, I visited Declan. Just in the short distance to his place, the houses had fewer ghost occupants. It felt odd. After letting me in, I noticed Declan walked slower and with care, but he insisted on pouring us iced tea. He seemed alright.

We rehashed the previous day's events. He asked

what I saw in my visions, details of the Native American clothing, etc. He wanted to figure out the exact tribes involved. I told him what little I could remember but I'd been focused on what was happening, not what they wore or the decorations in their houses. I was fine not knowing exactly who they were but not Declan. "You should have been a historian," I said. "Or a writer."

A wistful smile flickered across his face. "I had ideas when I was younger but there was no money for college." He paused. "Though it didn't much matter because I didn't believe in myself."

"Oh?"

"I've been thinking about this quite a bit. With all the ghosts, and you coming to town and helping me, and what happened at the lake, everything is changing. I'm changing. Can you imagine, at my age?"

I smiled.

He sipped his tea. "You taught me this ability to hear the spirits is a gift, not a curse."

I snorted. "There are days I'd disagree with you."

"Perhaps." He licked his lips. "You know, I've always been afraid of people. They're unpredictable and usually have these expectations I could never fulfill. Books were safer, more dependable. But I've enjoyed helping you with the research and, by extension, the town. It's rather nice to feel included. Right now, I'm learning, of course, but God gave me this gift and I'll not refuse it again. I'm looking forward to helping you as a ghost liaison. Because we both know if this town attracts ghosts, it's probably a magnet for other things as well. Foul things."

I didn't want to think that far ahead but nodded politely. I'd worry about it another day.

"And once you decide it's time to turn the job over to someone else, well, maybe I'll be ready to do it on my own."

To say I was totally blown away was an understatement of epic proportions. We chatted for a while longer, but he grew tired and I gave him a big hug before leaving.

"Now don't be a stranger, Kenna."

I grinned. "I won't. I promise."

Wondering what was happening with the town ghosts, I turned onto the service road and parked beside the warehouse. Outside, I didn't feel anything, but climbed in the window anyway. The room was empty and my footsteps echoed as I walked to the next room.

"Hello? Anyone here?"

Nothing. And no response in the other rooms, either. Disappointed, I went back to the window. Climbing the stack of pallets beneath it, I finally felt a presence and turned. Mitch stood in the middle of the room, smoking a cigarette.

"Hi," I said, happy to see him. Declan was right. Things were changing.

"What's going on?" he asked.

I climbed down. "I wanted to check on everyone. Yesterday, you said we lost some. Who?"

He frowned. "I don't know names. Wish I did. The boxer was one. You know, the one who gave you a hard time when you first came here?"

I felt a pang. "Muscles."

"That his name?"

"No, but it's what I called him. He fought hard." I remembered his battle cry across the fields.

Mitch took a drag on the cigarette. "They all did."

Smoke billowed out as he spoke. "There were farmers, shopkeepers, a nurse, school teacher, others. All gone."

"I'm sorry." I sighed. "That sounds so inadequate."

He blew out smoke. "Most of us are laying low for now."

"That must be why I haven't felt many ghosts today. Will you all be okay?"

"Oh, yeah. Just building back strength."

I breathed out, relieved. "Good." I hesitated. "Where did the others go? When the lake ghosts beat them and they disappeared?"

He shook his head. "Don't know."

This was so awkward. "Well, I just wanted to touch base, see how everyone was doing."

A tiny smile played around his mouth. "We're dead. How do you think we're doing?"

He had a point.

Driving around town, it seemed different. Weeds still grew in sidewalk cracks and building bricks still crumbled but something had changed. I couldn't quite put my finger on why, though.

Maybe it was all the cars parked on Main Street, more at one time than I'd seen the entire month I'd been in town. Brian's rust bucket of a pickup was one of them and he stood in front of the diner, talking to a guy holding a video camera. They were surrounded by a bunch of people wearing identical black t-shirts, though I couldn't see the logo. Must be TV news people again.

Leave it to Brian. The guy did like to talk.

36

I considered driving to the lake, but my stomach growled so I went to Hanley's instead. Trying to decide between the types of bagged salad greens, I felt a tap on my shoulder.

A young woman with lanky, blond hair stood behind me. She smelled of stale cigarettes. "Thanks for getting rid of those ghosts."

What a nice change. "You're welcome."

She twisted the handle on the grocery basket she held. "I was there and I know how bad they were."

Something clicked in my mind. "You were one of the kids partying at Rogers Lake?"

She half-smiled. "Yeah. Stupid, huh? But, I don't do that shit anymore. I just wanted you to know I'm really, really glad they're gone. So, thanks." She turned and walked away fast.

All through the store, people thanked me. It was beyond bizarre. In the parking lot, I froze when Mrs. Maglennon spotted me. She frowned, nodded, and walked on without saying a word. I wasn't sure whether that was good or bad.

At the house, I pulled shopping bags out of my trunk. "Hello."

I stifled a groan.

Gloria waved from the end of my driveway, Ralph straining at his leash.

I wondered what she was up to now. The Pomeranian reached me first. "Hi, there, Ralph." I leaned down to pet him and was covered in kisses. "Hi, Gloria," I said, with less enthusiasm.

She flashed a smile as if she didn't hear the difference. "So much happening in little, old Hurlbutt and you," she pointed at me, "are right in the thick of it. How exciting. In fact, I heard there's some of those ghost hunters in town right now."

Interesting. Probably the group I saw talking to Brian. Pretending tiredness, I stood up slowly, grunting. "That's nice. I'd love to stay and chat, but I'm wiped out and was about to take a nap."

"Oh, you poor thing. Why don't you stop by for coffee later?"

"I don't know. I've got to finish the house. I'm going back to Syracuse on Sunday and then I'll only be here on weekends."

Her smile never dimmed. "Well, you stop in any time. The coffee's always on." She waved, then bounced down the driveway.

"Thanks," I called.

Returning to the car, I grabbed the rest of the bags, and hurried to the house. The tomcat darted across the yard.

"I'm home, cat."

He head-butted my ankles.

I unlocked the door and he pushed ahead of me, charging up the stairs. After setting the bags on the counter, I pulled out a can of cat food and plopped a spoonful in his dish. He attacked it with gusto.

"I guess I'll have to take you back to Syracuse." He'd adopted me and I'd gotten used to the fur ball.

He gave me an unblinking stare then went back to eating.

My burning need to return to Syracuse had changed. I wanted to get back to work but it felt like a let-down now and I couldn't understand why.

Whatever. I'd figure it out tomorrow.

After I named the cat.

WANT TO KNOW WHAT HAPPENS NEXT?

Be the first to know what happens to Kenna and the residents of Hurlbutt, both living and dead, when the next book in the *Haunted Town* series comes out - and get reader exclusives!

Visit E.K.'s website and sign up for her Readers Group:
EKCarmel.com

ACKNOWLEDGMENTS

Beset by Ghosts wouldn't have been possible without the support of my family. They listened to me blather on about this story, read the different versions, and ate a lot of takeout dinners. You are the best and I love you!

Deep thanks to Angela McGill, Heiko Monsees, Diane Mills, and Mary Margaret Ripley for beta reading, asking questions, and pointing out plot holes big enough to drive a truck through. You all gave me the confidence to keep going.

To Holly Lisle, whose writing classes unlocked my stubborn brain and freed my Muse. And to the other writers on Holly's forums and the 20BooksTo50K, Smarter Artist, SPF-Genius, and Indie Author HQ Facebook groups for advice and encouragement.

To my friend and graphic designer, Laura Putorti, for creating a fantastic cover.

And thank **you**, my reader, for giving this book a chance. With all the other things you could be doing, watching, and playing, I can't tell you how grateful I am that you chose to take the time to read my novel. I hope you enjoyed it.

ABOUT THE AUTHOR

E.K. Carmel is an American fantasy writer living in a small town in western New York State.

She discovered the real world totally sucked to a kid with a big imagination. Books, TV, and movies transported her from her ordinary life to realms of magic, fantastic futures, and new worlds just by asking, "What if...?"

She grew up, graduated from college, worked, married her own personal MacGyver Man, and together they've raised two daughters.

Life was busy but good (she thought) until one day her creativity hitched a ride to the big city for some excitement. She found it in a dance club, doing shots and screaming, "WOOOOHOOOO!" Before it could run away with it's new besties, she persuaded it to return home with promises of homemade pie and more attention than the family cats.

E.K.'s favorite holiday is Halloween. For one night, the world runs amok! amok! amok! with ghosts, witches, and assorted monsters, transforming the strait-laced and normal into the haunted, the creepy, the fun. But how to make that feeling last longer than once a year and appease her restless creativity?

The truth is out there, and she found hers in writing

stories in small-town settings she knows so well, filled with quirky characters, supernatural elements, and occasional strong language.

www.EKCarmel.com
Eileen@EKCarmel.com